In the Land of Second Chances

In the Land of Second Chances

a novel by

George Shaffner

ALGONQUIN BOOKS OF CHAPEL HILL
2004

Published by
ALGONQUIN BOOKS OF CHAPEL HILL
Post Office Box 2225
Chapel Hill, North Carolina 27515-2225

a division of
Workman Publishing
708 Broadway
New York, New York 10003

Printed in the United States of America.
Published simultaneously in Canada by Thomas Allen & Son Limited.
Design by Anne Winslow.

Library of Congress Cataloging-in-Publication Data
Shaffner, George.
In the land of second chances : a novel / by George Shaffner.—1st ed.
p. cm.
ISBN 1-56512-440-5
1. Bed and breakfast accommodations—Fiction. 2. Eccentrics and eccentricities—Fiction. 3. Traveling sales personnel—Fiction. 4. City and town life—Fiction. 5. Life change events—Fiction. 6. Department stores—Fiction. 7. Nebraska—Fiction. I. Title.
PS3619.H345I5 2004
813'.6—dc22 2004046261

10 9 8 7 6 5 4 3 2 1
First Edition

For Mom and Dad

Many, many thanks to Jane and Miriam, Antonia, Kathy, and Grace.

Chapter 1

The Sad Edge of a Slippery Slope

My name is Wilma Porter. I own the Come Again Bed and Breakfast, which is the only B & B in Ebb, Nebraska, and the only one in Rutherford B. Hayes County that is recommended by two Internet directories. I bought the place from Clement Tucker, our very own Warren Buffett, who contracted an acute case of Midlife Crisis about five years ago and decided to build himself a modern house with all the latest conveniences.

The Come Again is a single-turreted, three-story Victorian mansion that was built by Silas Tucker the Second shortly after the Civil War. There's a single, grand oak tree in the front that antedates the house and a black asphalt driveway leading up to a formal porte-cochere and a little parking area for my guests. Last year, I had the house painted bone white except for the roof, which is black. I think the contrast is meaningful.

Clara Tucker Booth Yune, Clem Tucker's older sister and Ebb's most prominent recluse, occupies the entire third floor of the Come Again on a permanent basis. There are six bedrooms on the second floor. I live in the one that faces the back garden; the other five are for rent. Each bedroom has its own bathroom; the Cornhusker Suite even has a Jacuzzi. Downstairs, there's a living room the size of a tennis court, a parlor for the TV, a den, which I keep for myself as a rule, and a giant-sized dining room that will seat sixteen. Except for my kitchen, which is commercial grade, the entire house is decorated in beautiful old antiques that Clem Tucker left behind or I bought cheap at estate auctions and refinished myself in the basement.

Like most folks who live in Ebb, I was born right here, but about an hour after I got my high school diploma I jumped on a bus to North Platte. I came back with my two daughters after the divorce fifteen years later. Both girls are grown up and gone now. One is up in Omaha and the other is over in Council Bluffs, across the river.

By most measures, Ebb is a small town. It is the county seat, but only two thousand people live inside the city limits. There's not a lot to do here most of the time, and that's the way we like it. If we need some excitement, we can drive up to Lincoln. For twenty years, every politician in this area has been elected on the "No Wal-Mart, no how" platform. We take a similarly dim view of fast-food franchises, slow-food franchises, convenience-store franchises, and all other franchises with big, backlit signs in primary colors. The only exception is the new Starbucks on Main Street, but Ebb is so small that we only have the one.

All the rest of the stores on Main are unique and most of them have been in operation for more than fifty years. The biggest and most famous is Millet's, the last remaining department store in the tri-county region. Millet's, which is pronounced like "mill-it" and not like "mill-ay," sits right at the corner of Bean Street and Main, where it's been ever since Joshua Millet opened it up back in 1920. It has survived the Great Depression, rural flight, three bank bankruptcies, World War II, a flood, and God knows how many droughts and tornadoes. Now it is owned and managed by Calvin Millet, June and Joshua III's only child. Calvin is a smart, hardworking young man, and everybody in Hayes County shops at his store as if it was a patriotic duty, but we're all afraid that Millet's will not survive his run of terrible bad luck.

Calvin was a homely baby, bald and sort of wedge-headed, but he grew up to be tall and handsome in a gangly, fair-haired sort of way, kind of like Gary Cooper. He was too skinny to play high school football, a form of religion in these parts, but he studied hard and got good grades even though he worked in his father's store. After graduation, he went up to Lincoln and got himself a four-year degree in accounting, and then he joined the Air Force to see the world. They sent him to Bossier City, Louisiana.

Calvin had hardly been gone for any time at all when his parents were killed in a train accident. I could tell at the funeral that he had already started to lose his hearing. He's fine now; he wears tiny little hearing aids in both ears, but the Air Force had to give him a medical discharge so he came back home to run the family store. A year or so later, he married Mary Beth Tucker, Clem's only child and a bit of an airhead, but a real beauty and the catch of the county from a financial point of view. Six months after that, Lucy was born. I know what you're thinking, but the human gestation period in rural America is only six months for the first baby. After that, it's nine months.

When Lucy Millet was eight years old, she contracted some sort of neurological disorder. I hear it's similar to Lou Gehrig's disease, but more aggressive and unnaturally painful. Anyway, a real sick daughter was more than her momma could handle, so she pulled up and left for L.A. Just disappeared in the middle of the night. Took the Jeep and the dog and the George Foreman cooker and left Calvin a note saying she was real sorry.

Mary Beth's departure caused quite a buzz at the Quilting Circle. Most of us are divorcées ourselves, so we aren't inclined to be critical of any woman who leaves a man. In fact, we have a support system in place so that a woman can do it right: counselors, lawyers, day care, even police protection. But Mary Beth didn't use the system, and her husband and sick daughter suffered for it. She hasn't been welcome in these parts since.

Apparently, being a waitress to the stars was not keeping her in the manner to which she was accustomed, so Mary Beth came home anyway but just long enough to sue Calvin for divorce. Since she had only abandoned her husband and sick child in the dead of night, and taken the dog and the Jeep to boot, the court was sympathetic to her predicament. Calvin now pays her alimony. In case you were wondering, the judge is married to a Tucker, once removed.

Little Lucy Millet is the sweetest little blonde-haired girl you have ever seen and she is smart as a whip, but she isn't getting any better. For the last three years, Calvin has flown her all over the country looking for a doctor who can cure her, but all they've done is slow the disease down and, according to rumor, empty the Millet bank account. Calvin has health insurance through the farmer's co-op, just like everybody else in these parts, but most of Lucy's treatments have been experimental, and that means that the HMO won't pay for them. Unless somebody gets those insurance companies under control, I figure that two aspirin and a glass of water will count as a medical experiment before I'm dead.

The tornado hit last month while Calvin and Lucy were away at the Mayo Clinic. That was too early for tornadoes as a rule, but the weather has been unseasonably warm all year. Luckily, it was a tiny thing as twisters go. It missed the town and everything else in Rutherford B. Hayes County except for Rufus Bowe's grain silo and Calvin Millet's place. Actually, it tore the roof off of Rufus's silo and dropped it on Calvin's house—dead center. I drove out to see what happened with my best friend, Loretta Parsons, who is Ebb's sole resident black person and the owner of the Bold Cut Beauty Salon. Calvin's home was a sight to see. It looked like a pile of rubble with a great big aluminum teacup sitting in the middle of it. You wouldn't think that anybody's aim could be that good, not even God's.

After the tornado, Calvin and Lucy stayed with me at the Come Again for a few days until he found them a cracker-box of a house to rent in Carson, about fifteen minutes down the road toward the Kansas line. Calvin hasn't talked to Buzz Busby about rebuilding yet, even though that place is so small and so far away from town. I would know for sure if he had.

We're all sad for Calvin Millet and worried sick about poor Lucy—any caring person would be—but I have to tell you the honest truth: we're just as scared of rural America's variety of the domino theory. If Calvin's finances fall apart, then Millet's Department Store will fail. If Millet's goes under, then the county's political resolve will collapse and we'll get a Wal-Mart store one week later—in a ravine ten miles from nowhere because the land will be dirt cheap. The next thing you know, everybody in the county will be shopping for bargains in the ravine, so Loretta will have to shut her doors, and so will the Starbucks and every other place on Main except for the Corn Palace and the Yune Library. Then the girls won't bring their kids back after they get divorced and that will be the end of Ebb as we know it.

You may think that I'm exaggerating, but this town is perched on the sad edge of a slippery slope. I went to church and wished to God I could help in some way, but He sent us a salesman. That's right, a salesman. At least that's my theory. You be the judge.

Chapter 2

Mr. Moore Comes to Town

I WAS SITTING outside of Starbucks on the first day of spring, sharing some pound cake and swapping some tasty rumors with Loretta, when I got a call on my cell phone from a man who wanted to reserve a room at the Come Again. As usual, there was plenty of static, so the reception wasn't real good. It is my belief that our customer-centric telephone company bought exactly one cell for all of Hayes County and then they put it in the back of a pickup truck, so whenever it goes behind a hill or a big barn you can't hear a darned thing other than crackling air. Still, I could hear enough to determine that this man wanted a room that very evening, so I made my apologies to Loretta and went straight home to fix one up.

I was a bit unprepared because it was too early for visitors to Ebb. Excluding Clara, I get most of my guests two times a year:

at high school graduation and in the fall, right around harvest time and the county fair. Otherwise, I have visitors for funerals and holidays, but nobody had died recently, thank God, which meant I wasn't expecting.

The man said he would arrive around four o'clock, so I made a nice Darjeeling tea after I finished his room and then waited in the parlor where I have a panoramic view of my drive. My new boarder arrived shortly after that. He was driving an expensive, cranberry-colored station wagon, probably German, and that was fine with me. The men I don't like drive those poser pickup trucks, the great big, noisy ones with blown engines, huge wheels, and lots of decals. What in the world are they thinking? I know they're compensating, but I wish they would do it somewhere else, like Bolivia.

This man was special; you could see it right away. He was ruddy in complexion, probably in his mid- to late-forties, and trim but not skinny, with a head of dove-white, wind-mussed hair and a matching mustache that was well trimmed. He was wearing a snappy, double-breasted gray suit with a white-collared blue shirt and a colorful tie that I would ask him about later. His shoes were shined, too, which is always a good sign. Even pulling a great big roller suitcase in each hand, he stood ramrod straight and walked with a confident gait.

Before he could knock, I opened the door, smiled my best "welcome y'all" smile, and said, "Good evening, sir. My name is Wilma Porter and this is the Come Again Bed and Breakfast. Are you the man who called me earlier in the day?"

"Yes, ma'am," he said. "My name is Vernon Moore." His eyes were crystalline light blue, like a spring Nebraska sky, and they looked right into mine as he shook my hand with a strong grip. He smiled, too. I could see that he had excellent teeth. A country girl always checks the teeth.

"Please come in," I said. "May I help you with your luggage?"

"No thank you, Ms. Porter. I'm used to carrying it myself." He stepped inside the door and put his bags down on my carpet, a beautiful Persian thing that Clem Tucker didn't want when he left. I noticed that Mr. Moore wasn't wearing a wedding band, which a single girl checks whether she's from the country or not, even though she can never be certain that the data is reliable.

Mr. Moore stood in the foyer for a good half minute, just looking around at my antique furniture, my leaded-glass lamps, and all the pictures and mirrors on my flock-papered walls. Then he said, "This is a lovely house, ma'am. I appreciate your taking me in on such short notice."

"You're more than welcome," I answered. "If you'll be kind enough to sign the guest register, then I can show you to your room." About thirty minutes later, he came down the back stairs into the kitchen where I was slicing bacon for the next day. He was wearing creased jeans, white cross trainers, and a white, long-sleeved cotton shirt with a buttoned-down collar, as if he was a forty-year-old teenager straight out of the fifties.

I couldn't think of a thing to say that didn't sound too familiar, so I offered my new boarder a hot cup of tea. He asked politely for iced water instead and made himself comfortable at the kitchen table at my invitation.

After I had fixed him his drink, I embarked on standard B & B conversational protocol. It is right there in the owner's manual. You ask them if they like their room; they say yes. You ask them what they like for breakfast; they tell you. Men usually prefer eggs and bacon, but Mr. Moore asked for a waffle. You ask them if there is anything else they need; they practically always say no, but Mr. Moore asked for an ironing board and a radio. I resisted a teensy temptation to ask him if he ironed his clothes with a radio and agreed to bring them up to his room. Then I smiled sweetly and said, "That was a lovely tie you were wearing when you arrived."

He brightened up just like a man always does when a woman says something nice about his clothes. "Thank you, Ms. Porter," he responded. "It's a genuine Jerry Garcia."

"You mean the Jerry Garcia, as of the Grateful Dead?"

"The very same. Apparently, he designed some ties before he passed on."

I responded, "The pattern is unusual. I wonder what his body chemistry was like when he thought it up."

"I'm sure I don't know, Ms. Porter. The tie does have a fanciful design, but I like the colors and it goes with several of my outfits."

That sounded like a lead-in to me, and he seemed as if he was softened up enough, so I steered the conversation toward the Big Question. "Not many folks wear suits around here anymore.

Around this time of year, most of the businessmen in town start to dress in PGA Rural, which is pastel sweaters, clashing polo shirts, plaid pants, white socks, and tasseled loafers. There ought to be a law. If I may ask, what brings a man of your sartorial refinement to Ebb?"

Mr. Moore smiled right back at me. He had a warm, lovely smile with just a pinch of danger in it, like he was warning you that there might be hijinks ahead. He said, "I'm a traveling salesman, Ms. Porter. I sell games of chance. I have come to Ebb to sell games of chance."

I have to say that I was so startled by his answer that I had no idea what to say, but Mr. Moore just sipped his water and waited. I finally replied, "My, that is unusual. I don't remember seeing a traveling salesman in Ebb since I was a young girl. What kind of games do you sell, Mr. Moore?"

He answered, "I sell cards, dice, backgammon, traditional board games, any game that involves a fair measure of uncertainty. I specialize in cards. I carry decks from all over the world and in every conceivable price range."

He smiled again. It was that warning smile. "Do you like card games, Ms. Porter? Would you like to see a Siamese double deck in a mahogany box with inlaid mother-of-pearl?"

Well, there it was. One minute I was in complete control and asking the Big Question, and the very next minute I was on the pointy end of a sales pitch. After a few moments, I said, "You know, Mr. Moore, I do play some pinochle over at the Corn Palace on

Thursday nights. But that's only during the winter, and I don't know that they'll be needing many playing cards right now. Maybe they will."

Mr. Moore smiled again, sweetly this time if I may say so, and replied, "I'll stop by, but only to make a social call. I came to Ebb to visit Millet's. I understand that it's the biggest department store in the county . . . "

"It's the only department store in three counties," I said with pride, as if I had anything to do with it myself other than my regular custom.

"Well, that's just perfect," Mr. Moore replied. "If I'm a lucky man, then the proprietor will be interested in purchasing some of my games."

I turned back toward the counter for a minute, but not because I am impolite or because I had to slice more bacon. I just wanted to think a bit. Mr. Moore seemed like such an optimistic man, and I was sure he had driven a long way, but I doubted that Calvin Millet would be buying many old-fashioned games. On the other hand, I could not quite bring myself to believe that any man who dressed so well and drove such an expensive car was really a traveling salesman either.

Well, when was the last time you saw one?

I offered, "It's not my place to say, but I don't know how interested Calvin Millet will be in buying much right now. Things have not been going his way lately, to say the least."

Mr. Moore stirred the ice in his water with his finger and then he said, "Is that a fact, Ms. Porter? By inference, I assume that he is the owner of Millet's Department Store. I don't mean to pry, but I'd appreciate it if you could tell me about the man."

I sat down at the table with my tea and told him the entire sad tale. Mr. Moore listened quietly, as if he was taking notes in his head. He should give lessons to those commentators on TV; he didn't interrupt me one time. When I was done, he said, "It would be an understatement to say that Calvin Millet has been on a losing streak. What about his daughter, Lucy? How is she now?"

"We are all so worried about that sweet little girl," I replied. "Calvin brought her back from the Mayo Clinic right after the tornado—they even stayed with me for a while—but she hasn't returned to school, and a nurse has moved in with them down in Carson. If she's from hospice, and we all suspect she is, then he has finally given up."

Then Mr. Moore made a curious remark. He said, "That's not a very American thing to do, is it, Ms. Porter? Give up I mean."

I wanted to say, "Of course not," but I bit my tongue. He said it with such finality. It didn't seem proper to carry the matter further, so I went back to my chores.

Eventually, Mr. Moore said, "Would you be kind enough to introduce me to Mr. Millet tomorrow morning?"

Naturally, I agreed and then I left Mr. Moore to finish his iced water alone. He seemed to want it that way. He went on a walk right before sunset and didn't return until nine, which is when I lock the doors.

Yes, we lock the doors at night now. Even in Ebb.

Chapter 3

Mr. Moore Meets the Wrong Man

I CAME DOWN to fix breakfast at 6:30 A.M. and Mr. Moore was already sitting in the kitchen sipping some iced water and reading the local paper. He actually stood up when I came into the room—I can't remember the last time that happened—and then he offered me some hot tea. I was appreciative to be sure, but that was a bit more role reversal than I could stand with the lights on and I was afraid that he would want to cook the waffles next.

Since he was already there, I served breakfast in the kitchen. This is not consistent with best B & B business practice but he was so comfortable that I didn't want to ask him to move into the dining room. It seemed like it would be an imposition.

Mr. Moore had some fresh orange juice, a pecan waffle with real maple syrup that I order from Vermont on the Internet, and four strips of fresh bacon that I had sliced the day before. I had the same thing except I made Mr. Moore two waffles but he only wanted one. I hate to see good food go to waste; I always have. I suppose it shows a bit.

While we ate, we talked about the weather. We don't have a lot to crow about in southeast Nebraska, but one thing we do have is weather. The winters don't seem to be so harsh anymore, but there was a week back in January of 1972 when the high temperature in Ebb was minus twenty-two degrees Fahrenheit. That was the high for the whole week. The low was minus thirty-three, and I am not talking wind chill either.

Twenty years ago this May, Ebb got hit with two tornadoes at once. I was going to take the girls to the picture show, but one of the twisters knocked the theater down, and then the two of them churned out of town like they had been working together. Nobody had any electricity that night, so the girls and I stayed home and cooked marshmallows on the fire. The theater was never rebuilt. We have to drive up to Beatrice now.

Eventually, our conversation turned to the tornado that hit the Millet place, and that got us talking about Calvin and Lucy again. It seemed that he was more interested in Lucy this time but, not being a doctor, there was little that I could tell him about her condition. I did not say so to Mr. Moore, but I made a mental note to make some peanut butter cookies for Doc Wiley, who is the last remaining physician in Ebb. I know all about doctor-patient confidentiality, and so does Hank Wiley, but Lucy's condition is a matter of county health, too, and he won't open up to anybody else but me on the subject.

When we were just about finished, I said, "When would you like to walk over to Millet's, Mr. Moore?"

"When can you be ready to go?" he asked.

"Well," I said, "I still have to take Clara's breakfast up to her."

Mr. Moore's brow furrowed up, like it had been plowed by an intoxicated bug. Before he could ask, I replied, "Clara Tucker Booth Yune. She is my full-time lodger."

"You have a permanent tenant?"

"Yes. On the third floor. All of it. She always has the same thing for breakfast: oatmeal with soy milk and cinnamon, cranberry juice, and English Breakfast tea with honey. It will take me just a few minutes to make it."

"I take it she doesn't come down for breakfast."

I laughed and answered, "Clara doesn't come down for much of anything. She's a genuine recluse."

Mr. Moore sat forward and said, "Really? Why is that, Ms. Porter?"

I smiled and told Mr. Moore about Clara; everybody in Ebb likes to go on about Clara. "She's a Tucker. In these parts, that means she was born with a silver spoon in her mouth but, like poor Calvin Millet, she has not had a lucky life. When she was barely out of high school herself, and against the wishes of her family, Clara married the local high school math teacher, a man named Willard Booth. That must have been forty years ago, give or take. They had one child six months later, a boy, but he died in his crib before his first birthday, probably from what they now call Sudden Infant Death Syndrome. At that time, though, it was a complete mystery. Of course, Clara blamed herself; women always do, and she was just a teenaged girl at the time. A few months later, she found out that she couldn't have any more children. That was more than she could take, so she became a Born Again Christian.

"Several years later, her husband Willard was killed when the small plane he was flying in went down in a rainstorm near Olathe, Kansas. Apparently, he lived for about six hours after the crash, but they couldn't find the wreck in time. Clara blamed herself again because she was at a church meeting instead of with her husband. That was more than she could take, so she turned herself into an honest-to-God atheist."

Mr. Moore said, "Life seems to be hard here, Ms. Porter. I'm so sorry."

"I'm not done," I replied. "After twenty years of living by herself and hardly ever seeing anybody, Clara was swept off her feet by the local librarian, a real smart man named Nathan Yune. A few months after they got married, Nathan died of a heart attack. According to Doc Wiley, it was probably induced by sex. Poor old Nathan was a slight man and real, real shy. He had been a bachelor all his life, and the postmortem showed that he had a weak ticker. I guess you could say that sex broke his heart.

"Well, that was more than Clara could take. She went into

catatonic shock: she stopped talking; she stopped eating; she stopped bathing; she stopped brushing; she stopped doing anything. After a couple of weeks in Doc's clinic, he had to send her to a mental institution up in Lincoln.

"I figured she was never coming back, but about five years ago I got a letter from her lawyer proposing that she become a permanent resident of the Come Again. Hank went up to check her out and said she would be fine as long as I watched my P's and Q's, so I agreed. It took Buzz Busby nearly six months to remodel the third floor to her tastes, at her expense I should add, and then she checked out of the mental hospital and into the Come Again in the same afternoon. She came by limousine."

Mr. Moore said, "Does she ever come downstairs?"

"She does on the rare occasion, but it's usually because she's looking for sugar or dishwasher soap or something like that. She never, ever comes down when I have guests. Any time I have lodgers, I have to let her know immediately. It's in her agreement."

"Do you fix her lunch and dinner?"

"No. She has a kitchenette upstairs."

"What should I say if I meet her in the hall?"

"You won't, but if you do, don't worry about having too much of a conversation."

"Why's that?"

"Clara only says two words: yes and no. Even to me. If the place was burning to the ground, she would not yell 'fire.'"

"If I may ask . . ."

I said, "It is a tad out of the ordinary, but two words is a major improvement. When she first moved in, she wouldn't say a thing."

"Really? What happened?"

"Not long after she returned, Clara decided to put up the money for the new town library on the condition that it be named after her second husband. The plan, which made perfect sense to me and every other body in Ebb, was for it to be built on an empty lot on the far end of Main Street that was overrun with weeds. Naturally, she got sued for her good intentions. In fact, the entire Tucker Foundation got sued."

"Why? By whom?"

"The suit was filed by one of those big-city environmental groups. Apparently, they claimed that some sort of endangered insect lived in those weeds. Now, I have sympathy for endangered species, I really do, but have you ever driven down a country road in the summer in this state? You can't go five miles before your windshield is covered in green-and-yellow bug juice.

"Anyway, Clara refused to move the library, and then she refused to settle, and then she refused to testify, so the judge finally had to throw her into jail for contempt. Now, throwing a Tucker into jail for any reason whatsoever is not a career-enhancing move in these parts, so the parties negotiated a settlement, which was that Clara would answer yes and no on the stand. No more, no less."

Mr. Moore shook his head in disbelief. "Just yes and no? That's unbelievable. What happened?"

"Clara's brother, a very big man in Hayes County named Clement Tucker, hired some bug people of his own, and I guess they found the same endangered species in every other county in southeast Nebraska. Either that or they planted them there. Either way, that was the end of the lawsuit, but it was after Clara had testified."

"Really."

"You know, I was sure that that lawsuit would put Clara back on the road to ordinary conversation, I really was, but I was wrong. She stopped dead at yes and no. Doc Wiley says it's one of the devices that she uses to keep the real world at a safe distance. Anyway, she has never been much for doing what people expect of her, me included."

"If she lives here all the time, how do you two communicate? It must be difficult."

"As you might expect, conversation with Clara Yune is something of a chore. You have to fill in the blanks yourself. Luckily, we don't need to talk much. When we do, it's by email."

"So she writes."

"Yes. Her fingers have a full vocabulary. If the place was burning down, she might be kind enough to send me an email. That's why I check it so frequently."

"But she won't talk."

"Just yes and no."

"What an unusual story, Ms. Porter. What does she do with her time?"

"She watches TV—she must have ten TVs up there—and she surfs the Internet. She also exercises a lot. Buzz Busby turned half of my third floor into a gym, lacquered wood floors and exercise gear and all. Clara has a trainer in two times a week, a good-looking young man named Roberto Ling."

Mr. Moore frowned. "She does? How do they talk?"

"They don't. He's an exercise instructor at a special school for deaf mutes up in Lincoln, and he's deaf and mute himself. I suspect that he has taught Clara some sign language, but she has not sent me an email about it and I haven't asked. Even though she will write, Clara is not real fond of email either."

"Hmmm. You said Clara is well-to-do?"

"She's a Tucker, Mr. Moore. They're the richest family in southeast Nebraska by a country mile. The Tucker Foundation, which is run by her brother Clem, owns half the county. To my understanding, Clara is the second largest shareholder in the trust after Clem himself. I know for a fact that she drives him crazy because of it."

"Why?"

"Because she gives her money away from time to time, and when she does, she gives away lots of it. The Nathan Yune Library is just the most famous example. Whenever she does anything real expensive, like building a library or a high school auditorium, Clem has to divest something, and that makes him madder than a flaming Brahma bull—even when he doesn't get sued."

"This Clem Tucker, I take it, is not much of a philanthropist."

"Clement Tucker is a businessman, which is the dead opposite of a philanthropist."

That seemed to get him thinking, which concerned me some because I thought I might have insulted him, but he remarked, "And all she says is yes and no?"

"Yes."

"You know, that is just one word away from a salesman's dream."

"Mr. Moore . . ."

He smiled that dangerous little smile of his and said, "Don't you worry. I would never intrude on her privacy."

"Unless you sell exercise equipment or TVs, I don't think you need to worry too much. Like I said, having a conversation with Clara is a bit of a chore."

AT 9 A.M. SHARP, Mr. Moore and I met out front under the porte cochere. I was wearing a pretty white dress with a pleasant floral design, a red wool shawl, and my new Nike Air walkers. Mr. Moore was decked out in a blue blazer, a pink polo shirt, razor-creased khaki slacks, and spit-polished cordovan loafers. We could've been going to a dance instead of walking up to Main Street, except for my Airs, of course.

Mr. Moore stepped out into the morning sunlight, looked

around the grounds slowly, and took in a long, deep, almost wistful breath. You don't see that kind of appreciation much these days. Then we set off to Main Street at a brisk pace. While we walked, Mr. Moore asked me about my girls, Mona and Winona, which always gets my motor running. They're both fine girls, but Mona was on my mind at the time. Fifteen years ago this June, just one year before she was to graduate from college with a degree in dental hygiene, she married a pre-dent fraternity boy named Marvin Breck.

Mona gave birth to Matthew Breck right on time, which was six months later. Three Decembers after that, she gave birth to Mark. I guess Marv wanted to go for Luke next, but Mona started taking the pill and that was just fine with me, too.

Marv Breck is handsome and tall, and I guess he comes from a good Catholic family, but I have never liked that boy. I could tell from the get-go that he had more artificial ingredients than a Hostess Twinkie, especially that veneer of phony confidence that well-to-do boys get in high school when their daddy buys them a new car.

Marv has been a fully fledged dentist himself for a long time now. He works with his father in the family practice up in Omaha and Mona stays home with the kids. Four years ago, I drove up to the family store to get a front tooth fixed that had been chipped in a fist fight with Al, my ex-husband, back when Mona and Winona were little. What I remember most about the visit was that there were two Breck men in that office and a half-dozen women, all of them pretty young and pretty good-looking. It was like an office full of Barbies. No wonder Marv wanted to follow in his father's footsteps, but sometimes I wonder what happens to those girls when they lose their figures.

I would not have run off at the mouth about Marv so much but I knew Mona wasn't happy. She had called a few nights earlier to talk, and she did not say a word about her husband. All she talked about were her two boys, which is how I knew that something was wrong, so I called Winona because she always has the latest scoop. Don't ask me why, but when I want to know what is really going on with Mona, I have to call Winona, and vice versa. I've never understood it, but that's the way it is.

I was just telling Mr. Moore about Mona's little boys when we ran into Lulu Tiller, who is the town veterinarian. Lulu is a two-time divorcée and she can talk to the animals; I've seen her do it. That morning, she was taking six dogs to the park and not one of them was on a leash. When she stopped to say hello, the six of them sat down in a semicircle at the same time, like they were synchronized setters.

Now, Lulu is another person who can take some getting used to. She is friendly and smart, and she will volunteer for anything at all, but if she has an itch, she will scratch it right then and there, and it doesn't matter where she itches either. She can be in the middle of a sentence or in the middle of a dance or in the middle of Christmas dinner; it doesn't matter where she is or what she's doing. She seems to itch a lot, too. According to Doc Wiley, it's the animals. Like so many unlucky women, she is allergic to the thing she loves the most.

Well, I introduced her to Mr. Moore and we visited for a minute or two. Just when she was starting to scratch her bottom, though, the dogs got up and told Lulu that they had to go. At least that's what she said. Thank goodness she didn't have to scratch anything else; I hadn't had time to warn Mr. Moore.

We ran into several more woman friends of mine after that, and Mr. Moore was always gracious and friendly, but we eventually managed to work our way to Millet's Department Store. It's a rectangular, two-story building that runs along Main Street for an entire block, including the parking lot. At that particular time, the store's windows were full of big red Spring Sale signs. They had been there for nearly a month, even though spring was only two days old. I'm not a storekeeper, but my guess is that so many for sale signs for so long is not really a good sign.

Millet's has double glass doors at the main entrance. The left one says WELCOME and DEPARTMENT, one word right over the other, and the right one says TO MILLET'S and STORE. Just as Mr. Moore opened the WELCOME DEPARTMENT door for me, none other than Clem Tucker pushed his way out of the TO MILLET'S side. Instead of going on in, I stopped right there so I could make introductions. Clem stopped, too, and then he looked us both over like he was thinking about which one of us he was going to buy.

"Clement Tucker," I said, "I'd like you to meet Mr. Vernon Moore. He's staying with me at the Come Again for a while."

Mr. Moore put out his hand, smiled, and said, "Please call me Vernon. It's a pleasure to meet you. Ms. Porter has told me so much about you."

"Really? What has she said?" he replied.

"That you are the Duke of Hayes County."

"Wilma flatters me. I'm just a businessman trying to eke out a living in rural Nebraska."

The two of them stood there eye-to-eye, shaking hands for a bit longer than seemed natural to me. I suspected that it was because Clem rarely met a man whose wardrobe was on a par with his, but then he said, "Have we met before? Your name sounds familiar to me."

They finally stopped shaking and Mr. Moore replied, "I don't think so, Mr. Tucker. I don't believe we have. I'm sure I would remember you."

Clement smiled and said, "Call me Clem; everybody does. What brings you to our little town?"

"I'm a salesman, Clem. I sell games of chance. Ms. Porter has been kind enough to bring me over here to introduce me to Calvin Millet."

Mr. Moore had finished sizing Clem up, but Clem was still at it. He said, "Well, Vernon, I can see from your attire that you are good at what you do, but I've just met with Calvin myself and I can tell you that this may not be the best time for a sales call. Has Wilma said anything to you about his recent misfortunes?"

"She has, and I appreciate your advice. Perhaps Ms. Porter and I will just say hello and I'll come back another time."

Clem was silent for a moment and then he said, "I have another appointment right now but, before I go, may I have one of your business cards?"

"Of course." Mr. Moore brought a card out of his inside blazer pocket so fast that I had to rethink seeing it. Clem paused for a second, too, and that was how I noticed the card itself. The letters were embossed in navy blue and crimson on sand-colored, translucent rice paper. I don't think I've ever seen a prettier business card, and I have a thousand of them in my collection in the study at the Come Again.

Clem looked at Mr. Moore's card and then asked, "Do you carry a cell phone?"

"I don't anymore. I used to, but it went off three times one afternoon while I was hiking through the Cascade Mountains, so I heaved it into a deep ravine. I regret it now because I'm sure that it wasn't the ecologically sensible thing to do, but I haven't missed that contraption since. You can reach me during business hours through my answering service and anytime via email. If Ms. Porter doesn't mind, you can ring me at the Come Again, too."

Clem showed no reaction to Mr. Moore's admission of unbusinesslike behavior, which was a surprise. That man spends more time on the phone than a Hollywood agent. Instead, he handed Mr. Moore one of his own cards. It says "Clement Tucker" in the middle and then it just lists his business phone number, starting with a +1. I guess we're all supposed to know what he does for a living.

Clem said, "It was an unexpected pleasure to meet you, Vernon. I hope you enjoy your stay in Ebb. And it's always a great pleasure to see you, Wilma. You look just lovely, as always, except for those terrible shoes. What ever possessed you?"

Clem Tucker likes his women to be women, meaning either dressed to the nines or not at all. His inability to compromise in this regard, or any other, had contributed to the untimely end of our otherwise enjoyable and nearly secret affair. I replied sweetly, "If I had only known that we were going to meet, dear, I would have worn a low-cut black dress, fishnet hose, and spiked heels to walk all the way over here. In the morning."

Clem smiled and said, "Don't you lead me on, Wilma Porter. You know I am a weak and vulnerable man. I suppose you're taking good care of my great-great-great-grandfather's house."

"Oh I am," I said with a big grin. "He drifts in regularly to check on the place."

"I'm sure he does, Wilma, I'm sure he does. And how is my elder sister, Clara?"

"She's just fine. When I saw her this morning, she was chugging on the StairMaster and watching a Claudette Colbert movie on the TV at the same time. You should stop by and say hello."

"Really? Do you think Clara would want to visit, even for a minute?"

I batted my eyelashes and answered, "Not unless you've

started up a charity, dear, which we are all expecting any day. In the meantime, I might want to see you, if you behave like a gentleman."

Clem laughed out loud. "Would that be a veiled invitation to dinner, Wilma Porter?" Then he turned to Mr. Moore and added, "I have a personal chef, but she's only the second-best cook in the county."

I said, "I'm better company, too. Maybe I'll think about it."

Clem looked me in the eye and replied, with what appeared to be a pinch of actual sincerity, "Please do," then headed across the street toward the bank. Mr. Moore just gazed at me, but the question was all over his face.

I answered, "I was just kidding. I haven't seen old Silas the Second since I put in the Jacuzzi tub, and that was more than a year ago."

Without looking even a bit incredulous, Mr. Moore said, "But you have seen him? You're certain?"

"Oh yes. He first appeared when I moved in with the girls, and he stopped by again when I was remodeling the third floor for Clara."

"He's a ghost. Is that what you're saying?"

"That's right, but he seems to be an infrequent spirit. I think he just wants to keep an eye on his house."

Mr. Moore said, "That's very interesting. Very interesting indeed."

So many people, men in particular, think I'm off my rails when

I mention Silas the Second that I don't often talk about him, but Mr. Moore seemed genuinely intrigued. I started to ask him why, but he turned and held the Welcome Department door open so that I could go in the store. We worked our way slowly down the middle aisle toward the wooden, double-wide stairs at the back of the store. Mr. Moore stopped several times to check out a bottle of perfume or a small kitchen appliance or a canvas bag. He always looked at the sale price, too. I stopped at the cosmetics counter, but just for a second.

When we finally reached the second-floor administration offices, Lily Park was on station, just like always. Lily is a small Asian woman of Korean extraction, but she's a fourth-generation American, a third-generation Nebraskan, a two-time divorcée, a single mom, and two-time treasurer of the Quilting Circle. Her father was a field hand and she still talks like one. I don't know why, but it always makes me giggle when she says "Bull-shee-it" in a meeting, just like one of the good old boys.

Lily is Calvin's AA, which is administrative assistant for short, but like so many in her profession she is more of a sentry than a secretary. The way she protects Calvin, I wouldn't be surprised if she kept a Colt in her desk drawer. Lily is no danger to her friends, though, so I walked right up and introduced my new lodger. While I was doing the talking, he handed her his card, which she studied intently.

Mr. Moore said, "I'm a salesman, Ms. Park. I sell games of chance. I was hoping that you could find me a spot on Mr. Millet's calendar today. I won't need much of his time."

Calvin's door was shut. Lily looked at me with a question in her eyes. I smiled back; what else could I do? She replied flatly, as if her voice was a recording, "Mr. Millet is busy all day, Mr. Moore."

He responded, "Every good man I have ever known is busy during working hours, but a smart man can always find time for a good proposition. Is there a time in the afternoon when I can return?"

"I don't think so, Mr. Moore. This is the wrong time for sales, you know. Mr. Millet usually does his buying after the beginning of the month. On the Internet."

Mr. Moore nodded his head, as if in agreement, and then he said, "I can see he's a prudent man. By then, however, I will have been on my way. Is there any chance that you can find me an hour on his calendar tomorrow? It's a small amount of time and I am sure that he will find it profitably spent."

Lily looked Mr. Moore over carefully and sighed. "If you can hold your horses for a minute, I'll check his schedule." She turned sideways and began fiddling with the keyboard of her Apple. A few moments later, she turned back and said, "Mr. Millet has a thirty-minute slot tomorrow at ten-thirty, but that is all the time he has."

Mr. Moore smiled broadly and answered, "That will be perfect, Ms. Park. I appreciate it very much. Please take another one of my cards for your files."

Lily put her hand out and Mr. Moore took it in his, softly and just for a moment, while he looked her in the eyes. He said,

"Thank you again, Ms. Park," and then he gave her his card. I swear she blushed.

We walked out of Millet's the same way we walked in, but as soon as we were back on the street, Mr. Moore said to me, "I take it that the man we met coming in was the same Clem Tucker you mentioned this morning, Ms. Porter."

"The very," I said.

"Would you tell me more about him?"

"It was Clem's ancestors who first settled here back in 1825, and it was his great-great-great-grandfather Silas who originally built the Come Again as the family mansion. This used to be Tucker County, too, but Silas the Second changed it in order to get Rutherford B. Hayes to visit here during his first presidential campaign."

"Did it work? Did he come?"

"Yes. All of the Tucker men have been Republicans ever since, and they've all been wheeler-dealers. It is a genetic defect that is passed down from generation to generation. Clem's daddy even had the brass to try to change the county name back to Tucker about thirty years ago, and the state legislature actually bought it, if you get my meaning, but it was voted down in county referendum."

Mr. Moore nodded and remarked, "Well, the latest in the line of Tucker males seems to have survived the setback. I guess I would be correct in assuming that he is an influential man in this part of the state."

"Clement Tucker is an influential man in the whole state," I replied.

Before I could explain, Mr. Moore said, "I see a Starbucks down the street. Could we continue our conversation over coffee and a sticky bun?"

I couldn't remember the last time any man had offered to buy me anything other than aggravation. I was so tickled, I probably blushed myself. Just a little.

Chapter 4

What Everybody Ought to Know about Country Boys

AFTER TWO WAFFLES for breakfast, I thought a sticky bun would be too rich, so I had some chocolate biscotti with a cup of lemon tea. Mr. Moore ordered up a grande, no-whip coffee frappuccino. Can you imagine? At the time, I wasn't even sure what that was, but he offered me a sip and it tasted like a coffee smoothie. I drink it myself now, but with the whip.

You know, people in this country are always talking about visionaries, Mr. Visionary This and Mr. Visionary That, but I think that the greatest visionary in twentieth-century America was that man Howard at Starbucks. Who else could have ever predicted that normal people would pay four dollars for a cup of foo-foo coffee the size of Saskatchewan? I'm sure I don't know.

After we got our drinks, Mr. Moore and I sat down in a booth in the corner, and then he said, "Well it's not even ten-thirty and it's been an interesting day already. What else can you tell me about Clem Tucker?"

I was chewing on my biscotti so I couldn't answer right away, but it gave me time to organize my thoughts. As soon as I swallowed, I replied, "I don't mind, Mr. Moore, but why are you so interested in Clem? I don't think he'll be buying any games."

"I'm sure that's true, Ms. Porter, but the question goes both ways. Clem asked for my business card. Why? I sense that you two have something of a past, that you can tell me a lot more about him than most of the folks here in Ebb."

I blushed for the second time that morning and then answered, "Mr. Moore, would you please call me Wilma? Nobody over the age of eighteen ever calls me Ms. Porter. When you call me that, I am not always sure you're talking to me."

"Of course, and you must call me Vernon."

"I appreciate that, Mr. Moore, but I just wasn't raised that way. Every man I address by his first name is either a generation younger than I am, or I have known him very, very well. Do you understand?"

"Yes, Wilma, I do. You have a roundabout way of explaining things very succinctly."

"You will keep that item to yourself, Mr. Moore?"

"Of course I will. Please tell me about Clem."

"Okay, but if I do, will you tell me more about yourself? I feel as if I am always doing all the talking." That came out too fast and it made me shake my head. Every man I have ever known in the Biblical sense would have used it against me for a week.

Mr. Moore chuckled a bit but answered, "I'll try to do a better job of holding up my end of the conversation, Wilma. Please go on."

I had to quit chewing again, but then I wiped the edges of my mouth. "Well, Clement Tucker was born and raised right here in Ebb. Actually, he was raised in the Come Again back when it was still the Tucker manse. So was his sister Clara, which, according to Doc Wiley, is probably why she wanted to move back.

"For a rich boy, Clem is real smart. He was the salutatorian at Hayes High, and then he went to Grinnell over in Iowa, which I hear is a very good college. Then he took a boat over to London, England, to get himself a doctorate degree, but that was where he made his first big mistake: he got married. The second mistake he made was to was bring his English wife back to Ebb.

"There are two ways to live comfortably in this town. One is to go away and get married and then come back after you get divorced, which is popular with us town folk. The other is to marry somebody here and get divorced later, but without ever leaving town. That is the strategy most farmers seem to prefer. But the one thing you can't do is leave Ebb single, get married somewhere else, and then bring your spouse back here. That will not work. Clem tried to bring his snooty English bride home to Ebb, and he paid a handsome price for his poor judgment. She left him and went back to London not three years later, so Clem had to raise their daughter Mary Beth by himself. By his own admission, he was not very good at it, so when Mary Beth left Calvin Millet and their daughter Lucy, it was too déjà vu. I believe he has felt guilty about it ever since, as if he was the one who ran out on Calvin and Lucy instead of his child.

"When Mary Beth sued for divorce, Calvin refused to settle. Folks around here are not too fond of settling things out of court when it's a matter of principle, and everything around here is a matter of principle, so Mary Beth had to come back for the trial. About one hour before she arrived, her father flew a private plane up to Canada, ostensibly to do some hunting. Clem came back later to testify, for exactly one day, and he has kept his distance from Calvin and Lucy ever since. I was surprised to see him leaving Millet's today. I assume he was doing some shopping."

I took a sip of my tea and Mr. Moore said, "You may be right, in a manner of speaking. Tell me more."

"I don't want to give you the wrong impression about Clement Tucker. He is not a weak man. While he was living in England, his daddy, who was named Leon, and a local waitress were killed when the old man got drunk and wrapped Clem's '63 Corvette Split Window coupe around a telephone pole down toward the River House. Naturally, the waitress's parents sued the Tucker Foundation for a gazillion dollars. That's when Clem, who was the sole male heir, had to come home from England, new wife in tow.

"He got his daddy's automobile insurance company to take the weight on the wrongful death lawsuit and then he sued the phone company. I guess it was for unlawful placement of a telephone pole. Whatever it was, he won a seven-digit settlement from them—nobody can understand how to this very day—and he made it stick through about six appeals, too. In other words, Clem made money on the whole enchilada, a lot of it."

"What else can you tell me?"

"After Clem's wife left him and he finally got all of his lawsuits settled, he reorganized the Tuckers' business interests. First, he bought the local real estate company and then he converted the family from farmers into farm owners. Next, he took over the town bank and bought a controlling interest in the John Deere franchise which, with the possible exception of Millet's, are the two most important businesses in the county. A few years later, Buzz Busby sold Clem a fifty-one percent interest in his construction company. At the time, he was doing small-time work, what we used to call barnyard renovations around here. Now Buzz handles most of the civil engineering in southeast Nebraska and he is a rich man."

"Has Clem ever invested in Millet's, Wilma?"

"I don't think so. I'm not close to Calvin myself, but I think I would know if he did."

"I think you would, too. Do you have any idea why not?"

"Well, I don't suppose that Calvin would want to sell a controlling interest in the store, although that's what I thought about Buzz Busby, and Clem will not buy anything less. Maybe Clem thinks Millet's is a bad investment, or maybe he has been waiting until the price goes down."

"From what you've told me, the price may be pretty low right now, Wilma. I noticed that Clem had no bags or packages when he left the store this morning, and that may mean that he wasn't shopping there in the conventional sense. The question that comes to my mind is, What would he do with Millet's if he bought it?"

"What do you mean, Mr. Moore?"

"In the retail business, it used to be location, location, location. But everybody with any money has a car and a computer now, so the business is all about brands and fads and scale and price. That's why Wal-Mart can put a low-price superstore in the middle of nowhere, and why there are very few independent department stores left, even in the big cities. They just can't compete with the national chains."

"So what do you think Clem will do?"

"If Clem Tucker is the kind of businessman I think he is, then he'll do whatever is in his best interest. When we know what his best interest is, then we'll know what he's most likely to do."

I don't know why, but I started to tear up right there in Starbucks. Maybe it's the early onset of menopause, but I seem to cry a lot these days. Mr. Moore handed me his napkin and tried to divert my attention. He said, "Tell me, Wilma, is Clem Tucker a fair man?"

I regained my composure and replied, "I think he is, Mr. Moore, but don't be fooled. Mainly, he's a hard, tough man."

"You said something like that earlier, Wilma. I get the idea that you're trying to warn me. What is it?"

"A lot of city boys underestimate country boys, and I'll tell you why. Every country boy is in the 4-H, even the rich ones, because it keeps them busy after school, at least until they get old enough to play football. Most of the 4-H boys raise livestock to show at the county fair. They raise them from sucklings, they give them names, they feed them, and they wash them. Then a few days after the fair, those boys go home and find out that their pet pig or pet lamb or pet heifer is on the menu for dinner.

"Farming is a hard-hearted life. Country boys eat their pets. After that, everything else is easy."

Mr. Moore didn't say a word for some time. I was beginning to think it was my turn to ask some questions anyway, and I didn't want him digging into my past relationships, so I said, "Is that enough about Clem? What about you? What can you tell me about yourself?"

He was just about to answer my question when Loretta Parsons landed in our booth out of nowhere, right next to my new boarder. She winked at me and then turned her torso, which is the second best in Ebb, toward Mr. Moore and said sweetly, "Why Wilma Porter, I see you have been keeping a secret man in your private reserve. Will you introduce us, darlin'?"

That woman has absolutely no shame, which is one reason why she's my best friend. I said, "Loretta, dear, this is Father Vernon Moore. He is a Catholic priest, but he's in disguise because he's here on a secret mission. If you utter one word, then his life will be in peril and the Vatican will have you deported to Uruguay."

In a bad Irish brogue, Mr. Moore said, "Bless you my child. I presume that you are Loretta Parsons, owner of the Bold Cut Beauty Salon? When were you last at the confession?"

Loretta looked at me coolly and remarked, "This man is no priest. Just look at those clothes." Loretta turned back to Mr. Moore and continued, "Let me see your hands, darlin'."

Mr. Moore put both of his hands on the table, palms down, like he was going to type something. Loretta looked them over one at a time, carefully checking his nails. I could tell that she was checking for a wedding band, too. She said, "Your nails have been manicured but it's been a while. How long?"

"About three weeks," Mr. Moore said in a normal voice.

Next, she reached up and ran her immaculate, lipstick-red nails through the side of Mr. Moore's gorgeous white hair. "Umhmm. I can see that. And you need a trim, too." She winked at me again, and I had to put my hand to my mouth to avoid laughing out loud.

Mr. Moore said, "I'm happy to hear that your salon is so versatile, Loretta, but I think a manicure and a haircut would be enough."

Loretta looked at me out of the corner of her eye. "What time would be convenient for you?"

"Tell me, Loretta, will you be handling me personally?" This time, Mr. Moore winked at me. I was starting to feel like the judge at a winking contest.

Loretta made a little pout with her mouth and responded, "Is that what you prefer?"

He replied, "Well, I don't know, Loretta. I don't know anything about you except that you're a good friend of Wilma's."

Loretta batted her eyelashes like a cartoon harlot. "What would you like to know, darlin'?"

"Were you born around here? Where did you grow up?"

She smiled and answered, "Tell me, how many other black people have you seen in Ebb?"

I said, "Loretta moved here about ten years ago. Isn't that right?"

She continued, "That's a true fact. I was born and raised in North Omaha, which is the Midwest version of the great American ghetto."

"How did you become a beautician?" Mr. Moore asked.

"I earned my beautician's certificate after I graduated from Omaha North, and then I got myself a job over at the Crossroads cutting white women's hair. The reason I did was because I wanted to save enough money to open my own salon, and the big hair money was at the boutiques on the west side. It still is, I suspect."

"But why Ebb? Why a rural town?"

Loretta made another face and answered, "It's not normally my policy to be honest with a man. Most men don't like truthful women, but you're old enough to know better, so I'll give you the straight skinny. I moved here because I saw a news special about Ebb."

I smiled. Mr. Moore sat back a bit and said, "A what?"

"I remember it like it was yesterday. I was at home trying to make an airline reservation, and I had just spent thirty minutes on the phone trying to figure out how to get a special plane ticket that was advertised in the *World-Herald*. The first recording gave me eight options. Eight options! Can you believe that? I listened to them twice and then picked the one that I thought was right, and that got me eight more options. I thought I picked the right one again, but it was wrong so I had to start over. After two more tries, I picked the option that asked for personal assistance. What a hoot that was. I had been holding for about fifteen minutes when this TV news special came on.

"At that moment in time, Ebb had just passed a law banning automated teller machines, and there were lawsuits flying all over the place. I said to myself, 'Lo, honey, any town with no ATMs is your kind of town.' "

I said, "Go on, dear."

Loretta continued, "I got on the phone and found out that there was no beauty salon in Ebb, not even a barbershop, so I came down here for the weekend instead of flyin' down to San Antonio to see a former beau. Of course, I stayed at the Come Again and met Wilma. She walked me all over town and we became fast friends. I don't know how much she's told you, but Ebb is a very special place."

Mr. Moore looked at me and said, "Wilma has told me a lot, Loretta, but not much about the town. I'm sure it's because I haven't asked the right questions. Will you tell me?"

I answered, "It's not a state secret. Ebb is where women come after their divorces. Originally, it was just Ebb-born women, but then their friends came to visit and, pretty soon, some of them started moving here after they got divorced, too. Then we got together, and it turned out that we all wanted the same thing: we just wanted people to be pleasant to each other. So a few of us formed the Quilting Circle, a club that has two goals: the first is to preserve a rural American art form; the second is to make Ebb the nicest place on Earth the year round. While we're making our quilts at the clubhouse, we like to talk about what we can do to make things friendlier. Getting rid of ATMs was our first controversial move. It made perfect sense to us, but Clem's bank sued and so did the state banking commission, and the next thing you know, we were on Channel Five in Omaha."

Loretta chimed in, "That story made it to the newspapers and all the local radio shows, too. Wilma will never tell you herself, but she was even on NPR."

My boarder said, "Why Wilma, I had no idea you were famous. Tell me what happened. Who won the lawsuit?"

"It was a long fight, " I answered. "Clem Tucker won in the end, of course, but you can't find a single ATM in Ebb anyway."

"How is that?" Mr. Moore asked.

Loretta fluttered her eyelashes and said with a smile, "The Quilting Circle is not just a political force, Mr. Moore, it's also an economic force. Most of the stores on Main are owned by women, including the Starbucks franchise, both gas stations, the grocery store, and my salon. All of us, and two hundred more, belong to the Quilting Circle. When the law didn't work, we found another way to convince Mr. Tucker to dispose of his ATMs."

I picked right up where Lo left off. "Ebb is a woman's town, Mr. Moore. The Circle is a big, big part of it. We have six of the eight seats on the County Council. The mayor of Ebb has been a woman for eight straight years. We have the best public schools in the state because the superintendent of our schools is a woman. So is the county sheriff, and we don't have much crime here either. Mostly, though, Ebb is just a nice place to live."

Loretta said, "Which means people talk to people here, darlin'. Women talk to women, neighbors talk to neighbors, parents talk to children, and customers talk to proprietors, not to some damn machine."

Mr. Moore smiled and remarked, "It does sound as if you have things your way."

Loretta replied, "Not quite, darlin'. Othello had his Iago, Captain Ahab had his Moby-Dick, and we have Wilma's former flame, Clem Tucker, to deal with." Loretta put her hand on mine and continued, "It sure is a shame that those two broke up, because we used to have a real good idea of what that man was up to. We don't anymore, but as long as we have the Circle, we still have leverage."

"Are there any men in this Circle of yours?"

I started to answer but Loretta was faster to the punch. "Are you kidding? The next thing you know, we would have pool tables, fistfights, and titty nights. That's the last thing we want."

Mr. Moore sat forward and said, "I don't know why, but I sense that you have a certain attitude toward men. Are you a divorcée, too?"

Loretta chewed on his question for a second or two before she answered, "No I'm not, but I do have a certain attitude toward men. In fact, I have two of 'em. In the first place, I don't think that men should ever be allowed to meet in groups of six or more. When a bunch of men get together, especially a bunch of old white men, bad things always happen. No disrespect intended, but there ought to be a law against it."

"None taken. To the contrary, I agree."

Loretta went on as if my new lodger had not said a thing. "But one at a time, or even two, I have a different feeling altogether: I love men to death, or at least I want to. When I was a teenager, I loved tennis players, but that never worked out. Then I liked Air Force men for a time; there's a bunch of them in Omaha, but that didn't work either. For the last ten years, all I've wanted is a single, lone man with some civility, loyalty, and an IQ twice his age. I've been disappointed in my quest so far, but I haven't given up. How about you, Mr. Moore? Do you fit my needs?"

I started to choke on my biscotti and Mr. Moore laughed out loud; then he answered, "You're one hell of an attractive woman, Loretta, but I don't know if I do. For a man of my years, your IQ requirements may be a bit strenuous."

"Well, at least you seem to be able to carry on a conversation. Maybe I'll waive the IQ test pending a report on your manners."

"I am mightily relieved, ma'am."

Loretta looked at her watch, frowned, and said, "You still want that manicure and cut, darlin'?"

"Yes I do. My schedule is flexible for the rest of the day. What time would be convenient for you?"

"How about the end of the day, say five o'clock?"

"That would be perfect. And then perhaps you would join me for a walk to the Come Again, followed by dinner for the three of us at the Stake House in Nebraska City."

Loretta can be a hard and fast woman, but his invitation caught her as flat-footed as a wood duck. I was surprised, too. I hadn't been invited to an out-of-town dinner since the Cornhuskers' last game, which was more than four months past, but I managed to accept for both of us.

Well, Loretta and I had to discuss what we were going to wear right then and there. Once we had that all sorted out, she said, "Wilma darlin', we have got to talk about something else. Right this minute."

"What, dear?"

"It's Circle business, darlin'."

Mr. Moore said, "That must be my cue. I need to head off to the library anyway. I'll see you at five, Loretta. Thank you very much for all your help, Wilma, and for your company, too. It's been a lovely morning."

We both watched Mr. Moore leave the store. For a man of his age, he had nice buns.

Loretta was reading my mind. "My intuition tells me that there's something special about that one. How's Doc Wiley's supply of Viagra? I may be needin' a starter kit."

"Loretta Parsons, don't you even think about it. He's just passing through. You know he is."

"Wilma Porter, that man is no traveling salesman. His jacket is made of silk and those shoes are Ferragamos."

That made me pause for a minute. I said, "What do you think he does?"

"I don't know; I just arrived on the scene a few minutes ago. If he's staying at the Come Again, then that's your job."

"That's true, Loretta. It is my job, and I was just getting him to talk when you showed up and hijacked the conversation."

"Well, I'm not going to apologize. We can loosen his tongue tonight. If he can afford those shoes, he can spring for a decent bottle of wine. Afterward, we can cuddle in the backseat while you drive home."

"You're a bad, bad woman, Loretta Parsons. Now what was it that you just had to tell me in private?"

"Bett Loomis came in early this morning before she finished her route. I figured she wanted a massage, hauling all that mail around does seem to hurt her sacroiliac so, but all she wanted was a cigarette and a cup of decaf in the back room."

"Well, what did she say?"

"She delivered a big white envelope to Clem Tucker this morning. She said she couldn't be sure . . . "

"Bett opens those things up. You know she does. She has a jar of paste in the truck so she can seal them back up. I've seen her do it."

Loretta shrugged her shoulders and continued, "She said it was a financial report."

"Clem gets those things in the mail all the time."

"Does he get 'em from Wal-Mart?"

Chapter 5

Goin' Fishin'

ABOUT THE TIME that Loretta and I were visiting with Mr. Moore at Starbucks, Lily Park was in Calvin Millet's office going over his schedule. He seemed distracted, but when she handed him Mr. Moore's card he reacted sharply, "Vernon who? Who is this?"

"Wilma Porter marched him in. His name is Vernon Moore."

"Lily, this man's card says he is a traveling salesman. Those people went out with white bucks, string ties, and tail fins."

"I know."

"Did he have any sort of sample case with him?"

"Nope."

"Then he's not sellin' anything, Lily. What does he really want?"

"I don't know."

"Okay. Fine. Then why do I have an appointment with him?"

Lily hardly ever took her eyes off of her notepad when she talked to Calvin. "A woman's intuition," she replied.

Calvin sat there studying Mr. Moore's business card. Lily volunteered, "That card is not the only thing. He was expensively dressed, in a business casual sort of way. He stands straight as a rail, too, and he's polished, like a military man."

"So you think he wants something else. Do you think he could be a broker or a buyer? For God's sake, I haven't even put the ad in the paper yet. How could he know?"

"I don't know that he does, but he does seem sincere. Mostly, though, I don't think a man with his posture should be taken lightly."

"What else is there for tomorrow?"

"You have a meeting with the bank at two."

"Hmph. Clem didn't say a word to me about it, as if I should be surprised about that. Which one of his leeches is it?"

"It's Buford."

Lily was speaking of Buford Pickett. I've known him ever since we were in preschool together, but it's not as if we're good friends. He was an only child, Buford was, and not very friendly, even as a boy. He was never good-looking either, and that was before he acquired a stomach the size of a commercial seed bag and the longest comb-over in the Midwest.

Buford's appearance has been known to give people the wrong impression about him, but he's a bigwig at the bank and for only one reason: he always gets his money. I mean he always gets his money. I got behind on my payments a few times before Clara moved in, God bless her soul, and I can tell you that it's not a pleasant experience when Buford Pickett comes calling for his money. Any farmer in the area code will back me up on that.

Because of his success at the bank, Buford is very well-to-do, especially for a local boy who's not married to a Tucker. He buys himself a new Cadillac convertible every year, Cornhusker red of course, with a white top and white leather interior, but it never seems to help him from a social point of view. Loretta says he spends a lot of his time with one of her girls in the back room over at the Bold Cut.

Calvin said, "Buford Pickett! That's just great! What did he say he wants, as if I need to ask?"

"He said it's a general account review."

"Yeah, right. Just an hour ago, the owner of his bank was in here telling me why I should sell controlling interest in my family's store to him for forty cents on the dollar. He was a gentleman about it, too; he even asked me about Lucy. If he hadn't tried to steal my store first, I might have mistaken his interest in my daughter for genuine, grandfatherly concern.

"Tomorrow, Buford Pickett is going to explain to me what will happen if I don't settle up my debts, meaning sell to Clem Tucker, and he will be a perfect gentleman about it, too. He will never mention Clem's intentions. He will never threaten me with foreclosure either; he'll just speak in general terms. Very cold and businesslike. The thought makes me gag."

Lily didn't reply. She just kept her head down, as if she had found her Lamaze spot in the middle of her steno pad. This is something that all of us natural-birth mothers know how to do when we are under pressure. If you men will pay attention, you can sometimes seeing us taking slow, deep breaths through our noses, and then exhaling quietly through our mouths. Of course, you usually don't pay attention.

Calvin didn't either. After a while, he said, "Well, I suppose I have to see the man, don't I? Can you at least move the meeting to the morning? After opening, say nine o'clock."

"I'm sure I can."

"Good. Until further notice, I'll be spending my afternoons with Lucy. She doesn't have to see Doc Wiley this afternoon, so we're going out to the lake to do a little fishing."

"Do you think that's wise? For Lucy, I mean."

"It's what she wants, and from now on she gets anything she wants, except in the mornings because I have to mind the store. I'll need a lot of your help. I hope you don't mind."

Lily welled up a bit, but she kept her eyes on her notepad. "Hell no, Mr. Millet. Of course I don't."

"And you think I should see this Mr. Moore."

"It's a feeling, not a thought."

"That's just as good, Lily; I'll see him. But tomorrow my office is going to be a No Bullshit Zone, at least for one half day. I am all out of patience. I don't have any more time for the usual crap, so you may want to warn Buford and this Mr. Moore of yours. Right now, though, I'd appreciate it if you could let me have some time to myself before I have to drive home."

"Would you like a fresh cup of coffee?"

"What I'd really like, Lily, is a bottle of Tennessee sippin' whiskey and a square mile of a Rocky Mountain river valley all to myself. But I guess some coffee will have to do. Thank you."

Calvin left work about an hour later and drove straight home. By the time he arrived, Nurse Nelson had already made him and Lucy a picnic lunch. He changed into blue jeans and a tee-shirt with a smiley face on it while Nurse Nelson loaded up the Jeep. It was fire-engine red—you may have noticed a certain local preference there—with a black removable top. The day was partly cloudy and not too hot or humid, so Calvin took the top off before they left. When they pulled away, Little Lucy was perched on the front passenger's seat, all bundled up in a white blanket, a pink nightgown, fuzzy yellow slippers, a tan fishing hat, and granny sunglasses. I hear she was a sight to see.

When they arrived at the lake, Calvin picked out a nice spot in the grass under an old maple tree, and spread out the blanket; then he picked Lucy up, carried her over, and placed her in the shade. It took him three more trips to get the grocery bag with the utensils and plates and napkins in it, the cooler, all the food that Nurse Nelson had packed, Lucy's medicine kit, the bug spray, and the fishing gear.

It was a school day, so Calvin and Lucy were alone. Lucy didn't say very much while her father unloaded the Jeep; she just sat on the blanket and looked out over the dock to the water. Calvin didn't feel like interrupting either; Lucy hardly ever got to go outside and enjoy the day. After a while, though, he handed her a Coke and asked, "Are you ready for your medicine?"

She smiled and answered, "Okay, Daddy," and then she turned back toward the lake.

Calvin reached into her bag and pulled out her medicine tray, which by my actual count had fourteen different bottles in it, plus an inhaler and an armpit thermometer. Calvin got out Lucy's chart next. She took so many different pills at so many different times that it was necessary to keep track of it all on paper. After the sort of fussing that you would expect from a man, he handed her five pills. She took them one at a time, first putting her head up to let the pill fall toward the back of her mouth, and then looking back down before she took a sip of Coke and swallowed.

After she was done, Calvin handed her a peanut butter and honey sandwich, which was her favorite, and some potato chips on a paper plate.

She looked down at the plate and said, "I'm not very hungry right now."

He replied, "Why not, sweetheart?"

Without looking up she answered, "I'm a little worried, that's all."

Calvin moved over next to her and said, "About what? You're not worried about the house, are you?"

"No, Daddy, I'm not."

"You know I'm going to build another one. I just have to work some things out with the insurance company. That's all."

"I know."

"Then what's bothering you, sweetheart?"

With an innocence that could break the heart of a Chinese warlord, she said softly, "I'm just a little worried about me."

"Why, Lucy?"

She looked her father square in the eye and said, "Because you haven't told me I'm going to get better in a long time."

Calvin started to tear up because he knew it was time for him to tell her the truth about her condition, but he wasn't the least bit ready for it. He mustered up all the courage he could find, then he touched her cheek and said, "I thought Dr. Wiley already told you, honey. Of course you're getting better. You just can't tell yet."

"Is that true? Are you telling me the honest truth?"

Calvin forced out his very best retail smile and answered, "I promise, sweetheart. That's the straight scoop."

"Then why don't I feel better? How come my legs hurt so much? Why can't I walk without that stupid walker?"

"It will take some time for the new medicine to work. Dr. Wiley says you may even feel worse for a bit, but you will get better."

"When did he tell you that?"

"Last night, after you went to bed. Nurse Nelson said you looked better this morning, too."

Lucy turned back toward the lake. After a few seconds, she said, "Nurse Nelson always says I look better. I could be bleeding from my eyes and puking up my liver and Nurse Nelson would say I looked peachy. That's exactly what she would say: peachy."

Both Calvin and Lucy were quiet for a while, and then she said, "Do you miss your mother and father?"

"Yes. Of course. I miss them to this day."

Lucy mulled this over for a second and then asked, "Were they nice?"

Sometimes, even good men don't stop to think about the other person's situation before they speak. It's like their mouths are on autopilot. Calvin said, "Yes, sweetheart. They were both very nice, very special people. I'm sorry you never got a chance to meet them. You would have loved them both to death, just like I did."

Lucy turned her head slowly toward the lake again and asked, "Will you miss me if I die, Daddy?"

Calvin was caught off guard but he got himself together and answered firmly, "That's not a possibility. You can't die before I do. In fact, there's a law against it. I just read about it the other day. The law clearly states that no child can die before her parents. You don't want to break the law, do you?"

Lucy frowned and said, "That's the biggest fib I ever heard."

"It is not. You can check it on the Internet when we get home, but first you have to eat your sandwich. I won't have the gumption to face Nurse Nelson unless you eat the whole thing."

It took some cajoling, but Lucy ate her lunch. After she had taken a short nap in the shade, Calvin said, "Are you ready to go fishing?"

She smiled brightly and said, "Yes. Can I sit out at the end of the dock with you and watch?"

"Of course you can. That's why we came." Calvin took his gear to the end of the dock, and then he came back for Lucy. While he was carrying her out, she said in a whisper, "I hope we don't catch any."

He replied, "Me, too."

Chapter 6

A Zero-Sum Life

LATER THAT SAME EVENING, Loretta, Mr. Moore, and I were escorted to our reserved table at the Stake House overlooking the bluffs of the Missouri River. The setting was just lovely, and Mr. Moore actually held our chairs, mine first and then Loretta's. Our waitress was one of those sweet young things with perfect skin, rosy cheeks, and clear eyes, and she was altogether too innocent and solicitous. Do you know the type I mean? I always worry that those girls will end up marrying a God-fearing, church-going, sociopath of a serial killer; don't ask me why.

For the record, Mr. Moore did not drink anything except iced water and iced tea, but Loretta and I didn't feel even a smidge constrained. We each had a vodka whatever that was pink in color, and Loretta ordered us a bottle of red wine with the main course. She said it was a California Cabernet; I never asked how expensive it was.

During starters, we all talked about familiar things: the weather, the economy, politics, and such. But when the main course arrived, Loretta said, "Well, the purpose of this affair was to get to know you better, Mr. Vernon Moore. Tell us every single thing about yourself."

"What would you like to know?"

"Let's start with the most important item first. Are you married?"

I turned deep red and almost choked on the piece of USDA prime Nebraska filet mignon that I was chewing on. Mr. Moore just laughed and responded, "No."

"Have you ever been married? You don't look like a confirmed bachelor to me, and you don't look gay either."

"I've never been married, Loretta. And no, I'm not gay."

"So you like women?"

"Yes. Yes I do."

"Then how come you've never been married, Vern? Can I call you Vern?"

"Certainly. I guess I've just never found the right woman, Loretta."

"Well, you may be lookin' at her, Vern, but I have some more questions first."

Mr. Moore laughed again, thank goodness, and said, "Fire away. Do your worst."

"Do you have any children? Every black person in the world knows that havin' children and bein' married are two different things."

"No. I don't have any children."

"Good. Too much child support can eat a man up. But are you sure?"

"Yes."

"Are you sure you're sure? That worries me, Vern."

"Really. Why?"

"Do you like sex?"

Well, what is a woman supposed to do? I said, "Shame on you, Loretta Parsons. You get control of yourself."

She replied, "Look at this man, Wilma. He's as cool as a piña colada. He can take it." Then she turned toward Mr. Moore and repeated her last question, verbatim I might add.

Mr. Moore answered, "Yes. Yes, I do."

"Are you good at it? It's not rocket science, darlin'. That's something that a man should know."

Well, that did it. Mr. Moore turned redder than a Cornhusker hat. Loretta smiled and said, "That's all I needed to know, darlin'. You did real well. It's your turn, Wilma."

With considerable relief, I cleared my throat and said, "I hope you'll forgive Loretta. At her advanced age, the blessing of continued virginity can be discouraging, if you know what I mean."

Loretta started to object but I continued, "Tell us about your history. Where were you born?"

"Southern Ohio, Wilma. I was born in a town called New Boston."

"Did you go to school there?"

"Yes, and then I joined the military."

"Truly?" I said. "So did Calvin Millet. That's something that you two have in common. Were you ever sent overseas?"

"Yes."

"May I ask where?"

Loretta interrupted and said, "Wilma, you're just beatin' around the bush. Ask this man the question."

If you added up all the personality in Rutherford B. Hayes County, Loretta Parsons would have half of it, but sometimes that girl can get under my skin. The rest of the time she has the courage to say the things that normal folks won't.

Mr. Moore said, "What else would you like to know?"

Loretta replied, "We want to know what you do. You look a lot more like Ralph Lauren than Willie Loman, and nobody in Ebb, and I mean nobody, has seen a traveling salesman in thirty years."

"That may be true, Loretta, but I am a traveling salesman. I sell games of chance."

"Okay, darlin'. You're a salesman. You must be real good at it. How long have you been sellin' these games of chance?"

"About five years."

"Is that all?"

Before Mr. Moore could answer the obvious, I interrupted and asked, "What did you do before that, Mr. Moore?"

He answered, "I was in retail finance."

"Really? Now that sounds like an exciting job."

Loretta said, "Yes, it does. Why'd you give it up?"

Mr. Moore sat back from the table, as if he was deciding whether or not to answer Lo's question. Then he sat forward and said, "Until six years ago, I was a finance executive at a publicly held retailing conglomerate called RSA, Retail Stores of America. Have you ever heard of it?"

Loretta replied, "I think I have. Didn't they get themselves into hot water with the SEC a few years back?"

"They did, Loretta, and it was on my watch."

She said, "Well, darlin', tell us what happened. And we want the whole, unvarnished story, don't we, Wilma?"

Mr. Moore paused again, but then he said, "Are you sure that's what you want? Do you really want the whole story?"

Loretta answered, "Of course we do. Don't worry; we promise to keep it in complete confidence."

Mr. Moore shook his head and replied, "It's not a secret. In fact, the story was in the papers, all of them."

"Is that a fact?"

"It was. I was the controller, which is a big title for the head accountant, when the CEO retired and the board brought in a new man from the outside: a pretty-boy, Type A youngster named Junior Ray with an Ivy League MBA. Very quickly, I learned that Junior Ray cared about exactly three things: maximizing his personal fortune, minimizing the self-esteem of his subordinates, and exterminating any attempts at conservative accounting. Company performance, which had been thoroughly mediocre under his predecessor, quickly began to deteriorate."

"That's a shame," I said.

Mr. Moore went on, "I became less and less of a 'team player' because I refused to use fringe accounting methods to conceal RSA's troubles. Eventually, I was shuffled over to treasury, which is more of an investment management job than an accounting job. As soon as I was out of the way, Junior Ray cut reserves to practically zero and stopped writing down bad debt and obsolete inventory. After that, he slashed the capital spending budget for the older stores and dumped quality private label suppliers for nickel-and-dime vendors with no reputation, just because they would cut us a few extra points on margin."

Loretta said, "I get it. What happened next?"

"In January, just after Junior's second full year at the helm, the chief auditor came into my office and told me that we weren't going to get a signature on the annual report unless we made radical adjustments to the balance sheet and the P & L, which meant restating the entire year's earnings. Frankly, I was surprised that it had taken her that long to pull the plug. I also knew that it would do no good to see Junior, so I called up the chairman of the board and told him where we stood.

"In hindsight, that probably wasn't the most intelligent thing I could've done. Junior fired me the next morning but, before I left my office, I picked up the phone and called the SEC and the IRS. Five months later, RSA took a massive write-down, closed fifty-five stores, and laid off two thousand employees."

"Oh dear," I said. "That was a shame."

"Yes it was, Wilma. As a matter of fact, I was ashamed. I had never thought of myself as a coward, but I couldn't find the courage to blow the whistle on Junior Ray until a woman forced me to do it. That's always been my curse; I've never been able to quit. I lost every battle with that horse's ass, but I refused to give up. By hanging on too long, I damaged the lives of two thousand other people, and that's a cross I'll bear until my final days."

"What ever happened to that Junior Ray?" I asked.

"He went to jail. I don't know what happened to him after that."

"And what happened to RSA? Did the company survive?"

"It did, Wilma, and they eventually returned to profitability."

Loretta chimed in, "Well, doesn't that mean that you won, Vern?"

"I don't think so," Mr. Moore answered. "I certainly didn't win in time. Too many good people lost their jobs before Junior finally lost his."

"How about you? Did you go to jail?"

"No."

"Then why didn't you go back into retail finance?"

"I tried at first, but nobody, and I mean nobody, was looking for a highly qualified whistleblower."

"But there are a thousand other things that you could have done. Why become somethin' that nobody has seen since the invention of the portable hair dryer?"

"I thought about it for a long time. Maybe it was a midlife crisis, but I felt like I needed to write a new chapter in my life. I had always been interested in games, especially card games and board games that require a good understanding of probability. I didn't want to be a professional gambler, mind you, that's a zero-sum life, but I also promised myself that I would never work for another empty-hearted, pig-headed criminal like Junior Ray. I wanted to be my own boss, so I looked into the possibility of selling games for a living.

"It was hard at first, but I have a going concern now. I report to myself; I keep my own books; every day is a new day. I didn't know it at the beginning, but selling is rife with its own kind of uncertainty. That's the way I like it. Uncertainty is the spice of life."

Well, I had never heard of a notion like that. I guess Loretta hadn't either. It stopped the conversation in its tracks, at least until our innocent, soon-to-be-a-homicide-victim waitress came back to the table to clean up our dishes and offer us some dessert. Mr. Moore didn't want any but Loretta and I decided to share some chocolate cake with vanilla ice cream.

While we were waiting, Loretta said, "That was a sad, sad story, Vern. I'm sorry your career had to end that way."

"Me, too, but it was just a career. I like what I'm doing now a whole lot better."

She smiled at me and went on. "But those times must have been difficult to endure, especially since there was no Mrs. Moore to help you through it all."

Mr. Moore smiled. I'm sure he knew where she was headed.

He answered, "You're right, Loretta. It would have been much easier if I would have had a good woman at my side."

"Do you suppose you never got married because you were looking for the wrong woman?"

Mr. Moore's brow furrowed up and he said, "What does that mean? How could I be looking for the wrong woman?"

Loretta winked at me—I swear to God I thought she was going to start another winking contest—and then she said, "A lot of men do, darlin'; a lot of men do. Can I ask you a question?"

"Of course. Ask me anything you like."

"Now, we haven't known each other for very long, Vern. The question I'm about to ask you isn't going to be easy to answer."

"That's okay, Loretta. Fire away. Do your worst."

"Okay. What do you think of interracial marriage?" Loretta asked it like it was a dare.

I think Mr. Moore took it the same way. He looked at her, and then he looked at me, and then he looked at her again. After a few more seconds, he replied, "That's an easy one. It should be mandatory."

I'm not sure what everyone else in the restaurant was doing because at just that moment it seemed to me that the whole place went as quiet as a forest night during a soft, windless snowfall.

Loretta sat forward, her head cocked, and said, "What did you say?"

"It should be mandatory, Loretta. Compulsory. Like taking Phys Ed in the ninth grade."

I said, "That makes no sense. Why?"

"Because there is no more meaningless matter than the color of a person's skin, Wilma. Even so, humankind has been groping with the issue ever since the Egyptians, and we still can't seem to get the answer right. As trivial as it is, I think it's beyond our capacity as a species, so let's just throw in the towel and eliminate the problem at its source. After about a hundred years of mandatory intermarriage, I think that almost everybody would be a nice even shade of mocha brown, don't you?"

For once in her life, Loretta was incapable of responding. Mr. Moore continued, "It's a personal thing, too. Like many of my hue, I can get a sunburn from a flashbulb. When I was younger, in fact, I got so cooked by the sun that even my eyelids were burned to a crisp, on the inside. Frankly, I could have used a little of the pigment that you have in such abundance." He took a long drink from his iced water.

Loretta remained silent. I was silent. Mr. Moore was silent. I guess Lo couldn't stand it anymore, so she said exactly what I was thinking. "You know, Vern, you can't fool a country girl whether she's black or white or neon blue. There isn't a traveling salesman in the world who would have answered that question the way you just did, I don't care what he did before that. For a fact, there hasn't been a traveling salesman since Dwight David Eisenhower was in office. And even when there was, they didn't dress like European royalty, drive sixty-thousand-dollar cars, or talk like a college sociologist with a minor in black comedy."

Mr. Moore replied, rather smoothly, "Think what you will, Loretta, but there is at least one traveling salesman left."

Well, nobody wanted to talk much after that so Mr. Moore settled the bill and drove us home. It was a sharp, chilly night, but the sky was clear and the moon was near full, so he turned up the heat, opened up the sun roof and put an old doo wop CD on. Don't ask me why, but smack dab in the middle of "This Magic Moment" it became crystal clear to me that something important was going to happen in Ebb, and that Calvin, Clem, and Vernon Moore were all going to play a part in it, maybe even Loretta and yours truly, but I didn't have a clue what it was going to be.

Mr. Moore dropped Loretta off at her place and drove the two of us on to the Come Again. He went straight on up to bed, but I wasn't the slightest bit sleepy, so I went into my den and started to write this story down in my journal. A few hours later, I noticed Silas the Second wafting up the front staircase to the second floor, probably to check out my unusual lodger. I wished him well.

Chapter 7

First Call

THE NEXT DAY, Buford Pickett showed up at Calvin's office just after 9 A.M. He was wearing a pastel-yellow sweater, a flaming-red polo shirt, plaid slacks, white socks, and tasseled loafers. I kid you not. Lily said she darned near passed out at the sight, but I guess she managed to keep her amusement to herself long enough to usher him into Calvin's office. She didn't shut the office door when she excused herself afterward. Every good sentry leaves the door open unless told otherwise, in case her boss needs a rescue. That means, of course, that every good secretary has to eavesdrop. It's in the job description—and the Quilting Circle bylaws.

An antique mahogany desk sat in the middle of Calvin's office. It was always covered in papers and catalogs and brochures. Behind it were wall-to-wall, floor-to-ceiling shelves that were chock-full of books and reports and souvenirs from places like Las

Vegas and Los Angeles and New York. Calvin had some pretty Indian paintings on the side walls that were done by a Native American named Frank Howell, and he had a real Navajo rug under the two chairs in front of the desk. One of those chairs was hardwood with a cane back and seat; the other was dark green fabric and stuffed, like an easy chair. Calvin liked to see which one his visitors chose. After the two men shook hands, Buford picked the soft one and sat down. According to Calvin, most town folk did.

Calvin said, "This is an unexpected pleasure. How can I help you today?"

"I scheduled it yesterday morning with Lily . . ."

"I know, Buford. It's a figure of speech. How can I help you?"

"I'd like to take a few minutes to go over your current accounts at the bank."

"Is it just me, or do you seem to be in a hurry, Buford? What happened to establishing rapport with a valued customer? Wouldn't you like to talk about the weather first, or maybe the Spring Game?"

"No, I wouldn't. Not today."

"Well, that's very straightforward of you. Bravo. This is No Bullshit Day in my office and you score the first point. What's preying on your mind?"

"Your loan status."

"Fine. Okay. What would you like to know?"

"You owe us one hundred and eight thousand dollars on your

secured inventory line, and you are eighty-five days overdue on average, principal and interest included."

"You came here more than a week before the end of the month to tell me that my inventory line is eighty-five days past due?"

"Well, yes sir, I did."

"Buford, how long have you been the loan officer at the bank?"

"Since 1975, not too long after the bank reopened."

"That's a long time, even in these parts. You're a numbers man, aren't you? Isn't that your stock-in-trade?"

"Loaning money is a people business. You know that."

"Yeah, right, Buford, and Booth High Auditorium is going to host the next Hip Hop Music Awards. Tell me something: in the last ten years, what has been the average age of your outstanding receivables?"

"I don't have that number right at my fingertips."

"I don't need it to two decimal points. Just tell me what the answer is in whole numbers, and don't you tell me a tale either."

Buford didn't answer. Calvin said, "Are you sure you don't want some coffee?"

"No, I'm fine. I was just sorting out a few accounts in my head."

"Fine. You take your time."

In case you've never noticed, men of Buford's substantial girth cannot hem, they can only haw. After some hawing, Buford answered, "The average secured, non-farm commercial loan payment is usually about fifty-two days past due."

Calvin said, "Now let's add some seasoning. If fifty-two days is the average, what is it this time of year?"

Buford hawed a bit more and then answered, "More like sixty days, maybe a little bit more."

"Fine. Okay, so I'm only three and a half weeks worse than average."

"Until two years ago, you paid on time."

"That's right, but working capital has gotten scarcer since then. Here's another question for you: in the last ten years, how much interest have I paid the bank?"

Buford did some quick figuring and answered, "Just under one-point-two million dollars."

"During that time, how much of what you've loaned to Millet's or to me personally has been written off?"

"None of it."

"So, from a historical point of view, I must be very low risk. Isn't that true?"

"Yes. From a historical point of view."

"So what's your problem?"

"The problem, Mr. Millet, is that history is in the past."

"Excuse me?"

"Well sir, you have the fourth largest loan balance at the bank, but everybody knows about your recent troubles, and your personal accounts show it. According to our figures, the total value of your personal savings and investment accounts has gone down more than three hundred thousand dollars in the last twenty-four months. You have less than thirty thousand left, excluding the insurance money on your house."

"Well, I have some bad news there, Buford. There won't be any insurance money on the house."

Buford sat forward. "Didn't you have a tornado rider on your house, Mr. Millet? Everybody else does. I do. I thought you did."

"Nope. I canceled it after the divorce settlement. It was expensive and I needed the money for alimony and medical bills. I appealed to the insurance company anyway. I thought they might give me a break because I wasn't hit by that damn tornado; I was rammed by a flying silo. Turns out that I wasn't covered for kamikaze silos either, so they aren't going to pay me a dime."

"That's real bad luck, Mr. Millet. Real bad. Given your situation, how can you possibly bring your loan current?"

"Well, Buford, I don't have a clue. Who would know the answer to that question better than you?"

"But don't you have some other assets? Stocks? Bonds? Real estate? Something you can use to raise some cash?"

"They're long gone. Failure to cure a daughter of an incurable disease has gotten fairly expensive of late."

Buford squirmed around in the chair before saying, "I'm sorry about your little girl, Mr. Millet, I really am. Real sorry. But if you can't reduce the outstanding balance on your inventory line right away, then we're going have to compel you to pay."

"Exactly what does that mean?"

"That means that we'll have to pursue repayment in the courts."

"In other words, you will force me to sell the store."

"Or repair your loan situation in some other way. I won't have any choice."

"You listen to me, Buford Pickett . . ."

"Like I said, Mr. Millet, I don't have a choice."

Calvin considered his options for some time, then said calmly, "You know the farmers max out their credit cards this time of the year. They need time to pay off their bills, and that leaves me cash poor. Hell, I need another ten thousand dollars from you just to make payroll at the end of the month."

"That won't happen, Mr. . . ."

"It happens every damn year, Buford! Check your records. I always catch up in the fall, after harvest. By January, I'm rolling in cash."

"I know what happens every year, Mr. Millet, but you haven't been eighty-five days overdue every year. In fact, you've never been eighty-five days past due before."

"And what happens if Millet's goes under? Will that be good for the bank?"

Buford sat forward quickly and his eyes got real squinty. He asked, "Is that a practical possibility? Is that what you're saying to me?"

Calvin took a very deep breath and looked away. Without looking back, he replied, "No. The store is fine. My receivables problems are seasonal; my personal problems will be resolved within a few months, weeks maybe."

"I'm real glad to hear that, Mr. Millet. Real glad. So when can I expect a substantial payment on your loan? I have a portfolio review with the Loan Committee tomorrow morning. I have to tell them something positive. That was the point of this visit."

"I can't pay you a nickel, Buford. I need more money from you. Ten thousand dollars. Tell them that. It's the truth."

"The committee will refuse. And if you don't reduce your outstanding balance before the end of the month, then you may expect the bank to seek relief in the courts."

"Well, then I'll just have to see you there."

"You will, Mr. Millet. I regret it, but you will."

Calvin shook his head and said, "Did Clem Tucker send you here?"

"Mr. Tucker does not participate in the day-to-day running of the bank, sir."

"That's my understanding, too, but he stopped by himself yesterday morning. He said it was a social call, but he spent more time asking me about my store than about his granddaughter. Do you suppose that was a coincidence?"

"I don't know. Mr. Tucker and I are not on a first-name basis."

"Well, don't get your nose out of joint on that one. Clem Tucker's not the most congenial man in these parts, you know."

Calvin waited for a reply but none was forthcoming. "Are we done, Buford?"

"Yes sir. I guess we're done for now."

Calvin got up from his desk and opened the door to his office. He said, "Lily will show you out."

Calvin didn't feel like shaking hands, but he did it anyway because it was the polite thing to do. "And ask Lily to see me afterward," he said.

Lily walked into Calvin's office a few minutes later, notepad in hand, and sat down in the cane chair.

Calvin said, "Is there anything else on my calendar before your mysterious Mr. Moore shows up?"

"No, Mr. Millet. It's pretty quiet downstairs."

"It's Tuesday morning. What else would it be? I think I'll walk the floor for a while anyway; see if I can find a shopper and sell something expensive. If I miss your Mr. Moore, will you page me?"

"Yes, Mr. Millet."

"One more thing, Lily."

Calvin reached into his drawer, pulled out a checkbook and began writing. Lily waited quietly. When he was done, he said, "After Mr. Moore arrives, assuming he does, I want you take this check over to the bank and cash it."

She looked at it and remarked, "We don't have ten thousand dollars in the store's checking account, Mr. Millet."

"I know we don't, Lily. You go ahead and get it cashed anyway. If you have any trouble, you let me know."

"Yes sir. I'll let you know as soon as I get back."

Calvin stopped and gave Lily a little squeeze on her shoulder on his way out of his office. Lily never took her eyes off her notepad; she knew she would tear up if she did.

Later, Lily had lunch with her best friend, Lulu Tiller. You may remember Lulu; she's the town veterinarian who can talk to the animals. Afterward, Lulu went to visit Loretta at the Bold Cut, and then Loretta called me, so my information was *au courant* by the time Mr. Moore returned to the Come Again, which was at sunset. But I am getting ahead of myself.

Vernon Moore walked in the welcome department door of Millet's at 10:25 a.m. and went straight upstairs. He was wearing a jet-black, double-breasted blazer with gold buttons, a white shirt with gold cuff links, a neon-blue tie, and light-gray slacks, and he was carrying a small, expensive-looking leather briefcase. Lily got him some iced water and seated him in the office, then she paged Calvin, who came up a few minutes later.

When Calvin entered his office, he noticed that his visitor had moved the straight-backed chair closer to the desk. He put out his hand and said, "My name is Calvin Millet. Your name sounds familiar to me, Mr. Moore, but I can't place it. Have we met before?"

The two men shook hands. Mr. Moore replied, "No sir, I don't think we have. I'm sure I would remember you."

Calvin studied his caller's face for a few more seconds, and then took in his attire. "You dress like an investment banker, Mr.

Moore, but your card says you're a salesman. How can I help you today?"

"I appreciate the compliment, Mr. Millet, but I'm just a traveling salesman. I sell games of chance."

Both men sat down and Calvin continued, "Yesterday, Mr. Moore, I designated today, Tuesday, as official No Bullshit Day in my office, and it's already working. The loan officer from my bank was candid with me this morning, and I can't remember the last time that happened. So let me be candid with you: I haven't seen a traveling salesman since I was a kid and my grandfather was running this store. That was thirty years ago."

"I'm sure you're right, but I have a very profitable business."

"Really? Even in towns like Ebb?"

"I'm an independent, Mr. Millet. I go where my radar tells me to go."

"Well, I'm not sure that your intuition was in peak tune when you decided to come to Ebb. I'm not in much of a buying mood these days."

"I understand. These are not the best of times, but it won't take long for you to hear my proposition."

"Let me put it straight to you: I'm not a qualified prospect. I'm not the least bit interested in games right now, any kind of games."

"May I ask why? I've been through your store; it seems very well managed."

Calvin rolled his eyes and responded, "Spring is a poor time to call on rural department stores. I thought you might know that. The farmers and ranchers start to run low on credit this time of year, so they don't spend much on anything but necessities. If I were you, I would call again in the fall. Everybody is in more of a buying mood around then."

"I understand the seasonal aspect of your business, Mr. Millet. However, if you are interested in any of my games, then I can offer you very generous terms. If they sell well, then you'll find that your cash problems are relieved rather than intensified. If they don't sell, then you may return them to me without ever having risked even one Yankee dollar. What do you have to lose?"

Calvin laughed and replied, "Fine. Okay. I give. What kind of games do you sell? May I call you Vernon? And please call me Calvin. I'm not in favor of formality as a general rule."

"Me neither, Calvin. Thank you. As I was saying, I sell games of chance: cards, dice, traditional board games. I import them from all over the world . . . "

Calvin sat forward and put his elbows on his desk. "Don't you sell video games? You know that's what the kids want these days; their dads, too."

"No sir, I don't. I'm not in favor of them."

Calvin sat back again. "That's damn old-fashioned of you, Vernon. Why not?"

"Because those games don't teach our children one jot about real life. Instead, they lure them into a fantastic world that is too violent and too sensational all at once. Over time, I believe that repetitive use of video games programs our children to prefer very high rates of artificial stimulation, and it blurs the distinction between fantasy and real life in the weak-minded ones.

"Teachers and textbooks can't possibly compete. Attention deficit disorder is a plague among our young today, and I believe that there's a causal link to video games."

"So you think we should ban them?"

"Heavens no. I believe that we should provide our children with more educational alternatives."

Calvin opened his eyes up wide. "Like cards and dice? You think we should teach our children to gamble?"

Mr. Moore chuckled. "There are many, many card and dice games that have nothing to do with gambling, and they teach our children valuable lessons about the nature of uncertainty."

Calvin rocked back and forth in his chair for a few seconds and then said, "I suppose I agree with you about video games, Vernon, but there's no point in selling what my customers won't buy. Retail is not just a margin business these days. I have to get inventory turns to stay profitable."

"Isn't that the truth. Tell me, how are your turns right now, Calvin?"

"Sluggish. Like I said, this is the slowest time of the year."

"I see. If I may ask, do you carry many international goods here in Millet's?"

"Not many, no."

"May I ask why?"

"Rural folks still like to buy American, at least when they can."

"How about gifts?"

"That's a different story, but this is not the season."

"Don't a lot of the older folks still play cards in this part of the country?"

The last thing Calvin wanted to do was give his caller a positive answer. He said reluctantly, "I suppose that some of the Baby Boomers do. Not the Gen Xers and the kids, though. The Gen Xers watch TV and the kids play video games."

"What card games do your older customers play?"

"Pinochle at the Corn Palace is the big game in town, but people around here play some pitch and poker, too. I used to play some poker myself, but not anymore. I just don't have the time."

Calvin looked at his watch. Mr. Moore said, "I see. But given the inclinations of some of your more senior clientele, might you be interested in seeing some truly unusual card decks and accessories from overseas? It'll only take a minute or two and I promise you'll be pleased at what you see."

"I may be pleased, Vernon, but I don't see what difference your games can make to my business right now."

"You said your inventory turns were low. I suspect your foot traffic is the same. Am I right?"

"Yes. Like I said, it's the season."

"And how long have those sale signs been in the store windows?"

"A month, give or take."

"So what are you doing to pull traffic into the store?"

Calvin didn't answer. Mr. Moore said, "Well, how about a new, international product line that will entertain your customers but not set them back a bucketful of money?"

Calvin considered the cost of a negative answer and decided he didn't have the energy to pay for it. He answered, "Okay. Fine. I'll take a look. Why the hell not?"

Mr. Moore opened his briefcase on the far end of Calvin's desk and took out a catalog which he handed to Calvin. Calvin paged through it and was indeed surprised at what he saw: dozens of decks of cards from places like Italy, Russia, and Thailand; expertly carved cribbage boards in exotic woods; backgammon sets done in mahogany and white ash and bamboo; poker chips in hand-carved boxes; and elegant dice hand-cut from rare woods and stones.

"These are very unusual items. How do you find them?"

"I do it the old-fashioned way, Calvin; I go to the nation of origin. When I find things that are creative, well made, and suitably priced, I establish a personal relationship with the producer. Everything I sell is exclusive. You won't find anything in that catalog on the Internet, nor will your clientele."

"I see. You seem to have a discerning eye, Vernon, I'll say that, and your prices are reasonable. I might have been a qualified prospect for you a few months ago. Now, though, I'm afraid I'll have to pass. Perhaps another time."

Mr. Moore sat down again. "I'm sympathetic, Calvin. In my business, timing is everything. If I may ask, what has changed in the last sixty days?"

Calvin started down the list of polite, politically correct responses in his mind again, but he just couldn't bring himself to do it. He said, "This is No Bullshit Day, so I'll make a deal with you: I'll tell the truth if you will. It will be between us girls, and just for ten minutes. I don't want either one of us getting dizzy from too much unadulterated honesty."

"It's a deal," Mr. Moore answered.

"Fine. You first. Who are you really? And if you start down the 'I sell games' road again, then your five minutes will expire and this call will end immediately. I want to know what makes Vernon Moore tick."

"Fair enough, Calvin. To tell the truth, I used to be a finance executive. Retail Stores of America. Do you know of the name?"

"Of course; I'm in the trade myself. Didn't I read that they got themselves into trouble some time ago?"

"They did. I was the treasurer just before the company filed for bankruptcy protection and I was subsequently enjoined in the lawsuits filed by the SEC and every Shylock class-action lawyer in the lower forty-eight."

"That ended your career?"

"Yes it did."

"That was one hell of an admission, Vernon."

"It was one hell of an experience, Calvin, enough to change my life."

"I understand. But why sales?"

"That's a very good question. I love the uncertainty of life on the road. I revel in facing it myself, without any interference. If there's any one thing I've learned over the years, it's that uncertainty, squarely faced, is the true spice of life."

Calvin chewed on what he had heard for about a minute. Mr. Moore waited patiently. Eventually, Calvin said, "I've never thought about it in exactly those terms, Vernon, but now that I've mulled it over, I am absolutely certain that you're dead wrong—about uncertainty I mean. I would rather have ticks and boils."

"Is that so? Why?"

Calvin knew it was his turn to talk, but he was in no mood to switch from asker to askee. He replied, "Would you like some more water, or perhaps a cup of coffee? I know I would."

"Will it cut into our ten minutes of truth?"

"This is No Bullshit Day, so you'll get your quid pro quo. But let's get some coffee first. We can walk down the hall to the machine ourselves."

When they were settled in Calvin's office again, Mr. Moore said, "You were going to tell me about the store."

"The store is doing how it always does at this time of the year. Business is light, inventory turns have slowed to a crawl, and I'm short on cash. It's the nature of the business."

"For some reason, I sense that there's something unusual about the store this year."

Calvin replied, "You're a former RSA executive, so you know that our business is seasonal."

"I do. But I still feel as if there is something more here, that you are under atypical stress this year. If I'm prying, I'll withdraw the question, but I get the feeling that you would like to talk about it."

"Yet again, I'm afraid your intuition is not in peak tune. Millet's is fine; it's financial condition is standard for the season. That's it."

Mr. Moore sat back, closed his eyes and considered what he had heard, then he asked, "How about your daughter, Lucy."

Calvin shot forward, "My daughter, Lucy? Who told you about her? Never mind. It was Wilma Porter, wasn't it?"

"Yes."

"What in the hell did she tell you? Whatever it was, it's the accepted story all over town."

"She said that Lucy is very, very ill and that she's the light of your life."

Calvin bit his lower lip and then replied, "Have you ever lost a loved one?"

"Of course. Both of my parents passed on long ago."

"Parents are supposed to die first. That's the rule. What if you had a daughter who died before you did? What if you had to watch her waste away right before your very eyes?"

Mr. Moore thought about the question but he didn't answer.

"This is No Bullshit Day. How would you feel?"

"I'm sure I would be devastated. I can't imagine the despair."

Calvin bit his lip again. "You're right on the money. Lucy's doctor called me from the Mayo Clinic yesterday morning to tell me that they're out of ideas. All out. The tank is empty; the well's run dry; we're out of ammo. Doc Wiley confirmed the diagnosis last night. Do you know what that means? That means that the Mayo Clinic has given up on Lucy, the Mayo fucking Clinic, and they were our last hope."

Neither man spoke for several seconds, then Calvin started up again, "I'm sensitive to your past troubles, but I can see that you are up to them. I have no such confidence in myself; not when it comes to my daughter. For Christ's sake, she is only eleven years old, and she is terminally ill from a disease that nobody can even name!"

Calvin stood up and starting walking back and forth behind his desk. "There's no goddamn excuse! She's just eleven, for God's sake! No, I take that back. As of yesterday morning at 8:45 A.M. Central Standard Time, I am a confirmed, goddamned atheist. No God would ever allow this."

Mr. Moore asked, "How much time does she have left?"

"Two days, two weeks, two months. No one knows what will happen when they take her off the latest miracle medication. Naturally, it didn't do a damn thing except push her kidneys to the edge of collapse, so Doc Wiley started easing her off yesterday. Nobody knows how long she will last after that."

"Have you told her?"

"Yeah, right. Of course I did. Could you?"

"I'm sure it would be a very hard thing to do."

"Well, I had the chance yesterday, and I thought about telling her the truth—for about one millisecond. You know what I told her instead?"

"What?"

"I told her it was against the law for little girls to die before their daddies did. That's all I could think to say."

Mr. Moore sat forward and said, "That was creative, Calvin. Very creative. But tell me, are you absolutely sure that Lucy's life is over?"

"You're goddamn right I'm sure."

"What about the afterlife?"

"Afterlife? Did you say afterlife, Vernon? What a fucking joke! No God would ever allow my daughter to waste away into nothingness at the age of eleven! If there's no God, then there's no heaven. That's it; case closed."

Calvin stood behind his desk and began to cry softly. Mr. Moore came from a no-hug generation, so he tried to steer the conversation to a higher plane. "It's puzzling, Calvin. Only a benevolent God would create such a paradise on Earth, but no benevolent God would ever allow so much pain and suffering. That one little paradox, the Paradox of the Benevolent God, has created millions of late-blooming atheists and agnostics, just like you."

Mr. Moore's comment seemed to help. Calvin's crying switched to anger. "The goddamned atheists are right! There is no benevolent God nor any other kind of God! Life is an accident and a damn cruel one at that!"

"I understand why you feel that way, Calvin, I really do. But what if you're wrong?"

"I'm not. I don't see how any rational person could see things any differently."

Mr. Moore replied calmly, "As a matter of fact, I do."

Calvin stopped pacing back and forth and looked straight at Mr. Moore. "Now that's a revelation! You don't strike me as a religious person."

"I'm not, at least in the conventional sense."

"Another surprise. What the hell are you? Buddhist? Taoist? Zoroastrian?"

"No, Calvin, nor any other religion with a collection plate or a Web site. In matters of God, I usually keep my own counsel." Mr. Moore paused for a few seconds and then said, "But I think I may have a proposition for you."

"A proposition? From a salesman? I'm shocked! What is it?"

"What if I can convince you that there is a benevolent God?"

"Pardon me, Vernon, but why in the hell should I give even one little microscopic shit whether you can or not?"

"It's simple. If there is a benevolent God, then there is an afterlife. If there is life after life, then your Lucy has hope. Tell me, why did you lie to Lucy yesterday?"

Calvin didn't respond.

Mr. Moore answered the question for him. "Because you wanted her to have hope. Did she buy it?"

Again Calvin did not respond.

"Of course she didn't, because your story wasn't believable. Wouldn't you rather sell your daughter something she can believe?"

After several seconds of silence, Calvin said, "Of course I would. But how are you going to prove to me that there's an afterlife. Not with the usual religious claptrap; I'm sure as hell not buying any more of that. Besides, you said it yourself; you're not a religious man."

"I'm not. I think that the Paradox of the Benevolent God can be defeated by plain old common sense. A little empathy, too. I think we'll need some empathy."

"Empathy? For who?"

"For God, Calvin."

"Empathy for God! How in the hell can I have that? I don't even believe in Him."

"It won't be that difficult. Trust me."

"Trust you? What for? What's in it for me?"

"If I can prove to you that there's a benevolent God, Calvin, then you will be able to give your daughter genuine, honest-to-God hope."

Mr. Moore sipped his coffee. Calvin took a few seconds to make sure he understood the gravity of what the salesman had just said, then he responded, "My daughter could have hope. Real hope. Is that what you just said?"

"That's what I said."

"Because you can prove to me that there's an afterlife."

"I can prove that it is highly probable."

"Probable?"

"Very probable. You'll be convinced."

Calvin thought about it again for a second and then said, "Are you certain you can do this?"

Mr. Moore winced and then answered, "Yes."

"No religious claptrap?"

"Common sense, Calvin, and a pinch of empathy."

"Is this a lecture or a sermon or what?"

"It's a discussion; a dialogue."

"Is it complicated?"

"A bit. There are consequences. We should take our time."

"Consequences? What the hell do you mean by consequences, Vernon?"

"I'm offering your daughter hope. What do you have to lose?"

Calvin mulled his proposal over for a little and then said, "Fine. Okay. I don't see how you can convince me, but I may be willing to take a chance. Exactly how much of my time will you need for this secular journey to a nicer, sweeter God?"

"I'm not exactly sure. How much time do you have?"

Calvin looked across his desk and replied, "Confidentially, the store goes up for sale next Monday morning. What's left of my house, too. That means that all hell will break loose in Ebb. Assuming you can keep the big news to yourself, which means not telling Wilma Porter or any other woman over the age of twelve in a one-hundred-mile radius, then you can have one hour each morning until Saturday. I can't give you any more time than that; I don't have any more time than that. And if the first hour proves to be as confounding as this one has been, your time will be over. Is that fair?"

Mr. Moore considered his prospect for a minute, then he replied, "I'm offering your daughter life after life and you're offering me a few hours, Calvin? You act as if you're doing me some kind of favor. Why is that?"

Calvin broke off eye contact and shook his head for several seconds before responding, "I'm not sure, Vernon. I'm not sure who the hell you are or what you really want from me. I'm not sure what to tell my daughter, Lucy. I have no idea what I'm going to do with my life after she's gone. Hell, I don't know how much of my life will be left after she's gone. I'm not sure of a damn thing anymore."

"Then perhaps you could use some hope, too."

"That would be nice for a change, Vernon, but the Millet hope account ran bone dry yesterday morning at eight-forty-five. I don't have a drop left."

"Well, I have plenty in stock. With your indulgence, I'll sell you a measure in the next few days, enough for both you and your daughter."

Calvin asked, "And if you succeed in selling me some hope, what will you want in return?"

Mr. Moore shrugged and answered, "Nothing."

"Nothing? I thought you were a salesman?"

"If I can convince you that there is hope for Lucy, then I won't be offended if you buy some of my games. In fact, I will be grateful for it."

"My cash position is not at its zenith at the moment. I already told you that."

"I'm certain that we could work something out, Calvin."

"Fine. Okay. Do you have a specific figure in mind?"

"No. No, I don't. Let your conscience be your guide."

Calvin said, "That's a strange reply from a salesman, which means it bears a striking resemblance to everything else about this visit, but you have yourself a deal. If you can sell me some hope, then maybe I'll buy some cribbage boards and some poker chips—on credit—assuming I don't sell the store first."

"Fair enough, Calvin. One last question: is Clem Tucker a potential buyer?"

"Of the store?"

"Yes."

"I'm pretty sure he is, but how in the hell . . . ?"

"Just a guess. I didn't mean to pry. I very much appreciate your time."

Mr. Moore stood up and extended his hand across the desk. Calvin took it and remarked, "You're an unusual man, Vernon Moore, anyone can see that. But do you really think you can sell me some hope? That's a tall and strange order."

"We'll both know the answer in a few days. Between now and tomorrow morning you may want to do some thinking about arbitrary lines."

"Arbitrary lines?"

"Yes."

Calvin shook his head. "Okay, Vernon. Fine. I'll do some thinking about arbitrary lines. Lily should be back from the bank by now. On your way out, will you ask her to put our meeting on my schedule for tomorrow? And then will you ask her to come straight in here to see me? We have our own arbitrary line to discuss."

Mr. Moore smiled, they shook hands across the desk again, and then the salesman left Calvin's office without further ado.

Lily came in seconds later. Calvin said, "Well?"

"Annie took the check, Mr. Millet, but she wouldn't cash it. She looked at her computer and said that there was a temporary stop on our account."

"You mean she refused."

"Yes."

Lily said, "You don't seem surprised, Mr. Millet. We've had hard times before but they always cashed our checks."

Calvin remembered it was No Bullshit Day, but he also knew that there were times when A Little Bullshit was more appropriate. He answered, "Buford and I are playing a game of cat and mouse, Lily, that's all. He wants more money and I want more money. It's just a game. Like Annie said, the stop is temporary."

Lily is nobody's fool. She replied, "Will you tell me who wins your game, Mr. Millet?"

"Of course. In fact, I'll tell you right now. I'm going to win. I always do, don't I?"

Lily smiled weakly. "Yes, Mr. Millet. You always win."

"Yes I do. Now will you shut the door on your way out? And please hold all of my calls for at least a half hour. Can you do that?"

Lily responded in the affirmative and started to leave. As she reached the door, she turned and asked, "How was your visit with Mr. Moore? I've put him on the schedule again for tomorrow."

"Well, I don't know how it was. I don't even know what it was."

"What do you mean?"

"He's a financial man, Lily, and ex–retail executive. When was the last time you heard of a finance executive turning himself into a traveling salesman? Isn't that like a prince turning himself into a toad? Hell, when was the last time you saw a traveling salesman, period?"

"I don't know that I've ever seen one, Mr. Millet."

"Me neither, at least not since I was a kid. Maybe he's come here to take a look at the store. Some buyout companies will go to extraordinary lengths to get the inside story on a potential acquisition. If that's true, though, he has a curious way of going about his business."

"Should I take him off your calendar?"

"Hell no. If he's fronting for a buyer, which he probably is, then I definitely want him in the game. Besides, he's just about the only mystery I've got left. Everything else is just a matter of time."

Chapter 8

The State of Anxiety

LATER THAT SAME morning, I took some fresh, homemade peanut butter cookies over to Hank Wiley, the town doctor. Hank is a big, hairy bear of a man, maybe fifty-five or sixty years old; nobody knows for sure. He's also a widower; his wife, Emma, died from breast cancer about ten years ago. I know he blames himself. Why is it that so many of us blame ourselves for things that we can't ever fix, but we blame others for the things we can? I guess I will never know.

Doc Wiley moved to Ebb after a career as a military physician. To tell the truth, he was recruited here by the county council. They set him up in a big house with a built-in clinic that's about four blocks from my place. He converted one of the upstairs bedrooms into a shrine for his wife. He showed it to me once. It's chock-full of her pictures and her clothes and odd knickknacks from their life together, and it's probably the saddest room I've ever seen.

Like everybody else in this town, Hank has his peculiarities. One is his appetite. He can eat more food than any man I have ever met, farmers and ranch hands included, but it never seems to affect his weight. He has weighed about 275 pounds ever since I have known him, give or take.

Hank is not very good at making decisions either. You might think that that would be a handicap for a doctor, but he says that the decisions are never his anyway; he just has to be good at knowing the alternatives. I would be skeptical myself, except that his patients are hardly dropping off left and right—except for poor Lucy Millet, of course.

Anyway, Hank told me the dreadful news about Lucy that morning. I suppose I knew it was coming but still I had a good cry. He was close to tears himself, but he wouldn't let himself do it. He says that he would receive a written reprimand from the AMA if he did and I believe him.

We had tea and cookies and commiserated for a bit, then I headed over to the Corn Palace to meet Loretta for lunch. I was pretty late, I guess. By the time I arrived, she was on her third pitcher with six ranch hands from the Hereford Haven. That girl's liver is going to end up in the Internal Organ Hall of Fame. I had to drag her to a booth by the scruff of her neck so we could talk in private.

By the end of lunch, Loretta had the bad news on Lucy and I

had the bad news about Lily's trip to the bank. Loretta also told me that Mr. Moore had been to the Corn Palace for a bowl of chili and a Coke. She said she flirted with him for a while, which was probably the understatement of the Information Age, but he managed to escape her clutches before he spilled any beans about his visit with Calvin Millet.

That meant that the ball was in my court, so I went straight home to set up an ambush for him: homemade biscuits, homemade jam, and a pitcher of my best iced tea, the kind where each tea bag comes in its own little foil wrapper. But as soon as I got back, my telephone started ringing off the wall.

The first call was from my youngest daughter, Winona, who was in a state of high anxiety. Apparently, Mona had been over to see her that morning for coffee and had broken down completely. I must have talked about it with Winona for thirty minutes or more, which is not easy when you are also making biscuits from scratch. That put me into a state of anxiety, too, but I have been there before. In fact, I lived in the State of Anxiety the entire time I was married. I didn't like it there much either; the emotional taxes were too darn high and I had no time for myself. That's why I got divorced and moved back to Ebb. Then my girls grew up, got married, and moved straight back to Anxiety, especially my Mona. As I live and breathe.

It seems that everybody I know lives in one emotional state or another. My permanent boarder, Clara Tucker Booth Yune, lives in the State of Isolation. It's a very small state with no official language. Her brother lives next door, in a great big place in the State of Loneliness. My best friend Loretta lives in the State of Desire, at least when she doesn't have a man, and she doesn't have one right now. About two weeks after she gets one, she moves to the State of Disappointment for a while. That's not a fun state to visit.

Doc Wiley lives in the State of Melancholy, poor man, and Calvin Millet is living on the state line between Defeat and Sorrow. Lulu Tiller is the exception to the rule. Bless her soul, that woman lives in LaLa Land. I guess that can happen when your seventeen nearest friends are dogs and cats and farmyard critters.

When I find out what state Mr. Moore lives in, I'll let you know. So far, I don't have a clue.

Speaking of men, Clem Tucker called right after I got off the phone with Winona. Now, that was a bolt out of the blue. He hadn't called me himself since I squired him through his little bout with male menopause. Ever since then, he's had somebody else call on his behalf, which hasn't been often.

Clem is not much for beating around the bush; he never was, if you get my meaning. Without one word of introduction, he said, "I knew I had heard of your new lodger, Wilma. Now I know why."

Am I the only one who feels like this, or do some people have a way of making you feel suspicious right from the get-go? I answered, "He's not mine, Clem honey, he's just staying here. Should I be worried about his credit?"

"I doubt it, but it never hurts to check."

"He gave me a Visa Platinum card. The man is ironclad."

Now I have to tell you something that I figured out a long time ago. When you're the hub of a rural communications network, as I am, people sometimes tell you things for just one reason: they want you to spread it around. That is not my policy. I deal in information, not manure, and I'm also a patient woman, relatively speaking, so I waited for Clem to continue.

He said, "He may have his act together now, but apparently that hasn't always been the case. He was a central figure in the collapse of a large department store chain called Retail Stores of America some years ago."

"I know he was."

"He told you?"

"He told Loretta and me the whole story at the Stake House last night."

"Did he tell you he turned whistleblower?"

Well, I could just feel my hackles rising up. I said, "He told us that, too, but you make it sound like he was spying for the Russians. Is he a serial rapist, too?"

"Don't be flip, Wilma. What happened there was serious."

"You ought to be ashamed of yourself, Clement Tucker. You don't know a darn thing about what happened there; all you know is what the newspapers said. There's a big difference between the two. Of all people, you ought to know that."

"I suppose I do, Wilma, I suppose I do. Am I to take it that you like this Vernon Moore character?"

"He's a hard man to get to know, for sure, and he has some opinions that will curl your hair, but he's a smart and generous man. He has a certain air of confidence about him, too, as if he's beaten his demons to a bloody pulp. Not many men have done that."

Far be it for Clem T. Tucker to think that I might have been alluding to him. He said, "That's very interesting, Wilma. I appreciate your insight. Is he there now?"

"No," I said.

"When do you expect him back?"

I expected him back at any moment. I answered, "Before nine when I close up. He doesn't have a key."

"When he comes in, will you ask him to call me at the River House? I'd like to invite him over for breakfast."

I could only shake my head and wonder what shenanigans these men would get up to next. I inquired, "May I tell him why? Are you looking to hire a whistleblower to run the bank?"

"Maybe I am. You just ask him to give me a call. Okay?"

"I live for it, Clement. When was the last time you went to see your granddaughter?"

"I drove down to Carson this morning. Why do you think I stopped by Calvin's store yesterday? I wanted to let him know that I was going to pay her a visit."

Now that was another surprise. I couldn't remember the last time that Clem had visited Lucy and, believe me, if he had, I would have known about it in a heartbeat. I said, "You did? That was sweet. How is the poor thing?"

"She's not too good right now, but I'm still optimistic."

"We're all praying for her, Clem. Did you two have time for a chat?"

"We did. Of course we did. Now don't you forget to tell Vernon Moore to call me, hear?"

I had barely put the phone down when Mona, my eldest worry, called. We talked a bit about Matthew and Mark, but I knew for sure that there was more on her mind. Eventually, she said, "Mama, can I come down to see you tomorrow? I won't stay; I just want to talk for a while."

"Sure, sweetheart," I replied, "but you know it's a long way. What about the boys?"

"I'm sure that someone from Marv's office can pick them up after school."

"You mean one of the Barbies? Are any of them old enough to drive?"

Right then and there, I knew that I had said the wrong thing. Mona started to sob like a baby. There's nothing that breaks a mother's heart more than hearing her babies cry, so I tried to make her feel better. I wasn't very convincing—sympathy has never been my long suit—but Mona managed to pull herself together on her own. Then she said abruptly, "School is almost over, Mama. I've got to get off the phone. I'll see you tomorrow morning."

"Okay, sweetheart. You drive safely."

"I will, Mama. I love you."

"I love you, too, sweetheart."

After I hung up, I felt real guilty. It wasn't just the comment about the Barbies. I knew I was supposed to be feeling sympathetic for my daughter, too, but I was fantasizing about Vernon Moore instead. I know what you are thinking, but I was imagining that he was a hit man for hire and that he owed me a big favor, so I told him to drop the hammer on Marv Breck, his office full of lean, white-jacketed "assistants," and all my daughter's troubles.

Just then, Mr. Moore himself strolled right into my kitchen. I was so wrapped up in my little fantasy that I never heard the front door. His briefcase was in his left hand, his blazer was slung over his right shoulder, and there was just a smidge of sweat on his forehead. When I looked into those crystal-blue eyes of his, the plot line in my fantasy began to shift involuntarily.

I propositioned him right then and there. "If you can wait about fifteen minutes," I said, "I'll have fresh, homemade biscuits and jam for high tea."

"Thank you, Wilma," he replied. "That sounds just wonderful, and it'll give me just enough time to run upstairs and change into something more casual."

Well, my heart skipped a beat. For just a moment, I was sure he was going to say something more comfortable. I put the phone on automatic answer and went back to my cooking chores. Mr.

Moore came down the back stairs about twenty minutes later, dressed in blue jeans, hiking boots, and a tan, long-sleeved, cashmere sweater, looking as if he had just been scrubbed clean by my grandma. I felt grimy in comparison, like I needed a bath. Cooking and cleaning will do that to you.

Mr. Moore sat down at the kitchen table and I served him tea right away. The biscuits were just out of the oven but they still needed to cool, so I remained standing. I didn't want to keep jumping up and down in the middle of conversation. It's not polite.

Mr. Moore said, "Did I get any calls while I was away today?"

"Yes you did," I answered. "Just one, not even a half hour ago." Before he could ask, I volunteered, "It was Clem Tucker. Were you expecting him to call?"

"No, not really."

"But you aren't surprised, are you?"

"I suppose not. What did he want?

"Well, first he wanted to tell me your life story, the *Reader's Digest* version."

Mr. Moore smiled. "Is that so?"

"Yes it is, but then he wanted to ask you over to the River House tomorrow morning for breakfast. Do people often impugn your character to a third party and then invite you to a meal in the same phone call?"

"Not as a rule, no. Do you have his number?"

"Yes I do. He asked that you call him back as soon as possible."

Mr. Moore sipped his iced tea, but his mind went elsewhere. I said, "Well?"

"I haven't decided whether I'll go or not, Wilma. I think I'll ask him what he wants first."

I paused for just a minute to make sure I had considered what I was going to say, which is a precaution I should take more often, like twice-a-day more often, and then I said, "Can we speak in confidence for a minute?"

"Of course."

"Well, I certainly don't know for sure, but Clem's invitation may have something to do with an investment he just made."

"An investment?"

"Mind you, this information hasn't been corroborated, but the source is impeccable. Apparently, Clem Tucker has invested in Wal-Mart."

"Has he? Might I infer that investing in Wal-Mart is a bit controversial in this neck of the woods."

"It would be no different than if the U.S. Army bought stock in North Korea."

"I get the picture, Wilma. How sure are you that Clem has done this evil deed?"

"I don't know, Mr. Moore. Ninety-five percent at least."

"Do you know how much enemy stock he bought?"

"No I don't. I was hoping you could find that out tomorrow morning."

Mr. Moore mulled this over for a second or two and then replied, "Can I reveal the source of my information?"

"No. A nice divorcée would lose her job if Clem found out. Is that a problem? Do you have to know?"

"Probably not, Wilma. I was just interested myself."

"Then you will ask him about it?"

"Of course. It'll give us something to talk about besides the stock market."

"Can I get you the phone?"

"No thank you. I'll call him later on. How was your day?"

"Well, I took those peanut butter cookies over to Dr. Wiley just like I said I would."

"There was no good news there, was there?"

"How did you know?"

"I talked to Calvin about Lucy this morning."

"Calvin told you?"

"Yes. He's a sad, bitter man. I can't say I blame him one bit."

"Do you think he's going to be all right? Lucy is the only family he has left, and her days are numbered, poor thing."

"I don't know what he's going to do. He seems to be at the end of his tether."

"Then I don't suppose that Calvin bought many of your games?"

"No. No he didn't. That's not what he needed today. What he needed today was some hope."

"Isn't that the truth," I said.

Mr. Moore didn't say a thing while I stacked some biscuits on a silver tray that I picked up at an estate auction up in Hickman one time. The butter and the jam were already on the table, along with everything else we needed, so I sat down and said, "Will you be staying awhile? I've enjoyed your company so."

Mr. Moore started to butter one of my biscuits and answered, "I've enjoyed your company, too, Wilma. I can't stay long, but I don't expect to leave Ebb right away. I have to sell Calvin Millet some hope before I go."

Well, at just that second you could have shoved a piano leg in my mouth and not gotten a single splinter in my gums, but I guess that's another thing I should never say out loud. Instead I said, "Did you say hope?"

"Yes. That's what he needs."

"Well I never. How in the world are you going to do that?"

Mr. Moore swallowed and replied, "These biscuits are absolutely delicious, Wilma, and Calvin asked me the very same thing."

"Well, what did you tell him?" I asked.

"I told him that we're going to defeat the Paradox of the Benevolent God. That's not all of it, but it's where we'll start."

I suppose I should have said something like, "What on earth is that?" But I didn't have the nerve. All I could do was shake my head and wonder what kind of shenanigans these men would get up to next, and then have a hot biscuit myself.

Chapter 9

Bluff's Edge

THE TUCKER RIVER HOUSE was built as a hunting and fishing lodge by Clem's grandfather during the Depression. It's set in a copse of oak and maple on a bluff overlooking the Missouri River, and it may be the second prettiest place in southeast Nebraska. Thank heaven Clem hasn't had it modernized. All those dead animal heads in the dining hall would look pretty strange in that other house of his, the one in town with all the funny angles and odd-shaped windows.

Vernon Moore arrived at the River House five minutes early, which was his practice, and Clem answered the door himself, which was not his. Mr. Moore was dressed in his black blazer, a blue pin-striped shirt with a white collar, a red-and-black patterned tie, tan slacks, and black-and-cordovan saddle shoes. I am not kidding about the shoes. They looked pretty natty.

Clem was dressed in black slacks, black socks, black shoes,

and a black silk pullover. He did like to dress like a movie producer sometimes. He brought his personal chef along to the River House, a rotund Cajun woman named Marie Delacroix, which she pronounces "day-la-crah." She served them fresh mangoes and melon, chilled Pellegrino, eggs Benedict, Key-lime sorbet, and gourmet coffee for breakfast. Mr. Moore asked for iced tea instead of coffee. Marie, who has the distinction of being the fastest inductee into the Quilting Circle in its history, made a point of saying how polite he was.

The two businessmen discussed the usual niceties at first but, right after the fruit was served, Clem moved the conversation on to more substantial matters. "Tell me, how was your visit with Calvin Millet yesterday?"

Mr. Moore had to stop chewing first, but then he replied, "It went well. I think we made progress."

"Is that a fact? I must say I'm a bit mystified. I didn't think that Calvin would be a very good prospect for you."

"Really? We're meeting again this morning."

"Now that's extremely interesting. You must be a persuasive man."

"I'm not at all sure that that's the case. As salesmen go, I don't depend too much on my powers of persuasion. I'd rather ask questions and let the other person talk. I seem to learn a lot more that way."

"There's no doubt about that, Vernon; I adhere to the same principle myself. What did you learn from Calvin Millet?"

"He's your son-in-law, isn't he?"

"He's my former son-in-law."

"But he is the father of your grandchild."

"Yes."

"And I know you were there the other morning, so you already know how he is. He's a sad, bitter man who's badly in need of some hope."

"That's right, Vernon. Do you think that buying your games will help him?"

"No I don't. Not directly, anyway."

"Then I'm a tad confused. Didn't you just say that you two are meeting again today?"

"Yes I did."

Clem eats in the English style, which I find both pretentious and a bit disgusting. He put down his knife and his upside-down fork and said, "Why?"

Mr. Moore continued to chew for some time, then answered, "It seemed like the logical thing to do. It still does."

"That makes no sense to me at all."

"It makes perfect sense. Most folks think of selling as a one-time event. That may be the case on a used-car lot, but business-to-business selling is a process, a series of sequential events called a sales cycle."

"Even when you can't sell what you're selling?"

"One call does not a sales cycle make, Clem. That's my point."

"So you think you're going to sell some games today or tomorrow?"

"No. No, I don't."

Clem picked up his utensils again and said, "Am I going to get less confused following this line, Vernon, or more confused?"

"I think the latter outcome is the most likely."

"Well, then I would appreciate your help because I just can't seem to piece you together."

"Piece me together, Clem, like a puzzle?"

"Exactly. I've met you twice now, and I still don't understand why you're here. I hear you drive a high-zoot German car that I know you can't find parts for between Lincoln and Kansas City. You wear extremely expensive clothes. What's that jacket, an Armani?"

"No. It's a Zegna. I think he has an incredible sense of fabric, don't you?"

"How about that watch? Rolex?"

"Too clunky for my taste. It's an Omega."

Clem frowned and went on, "You see what I mean? And yet you claim to be a traveling games salesman. Is that right?"

"It is."

"Now, the icing on the cake is that the local department store owner is not interested in what you're selling, but you're seeing him again today anyway. Is that right, too?"

"On the nose."

"Well, I just don't see how that could be."

"I know you don't, but I think you'll see how it all fits together by the end of the week. In the meantime, I'm completely comfortable with the situation."

"Well I'm not."

"Why should you care? You're too big a man to bother with a small-time salesman like me."

"I would agree, Vernon, if you were a small-time salesman. There just happens to be another scenario that makes a whole lot more horse sense."

"Really? How interesting. What's that?"

"I know you were a retail executive. Ex-RSA. A numbers man. I had you checked out. It can't be a coincidence that a major-league retail man just happens to show up in Ebb right when Millet's Department Store is on the brink."

"Is Millet's on the brink? That's not what Calvin told me yesterday."

"Do you expect him to tell you that? To my understanding, it was your first meeting."

"You'd be surprised what people tell me. Sometimes, I'm amazed at it myself."

"Then I suppose he told you about my granddaughter, Lucy?"

"He did."

"How much?"

"All of it. The latest."

Clem yelled toward the kitchen, "Could you bring in some more coffee, Marie?" In a lower tone of voice he said, "How about you, Vernon? Is your tea okay?"

"I'm fine. Breakfast is excellent. My compliments."

"You're welcome. Marie is a first-class cook."

"How did you find her?"

"Through a recruiting firm in Atlanta that specializes in personal chefs."

"That's interesting. Did you have any trouble convincing her to move to Nebraska?"

"Heavens no. Her last two employers were professional athletes. I think she would have moved to Mongolia to work for an adult."

Marie came and went without remark, and then Clem said, "Since people seem to tell you so much, what else have you learned since your arrival in Ebb?"

Mr. Moore sipped on his iced tea and took an inventory of all the animal heads on the dining-hall wall. After he had counted all eighteen of them, he said, "I hear that you've invested in Wal-Mart."

Clem replied smoothly, "My investments are personal and confidential. Where did you hear that?"

"I can't say."

"Come on, you must have heard it somewhere."

"I did, but it was told to me in confidence, Clem. I can't divulge the source."

"Was it a woman? I bet it was somebody from that damn Circle."

"I don't know what the Circle is. I am curious, though. Based on what little I do know about this area, an investment in Wal-Mart would seem, well, unpatriotic."

"Politics and business are separate. You know that as well as I do."

"To the contrary, I know that they're irreparably intertwined. So do you."

Clem frowned again. "So you think I've committed some kind of economic treason?"

"I don't even know if you've invested in Wal-Mart. I was just following a train of thought."

Clement smiled and replied, "Well, that train has just come to the end of the line. If I may ask, where did you go to school?"

"Ohio. How about you?"

"Grinnell, then the London School of Economics."

"Really? Did you enjoy your time in England?"

"I did. If my dear departed daddy hadn't wrapped my vintage Corvette around a telephone pole, I might be there yet."

"My condolences. I like England myself, but I'm love with Italy."

"Are you? Why is that?"

"The Italians have an unmatched flair for life. It's infectious. I catch it again every time I go."

"Where do you like to stay?"

"Everywhere: Rome; Tuscany; Sardinia; the lake country. I suppose Naples is my favorite, though."

"Do you go there often?"

"At least once, maybe twice a year."

"Hmmm. That must cost you a pile of money."

"It's not the money. I don't care about the money."

Clem's eyes got real big and he said, "It's not the money? I've never heard a finance man say that in all in my life."

"I'm not in finance anymore. I haven't been for years."

"That may be so, but selling's a hard life. Haven't you ever thought about going back? I know I would have."

"I used to think about it. I used to think about it all the time. Why do you ask?"

"Are we speaking confidentially?"

"Of course."

"The Tucker family trust, of which I am custodian, now has more than seventy million dollars under investment. It's taking all my time to manage the damn thing, but I've reached a point in my life when there are other things that I want to do."

"Like return to England?"

"Perhaps, but just to visit. That phase of my life was over long ago, but now I want this phase of my life to be over, too. I'm just not sure what I want to replace it with yet."

Mr. Moore scanned the room and said, "Are you going to hunt, or are all these trophies from your predecessors?"

Clem answered proudly, "There are three generations of magnificent heads on these walls, Vernon. A third of them are mine. Do you hunt?"

"No. I could never see it as a sport."

"Is that a fact? Why not?"

"Because there's no real risk to the modern hunter, so there are only two practical outcomes: either the animal loses its life unnecessarily or it's a draw. I think overwhelming force has something to do with the imbalance. What do you think?"

Clem gritted his teeth and answered, "Don't you eat meat, Vernon? I thought I just saw you eat some Canadian bacon."

Mr. Moore looked around the hall for a few seconds and then responded, "I do eat meat, but I don't eat antelope, or bighorn sheep, or elk, or anything else you've got nailed to your wall. I don't know anybody who does."

"But you do eat lamb?"

"Yes I do, and I like it. But not bighorn. I draw the line before bighorn sheep."

"That may be where you draw the line. Other folks may choose to draw it elsewhere."

"They may, and it's one of the great things about this country: we have the freedom to draw our own lines. But where we draw the important ones is the litmus test of our humanity. When the hunters die at least one fourth of the time, then I'll reclassify it as a sport. Until then, I'll consider it a regrettable form of ego inflation."

"You know that you never once addressed me personally in that little tirade of yours, but I still feel insulted. Why is that?"

"I suspect it's because you're a hunter, in more ways than one."

"In more ways than one? What does that mean?"

Mr. Moore paused before answering, "Aren't you trying to buy Millet's Department Store yourself?"

"No. No, I'm not. Who gave you that idea?"

"I wouldn't exactly call it a leap of faith. First, you're the biggest investor in the region. Second, as you note, Calvin Millet is suffering through some difficult financial times at the moment; so is his store. Third, I saw you coming out of there yesterday morning after a meeting with the owner."

"I told you why I was there, Vernon. I was there to see the father of my granddaughter."

"Fourth, you invited me over here for breakfast. From what I hear, you don't normally dine in the company of itinerants. I can only think of one reason why you would: because you think I might be a buyer, too."

"You overestimate yourself. I invited you to breakfast so that I could get to know you better. I'm just about done, but you still haven't answered my question about returning to finance."

Mr. Moore looked down the length of the table and inquired, "Are you offering me a job, Clem?"

"Do I look like a dimwit to you? You know that an offer would be premature. If you were interested, though, then I might start the wheels of due diligence rolling and we could talk more later."

"I must say I'm flattered but, other than my dubious conversational skills, you know very little about me."

"I know a number of very important things about you. I know that you have a college education and that you've demonstrated the ability to handle very large investments under pressure. I also know that you're an honest, courageous man. If my information on the RSA situation is correct, then you were just trying to do what was right."

"Is that what you want to do? To do what's right? I've known dozens of big-time businessmen and politicians in my life. The vast majority of them had no interest whatsoever in doing what was right."

"I don't even know what you mean. My job is to preserve the family trust. What I want is someone who can help me ride herd over the investments in the family portfolio."

"And the paperwork?"

"There's that, too. You know there is."

Mr. Moore nodded and said, "I still don't understand why you're so interested in me."

"For a smart man, Vernon, you can be a bit thick on occasion. Look around you and tell me how many custom tailors and Michelin-starred restaurants you see. How often do you think a man of your pedigree passes through Ebb?"

"I suppose you've tried recruiting someone for this job already."

"I have. If I could have found one capable fund manager whose last two employers were NBA basketball players, we wouldn't be having this conversation."

"Can I think about this?"

Clem answered, "Don't you want to know about the money, or do you really not care?"

Mr. Moore thought about that question for a minute and then he said, "Before I answer that question, can I ask you one?"

"Sure. Shoot."

"What were the three most memorable moments of your life?"

It was Clement's turn to reflect for a bit. He answered, "Nobody has ever asked me that before, Vernon. Now that I've thought about it, though, I'd have to say that the three best moments of my life were the first time I had sex, the day I walked into the London School of Economics on my own two feet, and the day my daughter was born. That was the one and only time I have ever felt unconditional love."

"Didn't your wife leave you sometime later?"

Clem shook his head before answering flatly, "You're well informed, Vernon, and yes she did. My daughter also walked out on me and her family, and that was damn embarrassing, too. I wouldn't put either one of those episodes in my top three or anybody else's. Would you?"

"No. No I wouldn't. Tell me, then, was your first sexual experience with a hooker?"

"What? Hell no! I never . . . "

"Then which one of the moments you mentioned had a thing to do with money? Pick any one you like."

Clem took a moment before answering coldly, "None, obviously. Make your point, and then let's move on, briskly."

"Fair enough. Despite the fact that you're an extremely wealthy man, how much of your time do you spend in pursuit of more money, and how does that compare to the time you spend in pursuit of another memorable event like the ones you had before your wife and daughter left you? In fact, when was your last top-three event? Thirty, thirty-five years ago?"

Clem inhaled deeply and grumbled, "I get it." After a few more seconds, he brightened up and continued, "May I also conclude that you'll work cheap?"

Mr. Moore laughed and replied, "For you? Absolutely not."

"I didn't think so. When can I have an answer on my offer?"

"By this Friday. How's that?"

"I don't want a signed contract. All I want is an indication of your intentions. You appear to be a decisive man. Why not now?"

Mr. Moore smiled and said, "You know the consequences of an answer as well as I do. I do have a suggestion for tomorrow, though."

Clem said, "Shoot."

"Do you play cards? Cribbage or gin rummy, perhaps?"

"We play a lot of Hollywood gin up at the country club, Vernon. Why? Are you a player?"

"I am, and I think one man can learn a lot about another in a hard game of cards. How about it? Tomorrow?"

"I don't know. I have to drive up to Lincoln in the morning for a meeting with a few state legislators. I can never predict how long those things are going to last. I expect you know what I mean."

"I do, but I'm free all afternoon. Why don't you have your assistant call me when you become available?"

Clem smiled and wiped an imaginary crumb from each corner of his mouth; then he said, "I'll call you myself, Vernon, and that means our business is done, at least for this morning. I appreciate you coming over on such short notice."

Both men stood up and shook hands. Mr. Moore said, "The pleasure was mine, and Marie's breakfast was a joy. If I may, though, I do have one more small request."

Clem repeated, "Shoot."

"I noticed on the drive in that you have a beautiful view of the river here. Do you mind if I walk outside for a moment or two."

"Certainly not. Take as much time as you like. I suggest you go out the great room and through pappy's porch. That's the quickest way. I'd show you myself, but I have some calls to make."

Marie told me later that Mr. Moore walked over to the bluff's edge and stayed there for fifteen or twenty minutes before he went back to his car. Nobody knows what he was thinking about for sure. Maybe it was Clem's offer, but I never asked.

In the meantime, Clem called to ask me about a recent rumor concerning his investments. I disavowed any knowledge of it—"plausible deniability" I think it's called in Washington—but I don't think Clem was even a bit plaused by my denial. Still, he didn't seem too hot under the collar about it either. He just asked me to keep my mouth shut and to let him know if I heard anything else—for the good of the community, of course.

Clem called Buford Pickett at the bank right after he talked to me. He said, "Listen Buford, I don't know who this Vernon Moore is or why he's here, but I'm damn sure that he's no salesman. We should assume, therefore, that he may be a buyer. It's a bad time for that right now. We have Calvin Millet exactly where we want him; another bidder could cost me a pile of money."

"Yes sir, Mr. Tucker."

"I want you to drop whatever you're doing and devote yourself and your people one hundred percent to this man. I want to know everything. If he has the heartbreak of psoriasis, I want to know. If he has distant relatives in a Colombian jail, I want to know. Mostly, I want to know where he has been for the last six years and why he's in Ebb. Do you have any questions?"

Buford answered, "No sir."

"Good. Start in Ohio; that's where he said he went to college. If you have any problems, you call me personally. No one besides you and your assistants are to know of your little project. If you get asked by anybody at the bank, and I mean anybody, you just tell them that you're working on a special job for me. Is that understood?"

"Yes sir."

"Thank you, Buford. You're a good man. You let me know what you all learn about Vernon Moore—and do it yesterday."

Next, Clem called Dottie Hrnicek, who's our county sheriff. Her last name is pronounced "hern-uh-check." For some reason, there are a lot of Hrniceks in Nebraska, don't ask me why. They hail from one of those Eastern European countries that was so poor that it could not afford the entire alphabet, especially vowels.

Dot is a barrel-chested, wide-hipped, flat-butted fireplug of a woman with short red hair and bangs. She first came to Ebb as a teenager back in the eighties when her father tried to open up an ice cream store on Main Street. It went bust pretty fast, so they moved on to Broken Bow, which is where Dot graduated from school and got into law enforcement. Naturally, she moved back here after her divorce. In the last few years there have been rumors that her post-marital sexual tastes have switched. I don't care if they have or not. She is a fine peace officer and a hard-core member of the Circle.

Clem said, "Dottie, this is Clem Tucker. Can we speak confidentially?"

She answered, "Well, good morning to you, too, Clement. It's always a pleasure. What's on your mind, hon?" Dottie calls every man hon, lawful or criminal, including Clement Tucker. If the Pope came to town, she would call him hon.

Clem asked, "Have you heard of a new man in town named Vernon Moore?"

"Do you mean Wilma Porter's new lodger?"

"Yes. He's the one."

"Loretta told me about him this morning at Starbucks. I guess he made quite an impression. I haven't seen her so excited since she hired a bus to take forty of her closest friends to Grand Island for the rodeo."

"This is serious. Have you checked him out?"

"No, hon, I haven't. Should I? What have you heard?"

Clem answered, "He says he's a traveling salesman, but I just can't believe it. They're extinct as dinosaurs, which makes me worry that his intentions in Ebb may not be honorable. He was involved in a big retail scandal a few years back, you know."

"No, Clement. I didn't know. What are you tryin' to say?"

"Well, Dottie, you might be doing the town a big favor if you checked into this man's background. If he is a salesman, then he has to have a license of some kind, doesn't he?"

"All he has to have is a business license, hon. You must have about fifty of 'em yourself."

"I suppose I do. But would you check him out, make sure he has at least one?"

"I don't see any cause to. It's not like I got deputies hoverin' around the county courthouse lookin' for research work."

"It would be a favor to me."

"A favor? To you? And what would I get in return, hon?"

"What do you want?"

"How about your public support in the election this fall?"

That gave Clem some pause. He replied, "What about a campaign contribution instead? As you know, I try to stay out of local politics."

Dot said, "Uh-huh. Everybody knows that. You get back to me if you change your mind, okay? I got evildoers to incarcerate."

"Dottie . . ."

"You drive careful, hon. I don't want to hear about any low-flying Porsches today. Okay?"

"Damn it, Dottie . . ."

She hung up the telephone and called me straight away. We had a chat about Calvin and Lucy Millet while I got Mr. Moore's particulars for her, and then she got on with checking him out on her computer.

Meanwhile, Clem called Loretta. She said, "To what do I owe the pleasure? You're not due for a trim until next week."

"I understand from Wilma that you know Vernon Moore, Loretta."

"I do, and he's special, that's for sure. For a man of his vintage, he has a damn nice motor, too."

"What else?"

"Why do you want to know? What's goin' on?"

"I have reason to believe that he's not what he says he is. I'm trying to figure out what he really does for a living."

"Well, hell, Clem, why didn't you say so? Of course he's not what he says he is! Have you seen his clothes? He's smart, too, and he has peculiar opinions, too peculiar for a salesman."

"That's very interesting."

"Isn't that the truth? But why do you care, Clem darlin'? It must be something of economic significance or you wouldn't be calling me yourself. Is he planning a hostile takeover of the bank? Now that would be a Greek tragedy, wouldn't it?"

"This is my town. There won't be any takeovers here, hostile or otherwise. But I don't like men who can afford German cars and Italian outfits running around saying they're something they're not, at least until I know what they're up to."

"Is that it, Clem? There has to be more than that. I can't remember the last time you called me yourself. Did your administrative assistant quit, again?"

"There isn't anything else, not for now, anyway. You let me know if you learn something, hear?"

"Why Clem, you'll know the minute I know."

"Thank you."

"And I'll see you next week for your trim?"

"Of course. I'll be there." The moment they hung up, Loretta phoned to tell me the whole conversation and I told her about the call from Dottie Hrnicek. We were still talking when Dot called again, so I conferenced her in.

It turned out that Mr. Moore had a business license on file, just like he should have had, but Dot said that having a business license did not mean he was a salesman. It didn't even mean he was a businessman. It just meant that he could do business in Nebraska if he wanted to.

Dot also told Lo and me that Mr. Moore had no criminal record on file, not even a speeding ticket, and that he had a credit rating that would give a bank president goose bumps. She never told Clem, though. No one in the Circle ever would, at least without discussing it with me first.

Chapter 10

Empathy for God

FOR THE SECOND day in a row, Mr. Moore arrived at Lily's desk at 10:25 sharp. Calvin was already there, so he waved his guest on in. As soon as Mr. Moore walked into his office, Calvin said, "Good morning, Vernon," and extended his hand across his desk.

Mr. Moore shook it and answered, "It certainly is a beautiful day, isn't it? I was just at Clem Tucker's River House for breakfast and the view from his backyard was magnificent. If I'd had a good book and a sack lunch, I might be there yet."

"You were at the River House? That's a high social honor around here, Vernon. There aren't a dozen people in all of Hayes County who have dined there, myself included. What was the occasion, if I may ask?"

"I'm not sure I know. Maybe it was just a breakfast between two old men who overdress."

Calvin, who was wearing a blue denim work shirt, jeans, and cowboy boots, chose not to disagree. Instead, he checked his watch and asked, "Are you always early?"

"I have to admit I am. It stems from an observation I made in the military when I was a young man. I discovered that being on time was important but nearly impossible—that I was always either early or late. I also discovered that there were two kinds of people, the early people and the late people, and that the early people, especially drill sergeants, were constantly aggravated by the late people. For some reason, drill sergeants are particularly aggravated by tardiness. That's why I decided to join the early people. My life has been less stressful ever since."

Calvin smiled and asked, "Is that an example of what you call arbitrary lines?"

Mr. Moore replied, "I see that you've been doing your homework, Calvin, and yes it is. I decided to draw the line on the side of being early, which is a very large time interval, rather than attempting to draw it at on time, which is arbitrarily narrow and greatly increases the risk of being late."

"I see it's worked."

"It has."

Lily brought in some iced water for Mr. Moore. It was in a giant-sized "Go Huskers" mug. Mr. Moore thanked her, and Calvin looked at his watch again.

Mr. Moore took a sip of his water and said, "Is there some place you'd rather be?"

"No. No, there isn't. I'm just agitated. You talk about stress? I'm agitated all the damn time these days. Can we get on with it? You said you were going to sell me some hope. I'm a buyer. Let's get on with your pitch."

"Fair enough, but your use of the word 'pitch' gives me cause for concern. I'm not an old-time preacher who's going to mesmerize you with spiritual oratory. That's the road to blind faith. Our goal is reasoned faith, and that's a destination that can only be reached by logic."

"What happened to common sense?"

"I think the two are the same, don't you?"

"Fine. Okay. As I remember, our first stop is another Arbitrary Line. Right?"

"Not quite. First we need to examine the Paradox of the Benevolent God. Do you remember it?"

"I remember the gist of it, but not by heart."

"It goes like this, Calvin:

Only a benevolent God would create heaven and Earth;
But no benevolent God would allow so much pain and suffering on Earth;
Therefore, there is no benevolent God."

"Okay. I got it."

"Good. If we're going to defeat the paradox then, logically speaking, we have to start at the beginning. Fair enough?"

"What do you mean?"

"We have to begin with the first premise, Calvin: 'Only a benevolent God could create heaven and Earth.'"

"Why do we have to start there? I don't even agree with it."

"As I remember, the reason you don't agree with it is because your daughter has suffered so much pain and suffering at such a young age."

"That's exactly true."

"Well, that's the second statement. Like most folks, you seem to take it as axiomatic that no benevolent God would ever permit so much pain and suffering."

"He wouldn't; I'm sure of it."

"I understand your feeling, but it's more of an emotional reaction than a logical conclusion. Why don't we test the logic? That means you have to accept the first statement. Otherwise, we're stuck."

"Fine. I'll buy it. Only a benevolent God would create heaven and Earth. Let's move on."

"Good. Did you ever play baseball in Little League?"

Calvin shook his head but replied, "That question came right out of left field but yes, of course."

"Was your coach an ex–baseball player? I know mine was."

"Yes he was. As I remember, he played at Peru College."

"Good. Now let me ask you a question. What would have happened if he had put himself in to pitch every time your opposing team got runners on base?"

"What? That's preposterous!"

"Why?"

"It's perfectly obvious. We were just kids. We wouldn't have learned anything about teamwork, or hard work, or winning and losing, or fairness. The only thing we'd have learned was to call in the coach every time we got in a jam."

"You're absolutely right, which means that you're now qualified to go on to the next plateau."

"Which is what?"

"For the next few minutes, Calvin Millet, I would like you to be God."

Calvin grimaced at the thought and said, "This is the empathy part that you warned about yesterday, right?"

"Yes."

"Well it's quite a leap, but I guess it's a leap I'm willing to take." Calvin waved his right hand in front of him, as if he had a magic wand in it, and said, "Zip zap, shazam, my Lucy is cured."

"Not so fast, God."

"My predecessor did it for Lazarus and His own Son. I can do it for my daughter. What's more empathetic than that?"

"His Son only got a weekend pass, and you said it yourself: no religious claptrap."

Calvin sat back and folded his arms over his chest. Mr. Moore continued, "You're God now; you're all-powerful. You've created heaven and Earth, and now you have these tiny creatures running around who appear to show an occasional spark of intelligence. What are you going to do with them?"

"What do you mean?"

"Are you going to pitch for them every time they get in a jam?"

"No. Of course not."

"Are you going to feed them and care for them, like pets?"

Calvin considered the question for a moment, then answered, "No. They don't need it. They can feed themselves; even the bugs at the bottom of the food chain can feed themselves."

"That's correct, but there are other ways you can help. For instance, are you going to provide them with all the modern conveniences?"

"Maybe, Vernon. Come to think of it, no. No, I'm not. I want them to be different from the rest of the animals, to develop new things themselves. That's why I gave the critters some brains in the first place."

"Excellent. But I bet you would keep them from disease, wouldn't you?"

Calvin did not pause for one second. He said, "Yes, definitely. I can see where you're heading, Vernon, but I'm a benevolent God, the genuine article. I would eliminate all disease."

"So that's where you would draw the line. You would let human beings alone, except that you would eliminate disease."

"Yep. That's it."

"What about war? More than forty million people died in World War II alone, many of them under the most horrible conditions. Wouldn't you do something about war?"

"Yes. Definitely."

"What? Would you eliminate weapons? Then you would have

to eliminate invention, wouldn't you, because the line between peaceful and wartime use of so many things is blurry. Airplanes and knives come immediately to mind."

"Fine. Okay. I'll let the critters make war if they insist. But no disease."

"How about accidents? Could your people die or be maimed in accidents?"

"Hell, I guess I'd have to permit that, too. Otherwise I'd be tinkering again."

"That's true, but what about crime? Rape, murder, theft, child abuse?"

"No. I wouldn't permit any of that. I couldn't."

"Really? How on earth would you prevent it?"

Calvin replied, "I'd just reprogram everyone, men mostly, so that no one would want to hurt anyone anymore."

"Ah! Another excellent answer. In other words, you would exterminate free will."

This prompted a long pause, during which Calvin felt no compunction to answer.

Eventually, Mr. Moore said, "Of course, you could threaten your charges with eternal damnation if they were bad. Maybe that would stop some of the violence."

Calvin replied, "Fine. Okay. I would have to permit accidents and violence—but I'm still safe on disease. There will be no disease on my planet. If my critters never have any, then they'll never know what they're missing."

"Fair enough. You win. No disease."

Calvin sat forward and smiled. "I do? Great! That means you lose, Vernon."

"Do I, or have you simply redrawn the line?"

"What do you mean?"

"There is still pain and suffering on your world. There's a ton of it. You decided to allow war and crime and accidents on your world. How could you, a benevolent God, ever permit so much pain and suffering?"

"I had to; you made me. We went through it, step by step."

"Correct. You made your humans different from animals by giving them intelligence. So they could use that intelligence, you also gave them the gift of free will. But the moment you gave them free will, you couldn't prevent them from inflicting pain and suffering on themselves, either purposely or by accident."

"That's true, but I did eliminate a lot of pain and suffering because I eliminated disease. AIDS, too, that's out on my planet."

"Fair enough, but all you've done is redrawn the line. There's still a hell of a lot of pain and suffering on your planet, and there are two sides to that issue. I'm sure there could be less pain and suffering on Earth, but I'm equally sure that there could be a lot more, too."

"What do you mean?"

"What if we lived on a planet where the high temperature was minus fifteen and electricity hadn't been invented yet? What if we were hunted by rabid, flesh-eating bugs the size of lawn tractors?

What if we had nothing but gums after our baby teeth fell out, so that all we could eat was soup and yogurt after the age of eleven? On the pain and suffering scale, it seems to me that things could be a lot worse."

Calvin knew that simple logic obligated him to agree but he could not bring himself to do it. Mr. Moore waited. Calvin ultimately said, "Your point is that things could be worse here."

"Precisely. Things could be a hell of a lot worse. Of course, things could be better, too. What if there was no cold, no heat, no hunger, no disease, no war, no crime, no video games, no speed limits, and none of those damn jet skis that can raise the dead? Then the world would be a much, much better place, wouldn't it?"

Calvin remained resolutely mute. Mr. Moore said, "Well?"

Calvin said, "I give."

Mr. Moore said, "Exactly. In a world like that, we would be robbed of our senses, our emotions, and any hope of self-actualization. We would never know that we were warm because we would never be cold. We would never know that we were happy because we would never be sad. We would never be fulfilled because everything would be done for us. Our free will would be so confined that it would have to be relabeled. We'd have to call it something like partial free will or conditional free will."

Calvin answered, "I get it; I get it."

"Good. So you, as benevolent God for the day, have a choice: you can either give your critters free will, which will cause them a lot of pain and suffering; or you can eliminate their pain and suffering, but only at the expense of free will. You can't have it both ways. Which way do you choose?"

Calvin did not reply, so Mr. Moore answered his own question, "Free will is the greater gift but, in the interest of free will, a benevolent God would have to permit pain and suffering. The only question is where He would draw the line. In that regard, we have agreed that things could be a bit better but that they could also be a whole hell of a lot worse. In other words, our God has been, well, benevolent to us."

Calvin felt like he was getting a tooth pulled. He said softly, "I suppose so."

Mr. Moore went on. "The news isn't bad; it's good. It means that there may be a benevolent God out there."

"Okay. Fine. There may be a benevolent God, but He sure screwed my daughter in the process of being so damn nice to the rest of us."

"You're absolutely correct, Calvin."

Calvin sat forward and replied, "I am? Is that what you just said?"

"Yes. Life is unfair; it's very unfair."

"Damn right it is, which means we're right back to square one."

"Actually, Calvin, we're not. From a logical point of view, we have an entirely different problem. The existence of pain and suffering is no longer the dilemma; we now understand that to be a function of free will. Our new problem is the abject unfairness of living. How can we resolve the plight of an African child with no prospects and a life expectancy of forty-two disease-ridden, half-starved years against a man who is born to the aristocracy and lives fat, loose, and disease-free until the age of ninety-seven?"

Calvin said, "Amen, brother. Now I suppose you're going to tell me that a benevolent God would allow unfairness, aren't you? At this point, I wouldn't be surprised if you told me that He bathed in it."

"As a matter of fact, I'm not going to tell you that. Not this time. I don't believe that a benevolent God would be even remotely tolerant of unfairness."

Calvin shot back, "Then how in the hell do you explain Lucy?"

Before Mr. Moore could answer, Lily barged into Calvin's office with a worried look on her face and said, "Mr. Millet, there's a call for you on line one. It's Nurse Nelson. She says she needs to talk to you right now."

Calvin looked across his desk and said, "Could you two excuse me?"

Mr. Moore responded, "Of course." Lily shut the door on their way out and returned to her desk. Mr. Moore sat quietly in a chair nearby.

After only a few moments, Calvin came flying out of his office with his briefcase in one hand and said breathlessly, "I have to go straight home, Lily. Please take my messages for the rest of the day."

Mr. Moore stood up. Calvin looked him in the eye and said, "Your benevolent God is getting on my nerves, Vernon."

Mr. Moore replied, "There is a solution. I promise you. There is hope."

"Well, hope will have to wait because Lucy is in a hell of a lot of pain all of a sudden."

Mr. Moore said, "Tomorrow then?"

"Hell no. Hell, I don't know. I just don't know. Check with Lily in the morning. If I'm back at work, then we can meet again, but I won't be back if Lucy's not feeling a lot better."

Mr. Moore said forcefully, "Lucy deserves to know the truth. Either tell her today or be back here tomorrow."

Calvin said to Lily, "Mind the goddamn store." Then he scowled at Mr. Moore and sprinted down the stairs.

Like I told you earlier, Calvin had rented a tiny place in Carson, which is a dreary, half-empty hamlet on the edge of the county. The house itself is as square as a toilet tissue with faded green shingles, an old, gray composition roof, no dining room, no porch, and a one-car, detached garage at the end of a potholed, gravel driveway. There is an old broken swing, one scrawny tree, and a rusted-out natural gas tank in the backyard. The last time I saw the place, the lawn had not been mowed since the Reagan administration, and the folks next door raised chickens which, depending on the direction of the wind, sometimes gave the air a disagreeable smell.

When Calvin got there, Doc Wiley and Nurse Nelson were waiting for him in the front room. He came dashing through the door and said, "How is she? What's going on?"

Doc Wiley put his hand up and started to speak. Calvin interrupted him before he could say one word, "Don't you tell me to calm down, Hank; I'm not in the mood."

Nurse Nelson took over. "We have an important decision to make, Calvin, a very important decision about Lucy. You can either be calm or you can be in a tizzy. It's up to you."

Calvin sat down in a smelly, old stuffed chair that had once been an undeterminable shade of green.

Hank waited for a bit and then said, "She's in terrible pain . . . "

Calvin shot back, "Then make it go away, Doc."

Nurse Nelson said, "That's the decision we have to make. If the doctor gives her any more anesthetic, it will put her to sleep."

"So?"

"She will stay that way. She won't be able to wake up."

Calvin put his head in his hands. Nurse Nelson moved over, sat on the arm of his chair, and put her hand on his shoulder.

Doc Wiley started up again. "We have to make a decision, Calvin, but I don't see that there's really much of a choice. Lucy's in terrible pain right now. She's all curled up and sweaty and shivering. Her teeth are clenched so tight she can hardly speak."

Calvin stood up abruptly. "I have to see her," he said. Then he strode right into her room, Doc Wiley and Nurse Nelson in close pursuit.

Little Lucy slept in a special hospital bed, and she almost always had an IV running into one arm or the other—both of them were permanently bruised from the elbows down to the backs of her hands. Right then, she was lying on her side with her knees pulled up to her chest, shivering like a cold baby chickadee even though she was covered in a quilt and a pink wool blanket all the way up to her chin. Calvin sat down beside her and put his hand on her forehead.

Lucy looked up and said, "You f-fibbed, Daddy. I asked Nurse Na-Nelson. There's no such law that says ch-children can't die f-first."

Calvin replied, "It's a brand-new law, sweetheart. Nurse Nelson just hasn't heard about it yet. Isn't that true, Louise?"

Nurse Nelson tried to smile and said, "Your father is right, dear. Doc Wiley told me about it just this morning."

Lucy did not respond. Calvin said, "How do you feel, sweetheart?"

"I h-hurt. My legs and my b-back, they really, really h-hurt." She clenched her teeth and closed her eyes again.

"Do you want Doc Wiley to give you something to make the pain go away?"

"Ye-es."

"It will make you sleep. Is that okay?"

Lucy remained rigid in her bed, shivering like a leaf in a thunderstorm. All she could say was, "Uh-huh."

"Okay, sweetheart. We'll let you sleep. I'll check on you again later, okay?"

Lucy did not say another thing. Calvin ran his fingers through her hair, and then he nodded to Doc Wiley. Nurse Nelson stood up and turned a knob on Lucy's IV line, then she and Hank left Calvin alone with his daughter.

About twenty minutes later, he came back into the front room. "She's sound asleep," he said, and then he sat down again.

Nurse Nelson said gently, "I don't think there was any other choice."

"She's right, Calvin; we've run out of options."

Calvin's head shot up and he said, "What do you mean by that?"

"We're out of alternatives. You know it; I know it. Lucy is not going to get any better. If we let her wake up, then she'll be in at least as much pain as she was just now, maybe more."

"Are you sure, Hank? How can you be that sure? You don't even know what she has. How the hell can you be sure that we're out of options?"

"We've pushed the envelope about as far as we can push it, Calvin. You've tried harder to cure your daughter than any parent I ever saw, but we're done."

"Are you suggesting that I quit?"

"I'm suggesting that you pray. That's all we have left."

"Pray to who? I just spent an hour with a complete stranger who convinced me that a benevolent God would allow pain and suffering. Can you imagine? Hell, if God's behind all the pain and suffering, what's the point of prayer? What do I ask for, a ski boat?"

Doc Wiley didn't know what to say.

Nurse Nelson said, "Dr. Wiley has to go back to town, Calvin. Perhaps you two can discuss this again over the phone tonight. Would that be better?"

Calvin answered, "No problem. Lucy's sound asleep and I'm surly as hell. I'm sorry for being such a prick. I hope you understand."

"I do, Calvin. I do understand. Are you sleeping okay? Would you like something for your nerves?"

"No, I want to enjoy my pain and suffering, every goddamn minute of it." With that, Calvin Millet stormed out of the front door and jumped into his Jeep. Nobody knows where he went. Nobody ever asked.

Chapter 11

The Ebb Tribe

My daughter Mona arrived at the Come Again just after eleven, and I could tell from the front window that she wasn't right. She was dressed in old gray sweat clothes, floppy socks, and dirty tennis shoes, and her hair looked like two mangy old cats had just had a fight in it. No married woman who looks like that is interested in her man, at least not in any physical context, but a mother's love is independent of appearance. I intercepted her at the porte-cochere and gave her a great big hug, and then I led her into my kitchen for tea. Before we even sat down, she started to yammer on about the kids.

Your kids are your kids for life. I interrupted her on the spot. "Mona," I said, "you didn't drive all the way down here to tell me about the boys. I talked to your sister yesterday. I know that something disagreeable is going on up there. Is it that dentist?"

"No. Not really."

"Then what is it, sweetheart?"

"It's not Marv, Mama. Not really. I'm the problem."

That made me gnash my teeth. "We Porters are not Jewish people, Mona, and we aren't Irish either. We're Americans. That means we don't blame ourselves when something goes wrong, we blame somebody else. Now, what has Marv done?"

"Nothing, Mama, and that's the problem. Marv is exactly as advertised, and I am absolutely bored to tears with it."

It didn't seem like the best time to revisit premarital admonitions, so I said, "Explain yourself, Mona. No more beating around the bush."

"You know I love the kids, but . . . "

"This is not about the kids, Mona. Anyone can see that. Get on with it. Get it out."

"I am bored stiff, Mama. With Marv. All he does is fill cavities, watch TV sports, and play golf. He doesn't read except for the sports page and *Sports Illustrated*. He won't eat anything except red meat and potatoes. He won't talk about anything but sports and gum disease. If I have to sit through one more lecture on proper flossing technique at the dinner table, I'll blow a gasket. Every shelf in my house has at least one strand of Gore-Tex floss on it, as if he was marking it. We have sex on Sunday mornings, tee time permitting, of course, and it's always the same routine. He holes out while I'm still on the fairway.

"Marv's only idea of a vacation is going to the family cabin out on Lake McConaughy. We have done that every single year we've been married. Every single year. He wears the same white smock to work every day, only the color of his slacks changes. On the weekends, everything he wears above the waist says "Nebraska" or "Go Huskers" somewhere on it. We don't go to the movies; we buy DVDs. That way, Marv can watch them over and over again if there's enough sex and violence to hold his attention.

"I didn't marry a man, Mama, I married a rerun. In my mind, I've started calling him Rerun. Rerun Breck. The other day I let it slip, but he didn't notice because he wasn't listening."

"Have you thought about seeing another marriage counselor?"

"No. Not after that first experience. I still don't know who that man was more attracted to: Marv or me."

"How about a pastor?"

"A Catholic priest? Yeah, right. Did you see one before you left my dad?"

"Yes. As a matter of fact, we did."

"Well, I think I know the answer, but how did that work out?"

I answered factually, "It was very pious."

"Yep. Love, honor, and obey. What a bunch of anachronistic crap. You know, Mama, I'd settle for a walk, a talk, and a vegetarian recipe one night a week."

I could tell that I was running out of ammunition, which meant that I would have to be sympathetic. That is what we mothers are supposed to be but, as you know, it is not my strong suit, and Mona had just reminded me of my ex-husband to boot. With all the sympathy I could summon up, I said, "Boredom is a self-inflicted condition, sweetheart. In this case, you inflicted it upon yourself when you married that simple-minded, son-of-a-bicuspid. Now tell me the truth: how hard have you tried to break Marv out of this rerun behavior of his?"

"I took up Japanese cooking a few years ago, but Marv wouldn't touch it. I got a one-hundred-dollar makeover, a negligée, and a porno movie, but the sex was the same and the movie disappeared. I had to pay for it. Just a week ago, I took the kids over to Winona's and fixed Marv a candlelight dinner, but right after it was over he turned on a basketball game between two colleges that I've never even heard of. I think one of them was named Iona. I washed the dishes and went to bed by myself."

My daughter shook her head slowly and continued, "I never saw it until we moved up to Omaha, but you know what? Marv is a carbon copy of his dad. He's not even rerunning his own life; he's rerunning his father's. What's the point of living if everything you do is a rerun of a rerun?"

Somehow, I was getting the feeling that we had not reached the real heart of the matter. I said, "Tell me the truth. Has Marv been unfaithful to you?"

Mona didn't think about my question for one second. With no emotion whatsoever, she said, "I think he has, Mama. He comes home late from work a lot these days. To tell the truth, though,

I don't really care one way or the other. In fact, I hope he is having an affair, something illegal in a dental chair with laughing gas and blunt instruments, anything that would be a departure from the same old missionary crap. I swear to God, I'd pay the girl myself if he would do something interesting for a change."

When a woman no longer cares whether her husband is unfaithful or not, her marriage is pretty much done for. But I had to ask for final confirmation. "Do you love him, sweet . . .

"No, Mama."

Well, if there was even a tinge of equivocation in her reply, it flew right by me. I said, "How about Marv? Does he love you?"

"If he does, then his definition of love and my definition of household appliance are dangerously similar."

I thought about what she said for a second or two, and then I asked, "What do you want to . . . "

Apparently, she had already thought this out. Faster than you could blink an eye, she said, "I want to live in Europe, cross the equator and see Peru and New Zealand, visit the world's great art galleries, learn to scuba dive."

"What about Matthew and Mark?"

"They can come, too."

"Is that practical?"

"We're not gonna do it all at once. Don't be silly."

Once you become a fully fledged mother, you're issued a special, child-in-danger antenna to warn you when things like this are going to happen. It allows you to steel yourself in advance, but you can never quite imagine the feelings you will have when the poop finally hits the fan. I knew Mona's time was coming and I expected to be sad, even a bit remorseful, as if it was partially my fault, but I felt more like having a snack. I said, "How long have you felt this way, sweetheart?"

"More than five years. Ever since Mark started to school."

Five years sounds like a long time, but it's pretty close to par for suffering wives. I pressed on for a while anyway. In the back of my mind, though, I was wondering why we women ever let ourselves become so dependent on the institution of marriage in the first place.

When I was bringing up Mona and Winona in North Platte, my husband, Al, was nearly never at home. Even when he was, he wasn't, if you get my meaning. For all practical purposes, I had to raise my children alone, just like Mona does. That's what marriage means to a lot of women, working or not: it means raise your children alone. Here in Ebb, though, Mona's boys would be raised by an extended family. I would help, Loretta would help, Hank Wiley would help, Dot Hrnicek would help, Lulu Tiller would help, Buzz Busby would help, and so would the entire membership of the Quilting Circle. Every teacher from kindergarten through twelfth grade would know those boys by their first and last names, as would the whole Ebb tribe. By the time they graduated from high school, they would be so spoiled that we would be glad to put them on a bus out of town. In the meantime, though, they would be loved and cherished and watched over every minute. It may not take a village to raise a child, like the old saw says, but you sure do get a better result if you use one.

Presently, I brought out some chips and dips so Mona and I could munch our way through lunch. While we ate, our conversation drifted to Winona, who's not exactly thrilled with her situation either, and the latest news in Ebb. Mona was very interested in Calvin. He was a senior in high school when she was a freshman, so they hardly knew each other at all, but she had always admired him from afar. Of course, she already knew about his divorce and the tornado, but I hadn't told her the latest about Lucy.

I could see that Mona was starting to get melancholy around two o'clock, just as it was time for her to start back home. I was about to give her another big hug when I got a call from Hank Wiley. I could tell he wanted to talk, so I promised that I'd call him back. Then Vernon Moore came strolling into my kitchen, dressed for all the world like a Wall Street tycoon, except friendly looking. Mona dabbed at her eyes with the sleeve from her sweatshirt and we both stood up. It seemed like the proper thing to do.

Mr. Moore smiled, his eyes sparkled, and he said, "Good afternoon, Wilma. This must be your lovely daughter Mona of whom you have spoken so often."

I told you that she looked like something that the cat had dragged in, but he extended his hand. "It's a great pleasure to meet you."

Mona looked at me and shook his hand meekly without uttering a single word.

I said cheerfully, "Good afternoon, Mr. Moore. Please forgive the condition of my kitchen. I didn't expect to see you back so soon."

"Don't fret about it for even one minute," he said. "I came back to the house to change into something a bit less officious for the rest of the day."

Mona sat back down and stared at the bean dip. She still hadn't uttered a single word. Mr. Moore looked her over like an appraiser, but just for a split second, and then he said, "You have two sons, don't you, Mona?"

"Yes," she answered to the dip, although I could hardly hear her say it.

Unexpectedly, Mr. Moore sat down, too. "I thought so. I thought that was what your mother said. I'm a frustrated grandfather. Would you do me a small favor? Would you tell me a story about one of your boys? Just for a minute."

Mona turned toward me with a look on her face that said, *Is this man a nut ball?* I nodded my head but explained, "Mr. Moore is a salesman, Mona, or maybe he isn't. Whatever he is, he is a nice man and he is sincere. That's all you need to know."

Still looking at me, Mona asked, "What kind of story, Mr. Moore?"

"A funny story."

I nodded again, so Mona turned her eyes to Mr. Moore's electric blues. "Okay. I think I can do that.

"My two boys, Matthew and Mark, are fourteen and eleven. Ever since Matt was two, we've also had a Scottish terrier named Macbeth. Macbeth sleeps with me most of the time, meaning on my side of the bed. Years ago, I was awakened by a loud thunk in the middle of the night. Naturally, I woke right up, elbowed my husband, Marv, and asked, 'What was that?'

"Now Marv is not as fond of Macbeth as I am. He answered, 'Aw, that was just the dawg, honey. He crawled onto my side of the bed, so I heaved him off with my foot.'

" 'That's very interesting,' I replied, 'because Macbeth is lying right here next to me.' He was, too, stretched out just like a human being with his head on my pillow, but on my left side where Marv couldn't see him. Of course, Marv and I both jumped up and ran to the foot of the bed. There was Mark, who was just three years old at the time, lying on the floor. He was in his Blackshirt PJs, sucking his thumb and clutching his blanket, sleeping like a baby. He hadn't woken up, even though Marv had kicked him out of our bed."

Mr. Moore smiled and said, "I take it that no permanent damage was done."

"None that I could see. I just carried him back to his little bed and tucked him in."

"That was an excellent story. Thank you. But what about his brother, Matthew? He's a teenager now, isn't he? Tell me, what would you like him to be when he grows up?"

Mona paused before answering, "I want him to be intelligent

and considerate of others. After that, I don't care what he does in his life as long as there is an element of adventure in it. That's what I wish for both my sons."

"That's a very good wish."

Without skipping a beat, Mona said, "My grandfathers are both dead, Mr. Moore, and I haven't seen my own father in twenty years, so my boys suffer from a dearth of role models. Would you tell me a story about one good man who is not a board-certified dentist? Just for a minute, and then I have to go."

Mr. Moore smiled and answered, "Okay, I'll tell you about my grandfather, a man named Joe Moore. He was born to a dirt-poor family and got little education, so he grew up to become a sharecropper on exactly thirty-seven acres of Ohio river bottomland. When the owner died, he left it to my grandfather out of gratitude and kindness.

"Grandpa Joe was a skinny, frail-looking man but he made enough from that tiny acreage to support my grandmother for more than fifty years. He raised my father, who went on to become an influential educator in the state of Tennessee, and he fought and defeated tuberculosis before there were any drugs to help him do it.

"Then, at the age of ninety-one, Grandpa Joe contracted pneumonia, so my father took him to the local hospital for care. Grandpa Joe thought he was there to cheer up the other patients, but as soon as they put a gown on him he knew better. The moment my father left, he put his pants and shoes back on and snuck out. He forgot his socks.

"He bought six cows on his way home and drove them five miles, on foot. He died two years later with a smile on his face. The autopsy revealed that he had only one lung. He had coughed the other one up over the years because of his tuberculosis, but nobody ever knew about it because he never complained."

I asked, "Did you know him well?"

"Not well, Wilma. He was a quiet, stoic man. But like my father, I grew up in his shadow. Since then, I've known dozens of CEOs and financiers and politicians but, to this day, my Grandpa Joe was the strongest man I have ever known."

Mona said, "That must be pretty hard to live up to, Mr. Moore."

"I don't even try, Mona. He is beyond my reach. But every time I think my life is even a bit rough, I try to remember my Grandpa Joe. Even though I didn't know him well, he gave me the gift of perspective."

Mona stood up. "Thank you, Mr. Moore. That was nice. And it was a pleasure meeting you."

He stood, too, and replied, "The pleasure was mine. I wish you a safe trip back to Omaha this evening."

I said, "Tea, Mr. Moore? Around four?"

He smiled and answered, "That's a lovely offer, Wilma, but why don't you meet me at Starbucks instead? I'll miss your biscuits, but you won't have to clean up."

I accepted gratefully and walked Mona out to the guest parking area, where she got her big hug or I got mine, depending upon your point of view. Just before she pulled away, she stuck her head out the window of her SUV and said to me, "That man does have an outlook, Mama. What do you suppose he would advise me to do?"

"I don't know for sure. He's a hard man to read, but I think he did give you some advice."

"Are you sure, Mama?"

"No, sweetheart. I'm not even a tiny bit sure. You decide for yourself, and call me when you get home, so I will know you're safe."

I stood there in my parking lot after Mona had driven off, just thinking to myself, and I will tell you what was on my mind. If there are any boys and girls out there, I want you to pay attention.

Americans are blessed. When most of us are children, we are hardly ever faced with anything but opportunity: do we wear this dress or that one? do we play house or harass the boys? do we watch TV or go to the movies? Those are what Clem Tucker calls win–win decisions, and that's the way life is intended to be for children.

As we grow up, though, we start to be confronted with win–lose decisions: smoke or not; do our homework or not; have unprotected sex or not. These are some of the most important choices of our lives, but they aren't the hardest.

Sometimes adults have to face lose-lose decisions, meaning that there is not a positive alternative to be had. A single mother who is asked to do something sexual by her boss faces just such a dilemma. If she agrees, she loses her self-respect, and he loses his respect for her. If she refuses, she may lose her job. Men who are asked to break the law, like Mr. Moore once was, are put in the same boat. Lose-lose.

The test of adulthood is not to be paralyzed by the absence of a good alternative; it is to have the courage to make the least worst call. That's exactly the challenge that was facing my Mona. No matter what she did, her boys and her husband would be hurt, and she would be, too, but she still had to make the least worst decision.

I went back into the house to clean up my kitchen, but Hank Wiley called me back before I could get it done. I was right; he did want to talk. After hearing him explain his problem, I suggested that he meet Mr. Moore and me at Starbucks.

Chapter 12

The Doctor's Dilemma

WHEN I GOT to Starbucks, Mr. Moore was already sitting in the corner booth nursing a big, fat frappuccino and reading a skinny little book. He seemed all wrapped up in it, so I went to the counter and ordered myself a peppermint mocha that tasted like coffee with a hotel mint in it. As soon as I returned to the booth, he jumped up and said, "Hello, Wilma. Please have a seat."

I slid into the opposite side and said, "What are you reading?"

"Oh," he said. "It's a book by Hesse, an interesting item called *Demian.*"

I never got to go to college. At the age of nineteen, I was raising a baby girl, holding down a full-time job, and keeping up a house for a man who would black out whenever he heard the words *cook* or *clean,* so I've never read Hesse. If you would have asked me who he was, I would have guessed that he was a TV comedian. Better yet, I would have asked Loretta. She would know the right answer. That woman has read more books than two college professors. I asked innocently, "What's so interesting about it?"

Mr. Moore answered, "He had such an optimistic view of human potential. He was convinced that we were on the edge of greatness, but humanity's next great leaps were the Depression and World War II. I'm not sure that we've made any real progress since, either."

Well, what do you say after that? I'm sure that I don't know. With considerable relief, I watched Mr. Moore dog-ear the page he was reading and put the book aside. He said, "My apologies, Wilma. Sometimes I seem to lack the intestinal fortitude for philosophy. I'd probably be better off watching TV."

It occurred to me then that I had never seen Mr. Moore in the parlor at the Come Again, which is where my only TV set is. I said, "Do you watch any television?"

"I used to, but not anymore. Too much violence, too many commercials, too much artificial 'reality,' and too much repetition, especially too much repetition. I prefer the radio and a good book. When I listen to the radio or read a book, the song or the story appears in my mind. I can read in silence, too. There's a lot to be said for silence."

Well, I have another question for you. What do you say to a man who has just said that there is a lot to be said for silence? At the time, I had no idea so I just smiled and waited for him to go on. Naturally, he stopped right there, so all of a sudden we were two talkers short of a conversation. I don't know about you, but I have never been into body language much either. I think people should talk to each other and it makes me uncomfortable when they don't. I gave up and said, "I'm glad you got to meet my Mona."

"I am too, Wilma. She seems like an intelligent, caring woman."

"She is, but she's also very unhappy at the moment."

"I sensed that, but I'm sorry to hear that it is truly so."

"By the way," I said, "I thought you told Loretta and me that you never had any children. How could you have any grandchildren?"

Mr. Moore answered, "You have me. I don't have any grandchildren. At just that moment, though, it seemed to me that your daughter needed a distraction, so I created some atmosphere to help her talk about her boys."

I guess I shouldn't have been surprised, but I was. Still, it wasn't as if he was lying about the length of this or that. I said, "I suppose the end can justify the means but, just so I have my story straight, did you really have a grandfather named Joe?"

Mr. Moore grinned and replied, "Yes, and he was exactly as I described him."

"Did you have a special reason for telling Mona that story?"

"I can't say for sure. She asked for a role model, so a story about one of the felons of industry that I used to work for didn't seem appropriate."

"Did you mean to give her some advice? I think she read it that way."

"No I didn't, Wilma. I think free advice is overpriced, don't you?"

Well, I had to shake my head again. I thought all he ever did was give advice. I said, "Then I have to apologize, Mr. Moore. I invited Doc Wiley to join us here for tea because he has a problem and I thought you could help him with it."

"He's the town doctor, isn't he?"

"He is, and a close personal friend with a difficult dilemma."

Mr. Moore replied, "In my experience, it helps to talk about hard problems. If we just listen, and maybe ask a few good questions, then we may be able to help him out a little."

Just as I was shaking my head again, Loretta materialized out of nowhere with a latte in her hand. Before I could say a word, she dropped right into the booth on my side and pushed me into the corner with her hip so that she could be directly across from Mr. Moore. Once she was settled in my spot, she said with a big grin, "Why this is unexpected! What are you two up to? Is it something I can mess with?"

"No it's not, Loretta," I said with just a teeny bit of frost.

Loretta was wearing a brown V-neck sweater and no brassiere. I think I've already told you that she is shameless, and her choice of attire, or lack thereof, seemed to catch Mr. Moore's eye. To be fair, there was no way a man could miss it unless he was blind and dead. Being neither, Mr. Moore smiled and said, "You look particularly fetching today, Loretta."

She arched her back a bit and replied, "Yes I do, don't I? What's that you're readin', Vern?"

"Hesse."

"Ugh, ugh, ugh. Not my cup of tea, darlin'. Give me mystery and give me death. Give me James Lee Burke or Walter Mosley. Have you ever read *Devil in a Blue Dress* or *Black Betty*? How about *White Butterfly*?"

"Yes I have. All three."

"Good. I just wanted to make sure that you were well informed and not just pullin' my leg last night. I have a question for you, Mr. Mandatory Interracial Marriage."

"Do your worst," he said.

Loretta smiled and replied, "Will you marry me?"

Mr. Moore checked his watch before answering, "Yes. Of course I will. I have a meeting right now, but we could go over to the county courthouse tomorrow morning and get a license. How would that be?"

Loretta sat back in the booth and began to pout. By now, you've probably guessed that she is a kung fu pouter, but Mr. Moore ignored her and said to me, "Are wedding banns still required by law in this part of the country, Wilma?"

"I don't think so," I replied. "Not too many folks get married in Ebb anymore. They go somewhere else for that and then come back here after they've gotten it out of their system. I can tell you this, though: if you marry Loretta Parsons, you'll be breaking the hearts of half the men in Hayes County."

Loretta sat up and said, "Just half?"

I batted my eyelashes and replied, "The other half lust after me, honey. You know that."

At precisely that moment, Hank Wiley walked up to our table. He was wearing a ratty old brown tweed suit, cowboy boots, and a tan-colored Stetson with a permanent, inch-high sweat line running all the way around it. I once offered to have that thing cleaned and blocked, but he wouldn't have it.

Sweaty hat in hand, he said, "Hello, Wilma. Hello, Loretta. I wasn't expecting such a large get-together." There was no eye contact whatsoever between Hank and me, and I'm not sure that he had even noticed that Mr. Moore was in the booth. His eyes were locked on Loretta's chest.

Have you ever seen a cat catch sight of a bird? They go stone motionless for a minute, just sizing it up. You would think a doctor would know better, especially a man of his age, but Hank was stone motionless, staring at Lo's chest. He might have stood there for ten more minutes if I hadn't smiled and said, "Lo was just keeping your seat warm, Hank. She has to get back to the salon for a shampoo and a lobotomy. Isn't that right, honey?"

Ignoring me, Loretta looked at Mr. Moore and said, "You think about my proposal, Vern."

"But . . . "

"I know what you said, but you didn't mean it."

Mr. Moore smiled and replied, "Let's talk again tomorrow."

"Call me, darlin'." Loretta flashed a big smile at Hank as she got up from the booth but I think he missed it entirely. His eyes were still stuck on her torso—all the way to the door. Loretta was gracious enough to turn, pose, and wave just before she left; then I said, "Hank Wiley, it's time for you to meet Mr. Vernon Moore. He's the lodger at the Come Again I told you about."

Mr. Moore came out of the booth to shake hands, and then they both sat down, Hank next to me where Loretta had been. That didn't last too long, though, because Hank had forgotten to get himself something to drink. I went with him—he can get a bit confused by a lot of options—and Mr. Moore read some more while we were gone.

When we got back, I told Mr. Moore what I knew about Hank, which was a lot, and I told Hank what I knew about Mr. Moore, which was a whole lot less. Then Hank started talking about the weather, so I figured it was going to be up to me to get the ball rolling.

"Hank, dear," I said, "Tell Mr. Moore and me about your dilemma. He's a smart man with some unconventional but interesting views, and he won't say anything about what he hears at this table. You have my promise on that."

"Mine, too," said Mr. Moore. "Whatever you say will be confidential."

That seemed to loosen Hank up. He said, "I don't know why I need to talk about this. The problem I have is one we doctors face all the time."

"What's that?" I asked.

Hank's brow furrowed up and he starting wringing his hands on the tabletop. After several more seconds, he said, "I have a patient who is dying, Wilma, and all of a sudden she's in terrible pain. I have three choices. Today, I sedated her with so much painkiller that it put her into the drug-induced equivalent of sleep. Tomorrow, I could lower the dosage so she would be conscious of the things around her again, but then she'd probably be in terrible pain. She has very little time left, so my third choice would be to help her on her way.

"This isn't a hard decision to make for old folks. They've had their time, so the cost of going just a bit early doesn't seem very high. But this patient is a child of eleven years; she hasn't lived any life at all. I just don't know what to do."

Of course, I knew he was talking about little Lucy. It took every ounce of resolve I had to hold back my tears.

Mr. Moore gave me a sympathetic look and said, "That's a heartbreaking decision, Dr. Wiley, but is it really yours?"

Hank replied, "Thank heavens, no. It's her father's call. But I have to advise him and I don't know what to tell him to do."

I sat there mute. I was too choked up to speak. Mr. Moore continued, "Do you think that's right? Do you think that the girl's father should make the decision?"

"Of course I do. Who else could make it? Do you think I should?"

"No. No, I don't. But there is an alternative. What if the little girl made the decision herself?"

"What?"

"It's just a question, but it may be worth considering for a minute."

Hank looked at me and said, "He is a man with peculiar views." Then he continued, "She's only eleven years old, Mr. Moore."

He replied, "I can't convince Wilma to call me Vernon, but I wish you would. And I know your patient is only eleven years old, but isn't that the point?"

"I'm not following you at all, Vernon. I don't see how I could put a decision like that in the hands of a child."

"Is she a smart little girl?"

"Yes. Very."

"Does she know what kind of shape she's in? Is she aware that she is terminally ill?"

"No. At least I don't think so. I've discussed it with her father, but I certainly haven't told her, and I don't think he has either."

"Then what's your plan, Doctor? Is it to let her drift into a slow, foggy death without ever knowing?"

"I guess so. I guess that's it. Do you have a better idea?"

"Yes. Let her live the rest of her life."

"What exactly does that mean?"

"You said that she's nearing the end of her life and that there's a difficult decision to make. Why not let her live the last chapter of her life to the fullest? Why not let her make the final decision herself?"

"She's a minor, and she's under heavy sedation."

"Doesn't the sedation wear off? Isn't there a way to give her an endurable consciousness that would allow her to spend a few more days or a few more weeks with her father?"

"I don't know. I just don't know."

"Have you researched every single option? Isn't there some way?"

Hank crossed his arms and puckered his lips back and forth for a while, like a fish. After some number of puckers, he said, "Well, maybe. Maybe so. Maybe I could give her an epidural. It would stop the pain in her legs, but only for a while, and not in some of her back. It's darn expensive too, and not approved for this sort of condition, so Calvin's insurance won't pay for it. I don't think he can afford any more experimental treatments, and it won't do anything for Lucy's health either. That can only deteriorate from here."

"But shouldn't she be allowed to experience her last days? I can't speak for Lucy or her father, but if it was me, the thing I would want most would be to live out the last few days of my life with the person I loved the most; I don't care what the cost. And if it was me, the thing that I would hate the most would be for someone else to make my last, most important decision for me. That decision is at the core of human life. It is the final exercise of free will, one of God's greatest gifts to us. I don't believe that children are exempt."

Hank answered, "So I have to tell her that she's dying?"

"No. Her father has to do that, but you need to help him."

"That's what you advise?"

"I can only ask for empathy, Dr. Wiley. I can only ask you to see that your dilemma is really her dilemma, and that you see it through her eyes."

"But if I was in her shoes, I would be scared to death. Wouldn't you?"

Mr. Moore looked at Hank like he could see straight through him and he said, "That's really it, isn't it? It's not the pain you're anesthetizing; it's the fear."

Hank squinted and mumbled something that sounded a lot like, "Maybe."

Mr. Moore heard what I heard. He fixed his eyes on Hank again and said, "What if there was no reason for Lucy to be afraid?"

Well, that perked me right up. Hank said, "No reason to be afraid? She's going to die."

"I know."

"That makes no sense. None whatsoever. She should be scared to death. Heck, a Marine would be scared to death."

"No she shouldn't. No one should be afraid of death."

Hank looked me again and said, "Is this man some sort of religious fanatic?"

I shook my head, so Hank asked Mr. Moore, "Okay. Why not?"

"Hope is the antidote for fear, Dr. Wiley. If we can give her hope, then she won't be afraid."

"Hope? What kind of hope?"

"Rational hope; reasoned hope."

"What?" Hank looked at me again and said, "Do you get any of this at all, Wilma, because I sure don't. What do you mean by reasoned hope?"

Mr. Moore answered, "I can answer that question, but it takes time. How much do you have?"

"Me? Why? Why do you ask?"

"I have a proposition for you. If I can convince you that there is hope for Lucy, that it is logical to believe that there is life after life, would your dilemma be a little easier to solve?"

"It would, Vernon. I'm sure it would. But that would be a pretty tall order."

"I've heard that said before, but I don't intend to prove that the afterlife is certain; only that it's very likely. That's enough for hope, even for optimism. Would a strong dose of hope be worth a few hours of your time?"

I was ready to say yes, but Hank replied, "I don't know. I'm not a religious man."

"I'm not either, Doctor."

"You aren't. Then . . . "

"Common sense. That's all we're going to use."

The good doctor did not answer. Like I said, he's not very good with alternatives. Mr. Moore added, "What have you got to lose?"

Hank thought about Mr. Moore's proposal for a few seconds and then he turned to me and said, "Well, what do you think, Wilma?"

I thought to myself, *I'm going to smack you on the side of your head, Hank Wiley.* But I smiled sweetly and said out loud, "Why don't we all have dinner at the Come Again tonight? You two can sit in my kitchen and talk. That way, I can listen in while I cook. Maybe some spaghetti with meatballs. How does that sound?"

If there is any one man who truly thinks with his stomach, it is Henry Wiley, M.D. He answered, "Well, now that you put it that way, what *do* I have to lose?"

Hank showed up in my kitchen around seven o'clock. Mr. Moore was already there, of course. We talked all the way through dinner and into the night, right up until Calvin Millet paged Hank at around ten o'clock. Hank called him back from my kitchen phone. I never had to ask him what was said on the other end of the line because the conversation was plain simple to understand from our end.

Hank said into the phone: "Hi, Calvin. I got your page. I'm calling from the Come Again. I'm here having dinner with Wilma and Vernon Moore."

We sat there in silence while Hank listened to Calvin. Then he said: "Yes, he is a peculiar man. How's Lucy?"

Long silence at our end.

Hank: "That's good. That's the best we can do for her right now."

Silence.

Hank: "Yes, I'll tell him you can't make it, but do you think that's wise?"

Silence.

Hank: "The way she's medicated now, Calvin, she doesn't know whether you're in Carson or in Costa Rica. She won't miss you if you come into town for a while."

Silence.

Hank: "I know it's for your peace of mind, too, but I think your peace of mind will be better served if you visit with Vernon Moore."

Silence.

Hank: "What?"

Silence.

Hank: "No, we haven't discussed the details of her condition; that's privileged information. We've been discussing matters of philosophy. I wish you could have been here."

Silence.

Hank: "Get off your high horse, Calvin Millet, and just listen for a darn minute. If what he's saying is even half right, then there is hope for Lucy. Not the kind we both wish she could have, but there is hope."

Silence.

Hank: "We're discussing the second paradox, something called the Unfairness Corollary. Have you talked about that yet?"

Silence.

Hank: "Well, I think you should. The solution is never something I would have dreamed of myself, but the way he puts it makes some sense."

Silence.

Hank: "I know. He has another idea that we should talk about, too."

Silence.

Hank: "I don't want to say anything about it on the phone, but it's an interesting point. Three hours ago I would've told you it was an idiotic notion, but now I'm not so sure."

Silence.

Hank: "Well, why don't you just listen to the man?"

Silence.

Hank: "Okay. Why don't I bring him down to Carson tomorrow morning? Like I said, Lucy won't know what you're doing anyway. She's too heavily sedated and she'll stay that way unless we change her medication. That's what I think we need to talk about."

Silence.

Hank: "We can discuss it tomorrow. I'll bring Vernon along. I'm your doctor, too, and I think you're ill. You're sick with sadness. Here's my prescription: listen to Vernon Moore for one more hour."

Silence.

Hank: "One hour, Calvin. What have you got to lose?"

Silence.

Hank: "Just check her vitals on the monitor and then go to bed. If anything happens, Nurse Nelson will hear an alarm and she'll be in Lucy's room in two shakes."

Silence.

Hank: "Eight-thirty. I'll be there. You get some rest."

Silence.

Hank: "I know, but it won't do Lucy any good if you stay up all night. The next time I offer you a sedative, you might consider it for a minute. Remind me tomorrow and I'll leave you something that will put a rhino to sleep."

Silence.

Hank: "We'll be there at eight-thirty. Just go to bed."

After Hank got off the phone, he had a short chat with Mr. Moore and they agreed to drive down in separate cars after breakfast, which I volunteered to fix. Then the three of us went back to discussing philosophical matters and we didn't stop until 2 A.M. For the last two hours, Mr. Moore and I listened while Hank talked about his deceased wife, Emma, bless her soul. My Lord, he let it all hang out. It came in gushes. I have never seen a man cry like that, any man, but he felt a lot better by the time he got ready to go home. He said so himself.

Well, that got me thinking after he left, and not about him or Mona or Calvin or Lucy or Loretta or Clement. It got me to thinking that Mr. Moore should spend some time with Clara; that if anybody needed to visit with him, she did. Now, how in the world was I ever going arrange that?

Chapter 13

The Last Paradox

HANK ARRIVED AT the Come Again at 7 A.M., just like he said he would. He was darn near perky and Mr. Moore was sharp as a pin, just like always. After less than four hours of sleep, I felt like boiling some housecats myself. Over breakfast, Hank told Mr. Moore about his plan to consult with some pediatric anesthesiologists around the country, then the two men drove straight down to Carson. Once they got there, Calvin and Hank went into Lucy's room to talk, so Mr. Moore and Nurse Nelson went into the kitchen for some coffee.

The kitchen in that house is gloomy white. It has smudged-white cabinets, a chipped white-enamel stove, 1950s-era turquoise countertops that are curled up around the edges, and a checkerboard turquoise-and-white with waxy-build-up linoleum floor. The refrigerator is also white, and a dead giveaway that the house is a rental. It is so old that the freezer still has metal ice trays and there are no magnets or postcards on the door. Not a one. The kitchen table is painted white, too, although it usually has a tablecloth on it to cover up the spots, and there is barely enough room for three old aluminum chairs with plastic, turquoise seats.

If there is a remedy for that room, it's Nurse Nelson. Louise is a tiny thing; she can't be more than five feet tall, and she is skinny as a rail. I bet she wears a size two, if you can believe that. But she is full of energy and optimism and sass, and she can talk a blue streak.

It turns out that she also knows how to play cribbage. Mr. Moore challenged her to a game while Hank and Calvin were conferring in the front room. They didn't have a board, so Mr. Moore kept score on a yellow notepad. She won a dollar from him, but I wonder if he let her.

After the game, Nurse Nelson went into Lucy's room to consult with Hank, so Calvin went into the kitchen for some coffee. I heard later that Calvin looked like a refugee from the State of Distress. He was unshaven, his hair was dirty and mussed up, and he had big, dark bags under his eyes. His jeans and shirt looked like they'd been slept in, too, probably because they had.

I don't know how a normal salesman would react if he saw his prospect in such a sorry condition, but Mr. Moore looked Calvin over and said, "Do you plan on going with her?"

Calvin growled, "What does that mean?"

"I was just wondering if you're planning to check out with Lucy. You look like you're halfway there now."

"Why thank you, Vernon. That's very fucking sensitive of you. But if I understand you correctly, then there is life after death, so I'm not taking too much of a goddamn chance."

"What I said, Calvin, is that life after death is likely. And before you risk the one you have, I think we should discuss the consequences."

"Okay. Fine. I tell you what: let's talk about the consequences of my eleven-year-old daughter dying right under my nose when there's not a single thing I can do about it."

"I think we should. I think we should talk about exactly that, but we haven't finished establishing the possibility of life after life yet. We have to deal with the second paradox first."

"I don't recall any second paradox, Vernon."

"There isn't a second unless you get past the first, Calvin. You did. Now we need to move on to the second Paradox of the Benevolent God, something I like to call the Unfairness Corollary."

Calvin shook his head with an air of resignation and said, "Fine. Okay. You said something about that yesterday, didn't you? And then Hank mentioned the same thing last night. You're like a goddamn Beach Boy, Vernon, you get around."

"I'm a salesman. It's my job."

"Well, for a salesman you sell some unusual things, but Doc Wiley says he won't discuss any more options for Lucy until I talk to you. So let's talk about the second paradox. What did you call it, the Unfairness Corollary? I don't know what the hell it means, but I may be a hot prospect. I feel as if I'm in close personal touch with unfairness right now."

"I agree, Calvin. I think you are, too."

"That's interesting. Real interesting. As I remember, you said yesterday that no benevolent God would allow it."

"That's not what I said."

"Then what did you say? I want to know. I want to know how your God is going to be fair to my Lucy. You can't tell me that she's going to heaven either; that's off limits. No religious claptrap; that's the rule."

"That I did say, and I'll stick to it. Why don't we play some cards instead?"

Calvin laughed. "That's a fine idea. Didn't Nurse Nelson just tell me that she kicked your ass?"

"Yes, she did, but that was cribbage. Why don't we play some draw poker?" Mr. Moore picked up the deck of cards and began shuffling them silently, swiftly, and evenly.

Calvin watched his hands and said, "Do my eyes deceive me or have you done this before? Is this what you did with Hank and Wilma last night? You played cards?"

Mr. Moore answered, "For a while, yes. I even used the same deck. The Unfairness Corollary is a lot easier with cards. Are you game?"

"Sure. Why not? Deal the cards."

"I think I should state the Unfairness Corollary before we start."

"By all means. Let's state the fucking Unfairness Corollary."

Mr. Moore explained, "The Unfairness Corollary goes as follows:

Only a benevolent God would create heaven and Earth;
But no benevolent God would permit so much unfairness on Earth;
Therefore, there is no benevolent God."

Calvin listened as carefully as any man in his condition could and then he hoisted his coffee cup and said, "Well stated, and true as hell."

"Actually, Calvin, it's not, but the second paradox is exactly like the first. We cannot defeat it unless we accept its premise, which is that only a benevolent God would create heaven and Earth."

"I remember that, Vernon, and I'm still not sure I buy it entirely, but I don't want to get into another pissin' match this morning. Just go on."

"Fair enough. That means that we must attack the second statement rather than accepting it as axiomatic."

"I remember that, too. No problem. Let's attack unfairness. I'm all for beating unfairness into ugly green goo."

"But you also remember that we cannot prevent pain and suffering? That's an important precondition."

"Right, Vernon. I've got it. Now let's get on with it."

"Okay. How about a little five-card draw among friends?"

"That works for me, but aren't we going to bet something? I hear you're a mark."

"I think the stakes are high enough already, don't you?"

Calvin frowned and said, "Deal the cards. The clock is ticking."

Mr. Moore quickly dealt each man five cards. Calvin looked at his hand and said, "Since we're not betting, I guess I can tell you that this hand really sucks." At Mr. Moore's request, he turned it over on the table. It was a three, a five, a seven, a nine, and a queen. Only the three and the queen were of the same suit: spades.

Mr. Moore said, "You're right, Calvin. That's about as bad a hand as a person could get. Lucky for you, though, we're playing draw poker, so you have a second chance if you want it. Why don't you draw some cards? You can have as many as four."

Calvin said, "If four cards are all I can have, then give me four. Please give me four." He turned the three, five, seven, and nine over and passed them to Mr. Moore, who placed them in a little pile to his side.

Mr. Moore dealt Calvin four new cards: three queens and a king. Calvin had four queens just like that. Mr. Moore said, "I see that your luck has improved."

Calvin replied, "Yes it has. I'm betting the store on this hand, Vernon. What have you got?"

Mr. Moore turned over his cards, which were the three, four, five, six, and seven of hearts: a pat straight flush and an almost unbeatable hand. He said, "You would owe me one store except I know that you were kidding. I guess that luck can be pretty relative, can't it?"

Calvin said, "I'm beginning to get a little suspicious of your methods, Vernon. I'm beginning to suspect that you can deal just about anything you want. Is that the case?"

"If that were true, Calvin, then how could I lose to Nurse Nelson? Besides, we're not betting anything, so it's not as if you can really lose. Why don't we try again? This time, why don't you play a hand for Lucy?"

"Okay. Fine. That should be an experience. I just lost the store, so now I'm perfectly qualified to play for my dying daughter. Deal."

Mr. Moore dealt again and Calvin picked up a three, a four, a six, an eight, and a ten. Only the three and the eight were of the same suit, so there was no play for a flush. Calvin held the ten and took four cards. He received a two, another three, a five, and a seven, and said, "These are Lucy's cards all right. They're shit! What do you have?"

Mr. Moore replied, "It doesn't really matter." The he turned over three jacks and two aces and said, "Let's try again. You're still playing for Lucy."

"Is there a point to this?"

Mr. Moore said, "Yes," and dealt Calvin another hand. Once again, he held no pairs and had no practical opportunity for either a straight or a flush. Calvin turned in his four lowest cards, but their replacements provided no improvement.

"Deal again," Calvin said. Mr. Moore dealt four more hands that were remarkably similar in their lack of pattern or potential. Calvin said, "How long do we need to continue this? All you've done is convince me that you can deal any cards you want. What's the point?"

Mr. Moore replied, "You've played poker before, haven't you?"

"Yes."

"So you've had hands like the ones I just dealt you?"

"Yes, I'm sure I have. I don't remember having so many incredibly shitty hands in a row, though."

"Precisely, Calvin. That's exactly it! When the cards are dealt randomly, you get both good hands and bad hands. Your luck evens out over the long run."

Calvin did not reply. Mr. Moore pushed him. "Think about it, Calvin. You must've had some very good hands. Tell the truth. It's very important."

Calvin sat back and thought for a minute or so, then he shrugged and said, "You know, there've been times when I've wondered, but I have to admit that you're right. I've had some really putrid hands, a ton of them, but I've had some amazing hands, too."

"Do you remember any of them?"

"Sure, a few. When I was playing hold 'em at a retail show in Las Vegas a few years back, I had two sixes down and two more turned up in the flop. Best hand I ever had. I played it like three of a kind and won a bundle. I suppose I should be glad that you weren't in the game."

At just that moment, Doc Wiley stuck his head around the door and said, "Lucy is sleeping soundly, Calvin, and Nurse Nelson is keeping an eye on her. I have conference calls with several East Coast clinics today, so I'm going to drive back to Ebb. If anything happens, she'll page me and I'll come right back."

Calvin stood and shook the doctor's hand, then said, "Thanks, Doc. I'll try to be in a better state of mind when you return. When can we talk again?"

"You'll hear from me tonight, Calvin. We have a decision to make, you and me, and I think we should make it this evening."

"I still don't see why we can't make it now."

Dr. Wiley looked at Mr. Moore and said, "Because I need the consultations I've set up for this morning to make sure that I understand our options. Frankly, you need another consultation, too, with Mr. Moore there." Calvin began to protest and the doctor repeated, "This evening. No sooner, and that's assuming that you and Vernon finish your talk."

Calvin asked, "What in the hell is he going to tell me that I don't already know?"

"He's going to give you a new sense of perspective."

"What happened to hope? Where did that go?"

"That's the perspective. Now shut up and sit down. We'll talk again later."

Dr. Wiley disappeared and Calvin said, "Well, you've got him sold, Vernon. He's a different man. Maybe you should be selling him some games."

"He's not a qualified prospect. You are, and you were just telling me about your big hand. How much did you win with those four sixes?

Calvin sat down and answered, "As I recall, about seventy dollars."

"Is that the biggest pot you've ever won?"

"Oh, hell no. I used to play a lot at conventions in Las Vegas. I've won a dozen pots in the one-hundred- to two-hundred-dollar range, maybe more."

"Then I suspect you've lost some big ones, too?"

"Oh man, you bet I have. I remember a seven-card-stud hand in particular. A little old lady in a black dress and pearls beat my flush with a full house: tens over sevens. She pulled one of those tens out of the hole and I had the case ten down. I'll never forget it."

"How big was that pot?"

"A hundred dollars; maybe a hundred and fifty."

Mr. Moore leaned in a bit. "That was a tough loss, Calvin. Nevertheless, is it fair to say that your luck has evened out over time? Like I said, it's an extremely important point."

Calvin sighed and replied, "I suppose it has."

"Why?"

"Why? What do you mean 'why,' Vernon? The reason is obvious.

You just said so yourself. I've played hundreds and hundreds of hands of poker. Hell, I may have played a thousand hands. Of course I've had good luck and bad luck. Who wouldn't?"

"You're absolutely right, Calvin. That makes perfect sense, because Nature is perfectly fair in the long run. But now I'd like you to do me a favor."

"Why do I feel like I should be fastening my seatbelt? What favor?"

"I want you to judge your luck from just one hand of poker. I'm going to deal it to you now. If you want, you can deal it yourself."

"Don't bother, Vernon. That's an asinine request! Why would I judge my luck from a single hand when I've already played a thousand?"

Mr. Moore put his cards down and said, "Really? Are you absolutely sure?"

"Yes. Of course."

"Then why are you doing the same thing with Lucy?"

That stopped Calvin cold for a second, but then he answered, "You're going to have to help me out here, Vernon, because I just don't see the connection."

"That's okay. I didn't see it myself for a long time either, but I do now. In all matters of human behavior, there are always fluctuations in the short run. The way things get evened out is by multiple occurrences. We don't get a course grade based on one quiz; we take a bunch of them. We don't try to catch a fish by throwing the line in once; we do it over and over again. And we never play a single hand of poker, because one hand is no indication of either our skill or our luck. Isn't that true?"

"Yes. Of course it is."

"Well, if we're smart enough to figure that out, then don't you think that an omniscient God would be smart enough to figure it out, too?"

"What are you trying to say, Vernon?"

"Fairness cannot be delivered in the short run, Calvin, not in a universe designed for uncertainty. Ironically, though, fairness can be statistically guaranteed over the long run, but in only one way: by multiple occurrences. What if each of our lives is just a single poker hand?"

"Are you trying to tell me that we get multiple lives?"

"Yes."

"That's preposterous!"

"Why? What in the body of your extensive knowledge prevents the possibility of multiple lives? Tell me, and take your time. I'll wait."

Calvin got up from his chair and poured himself another cup of coffee. Mr. Moore sat silently in his chair. Calvin sat down again and said, "This sounds a lot like karma to me, and we said no religious claptrap."

"I don't remember quoting the Bhagavad-Gita, Calvin. We got

here with poker and, in fact, we've arrived at a different place. Karma suggests that you keep two cards from your last hand for the next deal. That might provide a certain measure of justice, but genuine fairness would require a fresh deal every time."

"Let me net this out, Vernon. You're saying that we each have multiple lives, right?"

"We started down this path, Calvin, because we could not reconcile the unfairness we see in life; one child born into abject poverty versus another born into European aristocracy; one child born with AIDS versus another born with the physical talents of a Michael Jordan; one child who will die from an unnamed neurological disease at the age of eleven versus a guilt-ridden father with a life expectancy of eighty-three years.

"In my mind, there are three possibilities. One is that this life is all there is; that this is all we get. But if that's the case, then life is damn unfair. Another is that people of blind faith are right and we'll go to heaven or hell for an eternity depending upon how we behave for a few incredibly short years. For a hundred reasons, that seems to be just as unfair, but there is a third choice. If we live multiple lives, then everything evens out over the long run: good luck and bad luck; war and peace; fortune and misfortune; happiness and sadness; sickness and health; premature death and extreme longevity."

Calvin said, "I take it that you believe in option c."

"Yes I do—because it's the only option that's truly fair."

"Then you believe in a benevolent God."

"Yes I do."

"I don't. That's the problem."

"Why?"

Calvin didn't answer. Eventually, Mr. Moore said, "Exactly, Calvin. Your original assertion was that no benevolent God would permit so much pain and suffering. However, we have since discovered that He would either have to permit pain and suffering or He would have to deny us free will which, in fact, no benevolent God would do. Therefore, a benevolent God would have to permit pain and suffering. It's only a matter of how much, meaning where He would draw the line.

"Then I proposed that no benevolent God would permit so much unfairness, a proposition that you enthusiastically supported. I have since demonstrated a simple method of guaranteeing fairness via multiple random occurrences. In large enough quantities, this method is mathematically certain and well within the power of an omnipotent God who has forever to be fair."

There was no response, so Mr. Moore continued, "Therefore, we have defeated the two most damning arguments against the existence of a benevolent God."

"That sounds smart, but it's not smart enough. I want some proof of an afterlife. All I have so far is a two-thousand-year-old book that describes exactly one return trip, plus a few esoteric arguments from an overdressed salesman. That's not much proof."

Mr. Moore sighed and replied, "If your belief in a benevolent God requires hard evidence, then you are doomed to a life of hopelessness because you'll never get it. With a few unverified exceptions, no mortal ever has, so it would seem that the odds of getting some personal proof of God are very, very long. I wouldn't bother checking your email."

Again there was no response. Mr. Moore said, "You don't suffer alone in this regard. I think there's no definitive proof of the existence of God because there never can be proof."

Calvin Millet looked up, rolled his eyes, and replied, "There can't ever be any proof of God's existence? Not any? Not ever? Is that what you just said?"

"Yes."

"Okay, this should be a good one. Fire away, Vernon. Why can't we have proof of the existence of God?"

"Well, we could. In fact, it would make perfect sense if we lived one life and then moved on to a higher or lower plane. If we live many lives, though, then we must never know."

"Really? Why?"

"Let's consider the alternative. What if we knew for certain that we would live many, many lives? Wouldn't each life be too cheap, a bit too much like a single poker hand? Wouldn't we be too tempted to just fold the bad lives, to cut them short?"

"What would be so bad about that?"

"Because we would be inclined to quit whenever things got tough. Worse, we could avoid the consequences of our actions."

"Explain please."

"Fair enough. Let's say I get tired of trying to explain all of this philosophical twaddle so I kill you, I rape Nurse Nelson, and I leave Lucy to die of inattention. Then, after I'm done, I decide that I don't want to spend the rest of my life in a federal penitentiary, so I pull the plug. I commit suicide. Why the hell not? I'm going to get some more lives, probably lots of them."

Just then, Calvin and Mr. Moore heard a rapping on the doorjamb. As they looked up, Nurse Nelson bounced into the kitchen and said, "Yoo hoo! Am I interrupting something?"

While she was filling her coffee cup, Calvin replied, "Yes. As a matter of fact, Mr. Vernon Moore was just describing how he could force himself upon you and get away with it, scot-free. Weren't you, Vernon?"

Before he could answer, Nurse Nelson said, "Don't be a boob, Calvin! Just look at that man. He's never had to force himself on any woman. Isn't that right, Mr. Moore?"

"You're too kind, Louise."

"Am I? If you're thinking seriously about forcing yourself on a woman, Mr. Moore, would you please get my number before you leave?"

Calvin said, "Did you know that this man is a cardsharp, too? I've seen him do it. He can deal any hand of cards he wants."

Nurse Nelson asked, "Is that true?"

Mr. Moore answered, "It is, but the existence of a skill does not necessarily imply its use. For selfish reasons, I would never use my abilities to manipulate a deck of cards in an actual game. It would deny me the uncertainty of a fair contest, meaning any sense of challenge, excitement, or achievement."

Nurse Nelson pinched Mr. Moore on his cheek and said, "I knew that's what you'd say, dear." With that, she bounced out of the room.

Calvin said, "Do you always have that effect on women?"

Mr. Moore replied, "It's the clothes; they seem to love the clothes. Whatever it is, I must admit I like the attention, even at my advanced age."

"You can't be that old, Vernon. How old are you? Forty? Forty-five tops?"

"I'm older than that, and I believe that God wants me to experience the absolute fullness of my life to my very last breath. Do you agree? It's another important point."

Calvin answered, "Now that's a concept I can live with. I think we all should live our lives to the fullest. I just want my Lucy to have a fullest. Hell, I'd settle for a full, even a half full."

Mr. Moore sat forward. "Then you must see why we can never have proof of life after death."

Calvin replied, "Okay. Fine. I get it. If we were certain that there were more lives after death, we would be too tempted to 'fold' bad lives."

Mr. Moore continued, "Correct. That, in fact, is the third and final Paradox of the Benevolent God. It goes like this:

Only a benevolent God would create life after life;
But no benevolent God would ever reveal life after life;
Therefore, we can never know for sure if there is life after life."

"That's the third paradox?"

"Yes."

"We can never know for sure?"

"Yes."

"Okay. What's the solution?"

"The third paradox is the solution, Calvin. A benevolent God could never let us know for sure because He would deny us the fullness of life—a life that has been carefully constructed on a flat, even foundation of uncertainty."

Calvin thought about what Mr. Moore had said for a while and then replied, "I suppose you have me in a corner, Vernon. I can see why we shouldn't fold bad lives, so I have to agree. But I still don't like it."

"Fair enough. But if you could see Lucy living a thousand times, at least ten of them in the lap of extravagant luxury until the age of one hundred and nine, would that improve your disposition?"

"Yes."

"Then see them, because, in extremis, that's exactly the kind of potential that we're talking about."

"You are a card-carrying heretic, Vernon Moore."

"I know I am, but I'm an old, scared heretic. If I can't have proof of life after life, then I want hope."

Calvin began to rock back and forth on the back two legs of his chair. It was obvious that he was no longer in the mood to explore philosophical phenomena. Mr. Moore said, "Yesterday, I asked you to be God for a day and you did a fine job. Would you like to know what I would do if I was in God's shoes?"

Calvin looked up and said, "This should be weird. Tell me. What would you do?"

"If I was all-powerful and all-knowing, then the one thing I would crave would be excitement, some surprise. So the first thing I would do is create an infinite universe. Second, I would embed in its physics the very essence of uncertainty. Third, I would create a paradise of diversity, or perhaps thousands or millions of them, just like planet Earth. Last, I would create an intelligent species, or perhaps thousands or millions of them, and I would give them an unfettered will. Then I could be surprised and excited and saddened and appalled every millisecond of every day. That's what I would do."

Calvin said, "It sounds to me like you would need more than a day to build all of that. How much time do you think it would take?"

"If I was all-powerful, nearly a week. I think I'd need about six days."

Calvin smiled but didn't reply.

"Are we done for today? You look beat."

"I am, Vernon. I'm bushed, and I need some time to let all of this sink in. Do we have more to discuss?"

"A little more. What if I come back tomorrow morning?"

"More? You're kidding. You said that the third paradox was the last one."

"It is. We're almost done. There's just a little bit more."

"Promise?"

"Cross my heart. We're almost home."

"Fine, Vernon. Okay. How about the same time tomorrow?"

"I'll be here at eight-thirty."

Calvin remained pensive and showed no signs of movement. Mr. Moore said, "I know that this is not the best time to ask, but how are your discussions with Clem Tucker?"

"With Clem? About what? Lucy?"

"About selling the store."

"That, Vernon, is still none of your business."

"I don't mean to pry. I just thought I might be able to help."

"Don't I recall that you identified yourself as a simple salesman, even though we haven't talked about your products for more than what, five minutes? Anyway, I don't need your help. I have this poker game well in hand."

"Are you sure? He's a pretty cagey player with a pile of money."

"Hell yes, I'm sure. I'm very sure."

"Why?"

"Because I'm going to sell the store. I'm going to get out. It's to my advantage that Clem is a potential buyer."

"Then you don't care if he buys a controlling interest."

"Not as long as it's one hundred percent."

"My understanding is that Clem usually buys fifty-one percent."

"Well, that won't work. If he wants to control the store, then he's going to have to buy the whole damn thing, and on my terms."

"Really? How can you be so certain?"

"Because I can."

"That's very masculine of you, but what if his bank pushes you into receivership? I would think that even the threat of bankruptcy would cause the price of the store to plunge."

Calvin sat dead still, like he was a stone statue. Mr. Moore waited. After a while, Calvin said, "You may be right, Vernon, but I doubt it. If Clem pushes me into bankruptcy, he risks enormous loss."

"How?"

"Play the hand out. It's simple: I don't sell; I fold. I just let the store slip into Chapter Seven. Kaput. Finis. Then all Clem's bank will get is leftover inventory, a huge unpaid debt, and an empty building that nobody will lease for three dollars a month. I wonder how that will look on their books. My guess is that it won't be a pretty sight."

"You'd do that?"

"It's a poker game, and I might because, ultimately, I just don't give a shit."

"Really? You don't strike me as the kind of man who would give up, especially something as important as the family business."

"Why the hell not? I'm all out of cash and pretty soon I'll be all out of family. But between now and then, all I will give even one subatomic shit about is my daughter, Lucy. And maybe getting some sleep. Right now, I could use about forty thousand winks. I don't suppose you're selling winks today."

Mr. Moore smiled. "I would if I had any in stock, Calvin. Why don't I show myself out and let you get some sleep? If I'm very quiet, do you mind if I see Lucy on my way? I won't wake her up."

"I don't see why not. And don't worry, you couldn't wake up Lucy if you had a cowbell and a chain saw. Just check with Louise first."

Nurse Nelson showed Mr. Moore into Lucy's room. It was softly lit by a single pink table lamp in the far corner, and Lucy was sound asleep. Except for her left arm, she was covered up to the neck. All Mr. Moore could see was that one skinny, bruised arm and a tiny, drawn face under long strands of brittle, blond hair. There was no pain in her expression, but there was no life in it either, and Mr. Moore could see no movement of any kind, not even the heaving of her chest. Still, he stood silently at the foot of her bed for fifteen or twenty minutes. After that, he gently touched the foot of her blanket, and then he nodded at Nurse Nelson and walked out.

Chapter 14

War and Gin at the Come Again

I GOT OUT of bed for the second time that morning at around nine-thirty. I don't know if I felt any better, but at least I had had some sleep. After I cleaned up the kitchen, I sat down at my computer to check my email. There was a note from Clara, asking me why Mona came to visit by herself.

Well, I wrote Clara a long response telling her about Mona's troubles, Calvin's troubles, Lucy's troubles, Clem's shenanigans, and Hank's dilemma. Of course, I told her the latest about my new lodger, too. He seemed to be in everybody's business, but in a good way. I even tried to explain what Mr. Moore had said about the three paradoxes of the Benevolent God and how they had helped Hank so much, but I didn't do a very good job. In the end, I suggested that she meet him herself. That was the very first time that I had ever asked Clara to meet anybody.

Mr. Moore got back to the Come Again around eleven. I was still in the den, so I didn't actually see him come in, but I heard him go upstairs. He changed into some walking clothes and came down the back stairs into the kitchen, where I was just starting to make Hank Wiley some banana nut bread. Naturally, I invited him to sit a spell and tell me all about his trip down to Carson.

While I was fixing him some iced tea, I asked, "How was Lucy, Mr. Moore? How did she look? Did you see her?"

"I went into her room for a few minutes, but she didn't know I was there. She is heavily sedated now, you know. She looked small and pale and very frail, but peaceful."

"I don't suppose the outlook for her has changed any?"

"No. No it hasn't."

"Did Hank and Calvin talk about what they were going to do?"

"I think so, but I'm not sure. When I left, nothing had changed."

"Did you meet Louise Nelson, Lucy's nurse?"

"I did, yes. We even played some cards while Hank and Calvin were talking."

"She is a sparkly little thing, isn't she?"

"She is, even under the saddest of circumstances. I suppose it's her way of maintaining balance. God knows, she has a difficult job."

I said, "Isn't that the truth," and then I heard a loud noise in the front of the house, the kind of "kerplunk" that makes you think someone has dropped something heavy on the carpet. I wiped my hands on my apron and headed toward the foyer. Mr. Moore came along behind, tea glass in hand.

Mark Breck, Mona's eleven-year-old, was standing in my parlor between two suitcases with a great big grin on his face. He came running right up to me and threw his arms around my waist and said, "Hi, Gramma! We've come to visit! We even get to miss school today!"

I gave him a great big hug and a kiss, and then I looked out to the parking area, which wasn't too tricky because the front door was wide open. There was Mona and Matthew unloading the back of their SUV. Mona drives an SUV that's bigger than a John Deere harvester, probably heavier, too. No woman needs a rig that big unless she has to tow livestock, but Marv bought that thing for her so that he could take it out hunting.

While I was standing there hugging little Mark, Mr. Moore put his tea glass down and went out to help Mona and Matthew with their bags. I should have gone out, too, but I was in a state of shock, I guess.

A few seconds later, Matthew came in carrying a backpack and towing a big roller suitcase. He said, "Like, where do I put these, Gramma?" The way he said it, I could have been the concierge.

In case you don't remember, Matthew is a teenager. As any mother will tell you, God invented teenagers so we wouldn't feel so bad when they left the nest. I let Mark go and said to Matt, "Is that any way to greet your Gramma?" Then I took a step toward him.

He took two steps back and held out his hand, as if I was actually going to shake it. At a whopping fourteen years of age, he was already too manly to be hugged by his Gramma, especially in front of a stranger. Being the sensitive, understanding grandmother that I am, I faked the shake, grabbed him around the neck and mussed his hair up real good, and then I gave him a proper hug and a big sloppy kiss on his cheek.

Matthew was beginning to untangle himself from my grip when his momma came in the door looking all the world like she had just been voted off the island. Before he could say one word, she said, "Shut up, Matt, and help Mr. Moore bring the rest of the suitcases into the foyer. I need to talk to your Gramma alone for a minute." Then she said to Mark, who had been watching me mug his brother with considerable interest, "You go help your brother."

Matthew just stood there, but his little brother said, "C'mon pimple face. Let's go help the geezer," and off they went. I just love little boys. It is such a shame that they have to turn into teenagers.

I gave Mona a big hug, took her by the arm, and said, "Come on into my kitchen, sweetheart."

Mr. Moore followed us into the kitchen a minute or two later and said, "Where should we put the luggage?"

I replied, "Could you put Mona's in the back corner bedroom

with the white canopy bed? You know the one; it is just two doors down from your room. And put the boys' things in the room on the other side of hers, the one with two singles." I looked at Mona for a second before continuing, "Why don't you tell them to unpack their things, too."

Mr. Moore looked Mona over and said, "That won't take very long, Wilma. How much time do you think you two will need?"

Mona started to answer, but I said, "I think we'll need about an hour, don't you, sweetheart?"

Mr. Moore replied, "That's no problem at all. I'll stop back in an hour to see if you need more time." Before Mona or I could say a word, he did an about-face and left the kitchen.

I made a note to myself to ask him what his favorite dinner was, and then I said to Mona, "Well?"

Well, she just sat down at my kitchen table and began to sob. That was good enough for me. I got her some Kleenex, and then I rubbed her on the neck and murmured some of those reassuring things that we mothers are required by law to murmur at such times, and then I made us some hot tea.

Well, Mona had herself a good, long cry. I wanted to join in, I really did, but I was wearing makeup. Anyway, I couldn't bring myself to go down that road because I figured that the right thing had happened, only a tad sooner than I'd expected.

Mona was just starting to come around when the telephone rang. It was Clem Tucker. Judging from the static, I figured that he was calling from his vehicle of the day.

I said, "Good morning, Clem. This is two days in a row. People will talk."

"I'm calling for Vernon, Wilma. Is he there?"

I considered my options carefully and then answered cheerfully, "He is, dear. I'll see if I can get him to pick up the phone."

"That won't be necessary. That's all I need to know." The line went dead, so I guessed that he had hung up, which was fine because Mona blew her nose right then, very loudly, and then she grabbed another handful of tissues. A pile of wet Kleenexes was already on the table, so I checked the box, but there seemed to be enough inventory left to get us through to the crisis at hand. I was just about to throw the gooey ones in the trash when Hank Wiley walked into the kitchen.

"Did you know that your front door was wide open?" Then he noticed Mona and said, "Mona, is that you? Is that your big SUV out front? What brings you to Ebb?"

Mona started to cry again. Now, crying women trouble men greatly, even doctors, and especially Hank Wiley. He looked at me with one of those little boy, "what-did-I-do-mommy?" expressions on his face, so I took him by the elbow and led him into the dining room to explain. Just then, Mark showed up out of nowhere and tried to walk right past me and Hank into the kitchen. I grabbed him by the shirt and said, "Not so fast, hot stuff. The kitchen is off limits. I am making a secret potion that turns nasty little boys into sweet little girls, and the fumes are everywhere."

Mark replied, "Yeah right, Gramma. Why don't you make something for the zits on Matt's face. I wanna see my momma."

That's when Mr. Moore came into the dining room with Matt in tow. He said, "Sorry, Wilma, I guess I lost one."

Hank said, "Hello, Vernon. How was your visit with Calvin?"

Mark attempted to free himself from my grasp, futilely I might add, and said, "I wanna see my momma."

Matt walked up and said, "Like, don't you have cable, Gramma?"

Mr. Moore said, "We made progress, but we didn't reach a conclusion. Let's talk a bit later. Right now, I have another chore." Then Mr. Moore looked down at Mark and said, "Do you like cars?"

Matt answered for him, "Yeah. Is that, like, your Audi out front?"

Mr. Moore said, "Yes, it is."

Little Mark said, "We don't like station wagons. They're for girls. My dad drives a Corvette."

Mr. Moore said, "A Corvette is a fast car, but I wonder how fast a station wagon would be if it had three-hundred-and-forty horsepower, all-wheel-drive, and a six-speed manual transmission?"

With that unmistakable male air of automotive authority, Matt replied, "Like, that is complete bullshit."

Vernon smiled and said, "Do you have a dollar, young man?"

"Yeah. Like, why?"

"Because I'll bet you one dollar that I drive a three-hundred-and-forty-horsepower station wagon with a six-speed transmission."

Mark said, "How're you gonna prove it?"

Mr. Moore answered, "Let's go out and look. I think the transmission will probably speak for itself. Then we can check under the hood and take a test drive down a nice twisty road I know. If you're still not convinced, you can read the owner's manual. After you pay me my dollar, I'll spring for something to drink at Starbucks on the way back. Like, how's that?"

Being a teenager, Matt tried to look as bored as he could, but I could tell he was hooked. Both boys headed for the front door at a canter with Mr. Moore bringing up the rear.

Hank frowned and said, "Is anything wrong with Mona? Is there something I can do?"

"Not this minute," I said. "But why don't you come back in an hour for lunch. By then, I expect that Mona will be glad to have some company. I know I will."

Hank put his Stetson on and headed out the door. I went back in the kitchen to find Mona rinsing dishes and putting them in the washer. I knew she would start talking when she was ready, so I poked my head into the refrigerator to see what I had on hand that could feed two men, two women, and two boys for lunch. I checked high and low, but I had no loaves and no fishes, so I knew I'd have to go to the grocery store. Remember, there's no fast food in Ebb.

I was just about to ask Mona if she would want to go along

when Loretta strolled into my kitchen. "Hello, darlin'," she said. "Mona, is that you? What are you doing here, honey?"

Mona turned around and I could tell that she was tearing up, so I grabbed Loretta by the elbow and hauled her into the dining room. As she was backpedaling, she whispered, "Is Mona alright? That girl looks like she's been cryin'. And what happened to her hair? She usually has such pretty hair."

When we were out of earshot, I answered, "Did you come over here for lunch?"

Loretta answered, "That depends, darlin'. I don't want to get in the way of you and Mona. To tell the truth, I had an empty couple of hours on my schedule so I wanted to flirt with Vern. Is he around?"

"He's off with Mona's boys in that foreign car of his. They won't be back for an hour or so, which is when I plan to have lunch ready. Can you stay?"

"Of course," she said.

"Good. We have to drive to the grocery store this minute and get enough lunch meat and sandwich bread for seven people."

I thought Mona could use the time to herself; sad women need their privacy, so I told her what we were doing, and then Loretta and I drove off to the store. An hour later, we pulled around to the back of the house and came in through the kitchen door with two bags each. Mona had polished my kitchen to a high sheen and she was sitting at the table nursing a glass of cranberry juice with none other than Clement Tucker.

Those two were a sight. She was dressed in a cheap red sweat shirt with black paint stains and dog hair on it, gray sweat pants, floppy socks, and dirty tennis shoes. Clem was dressed in creased designer jeans, a silver-studded cowboy belt, endangered-species cowboy boots with silver toes, an off-white silk cowboy shirt with pearl buttons, and a custom-cut tweed jacket with suede trim that must have cost a gazillion dollars by itself.

I said, "Why hello, Clem. Are you staying for lunch?"

Mona answered, "I already offered, Mama. He said he's come to see Vernon Moore."

Loretta said, "Does that mean you can't have lunch with us common folk, Mr. Big Shot? Wilma bought enough food to feed the multitudes."

With characteristic gratitude, Clem grunted something unintelligible that sounded like, "What are you havin'?"

Loretta answered, "Good food and good company. Vernon Moore will be joining us, too, you may be interested to know. So will Mona's boys and Hank Wiley. Have you ever met Mona's boys, Clem?"

Mona shook her head. Clem replied candidly, "I'm sure I have."

Loretta rolled her eyes and asked politely, "What kind of sandwich do you want, Big Shot?" After determining his options, Clem gave us very specific instructions and then Loretta ordered him out of the kitchen.

Hank Wiley came in the kitchen a few minutes later, followed by the two boys. Their eyes were bigger than boiled eggs, which bothered me some. I always worry when boys show off their toys. I was making a note to ask Mr. Moore about it later when he walked into the kitchen.

Hank said, “Do you have a minute or two before lunch, Vernon? We need to chat.”

Loretta made that pouty look of hers and said, “Girls first, Hank. I came here to see Vern, too.” Then she smiled at Mr. Moore and said, “We do have some unfinished business, don’t we darlin’?”

Clem said, “I thought we had a date for of a game of gin, Vernon, but I see that the queue’s gettin’ pretty long in here.”

Well, I couldn’t help any of them so I shooed everybody out of my kitchen, except Mona of course. I guess everything got settled because they all filed back into the dining room after I hollered, “Lunch!”

As soon as we sat down, Hank started droning on about the warm weather, but before he could get very far, Loretta said to Clem, “What in the hell are you wearing on your feet?”

Clem wasn’t exactly forthright in his answer, so it got to be a big guessing game for everybody else at the table. We were getting nowhere fast until Mark walked around to the head of the table where Clem was sitting and asked him to take one boot off so that we could all see it. Well, I don’t know what got into that man, but he did just that, and then he put it right on top of the table. Men will do the oddest things at the dinner table. It turned out that his boots were made from the underbelly of a Chinese alligator, which put a bit of a damper on my appetite, I have to say. It didn't seem to bother any of the males at the table, though, except maybe Mr. Moore.

Once the Mystery of the Duke's Boots had been solved, the men started talking about cars. Actually, it was the boys who got them going because they were still wild-eyed from their ride with Mr. Moore. In the process, Matt managed to use the word *like* five times in a single sentence. I counted them up as he went, and not one was a verb. I do worry about that boy. At the end of lunch, Clem offered to take Matt and Mark for a ride in his Porsche. I worry about that boy, too.

After lunch, Matthew and Mark went into the parlor to hook up their video game set to the TV. Loretta had to go back to the Bold Cut, but she wanted to talk to Mona for a minute before she left, so they went off into the kitchen together. Meanwhile, Mr. Moore walked Hank to the front door, where they had a short talk. Then Loretta came out of the kitchen and Mr. Moore walked her to the front door, too, where they talked a bit. I thought Clem Tucker would be next, but he volunteered to help clean up. I know. You could have knocked me over with a feather. Clem and Mr. Moore cleared the table, all by themselves. I wish I had a camera.

While Mona and I washed the dishes and put everything away, the two men went back into the dining room and sat down catty-corner from each other. Clem said, "Did you know that I was raised in this house, Vernon?"

"I did. Wilma told me. It must have been a wonderful place to grow up."

"It was. There are a thousand places to hide in this old mansion. They don't make them like this anymore."

"That's true. Why did you move out?"

"My last few years were not happy here, Vernon. It seems like I was in a pitched battle with my father every day. He kept me from going to Claremont, you know, which is where I wanted to go to school, and then he tried to dissuade me from going to London to get my graduate degree by withholding family funds. He said it was too far away. As far I was concerned, that was the whole idea, and I had a scholarship anyway. After he killed himself with my Corvette, I brought my wife back here, and that didn't work out, either. She went back to England, so I was left all alone in this big place, except for my baby daughter. I guess I just needed a change."

"But not the River House."

"The River House is a lovely, lovely place, but it's too far from town to keep as a primary residence. One thing you don't need in the country is a twenty-minute commute every day; that's just a waste of time. So I built a new house on some land I own on the other side of town. It's not as big as this, but it's quite a place nonetheless. You should come over some time and visit."

Mr. Moore said, "We have a date for a game of gin rummy. Why don't we go over there right now?"

Clem replied, "I have to be at the bank at three o'clock. Can we play here instead? I don't know why, but my intuition tells me that you have some cards handy."

"I do. I'll get an official score sheet too."

While Mr. Moore went up to his room to fetch the cards, Clem came into the kitchen and poured himself some coffee. We talked about old times for a minute, but then he went back into the dining room when he saw Mr. Moore.

Clem took off his tweed jacket before he sat down, as if he was a matador removing his cape. Mr. Moore removed the wrappings from a fresh deck of blue-backed cards, began to shuffle them, and said cheerfully, "What shall we play for? How about a dollar a game?"

"A dollar a game? I figured you for a high roller."

"It's not the money, Clem. How high would the stakes have to be before you got hurt? It's the competition; the thrill of the hunt. All I need to affirm my victory is the head of one George Washington."

Clem grinned. "That's okay with me. But if I win it, I'm going to have it mounted and hung on my wall in the River House."

Mr. Moore put the cards on the table and said, "Cut for deal."

From the kitchen, that game looked pretty serious. You know that some of the games men play aren't about money or winning or even keeping score; they're about superiority. When men are playing for superiority, it's best to give them a wide berth. That gave Mona and me a chance to talk, and she seemed to be in a better frame of mind. I guess things had just unraveled completely the night before. Marv didn't come home until after ten, and then he and Mona started yelling at each other, so she slept in the guest room after the boys went to bed, and he didn't even notice until the morning. That was when she decided that enough was enough.

There was no regret in Mona's voice, not any, except for leaving Macbeth behind. She knew my rule about no pets being allowed at the Come Again, so she put him in a kennel before she came down. I told her she should have called Lulu Tiller first, but Mona said she just wanted to get on with it, and she didn't want any contingencies in her way.

Of course, I had to ask her what she had shared with the boys. Mona was not particularly candid, I guess, which made Matt moody and suspicious. Moody and suspicious is a working definition for a teenager anyway, and we both knew that the boys would just have to adapt if we were ever going to save them from a life of dental floss and same lake vacations. We were starting to talk divorce lawyers—everybody in Ebb knows at least three of them—when Mark walked into the kitchen and asked what the men were doing in the dining room. I guess he had never seen anybody playing cards before.

Well, Mona wanted to go over to the Bold Cut, so I offered to teach little Mark how to play war, which is the simplest card game I know. That's what we did until Clem came into the kitchen about an hour and a half later. He said, "My gin game notwithstanding, I want to thank you for having me over for lunch, Wilma. I had an excellent time. Mark, you and your brother meet me out front at nine tomorrow morning. As long as it's okay with your momma, we'll go for a ride down to the River House. How would that be?"

Mark looked up at me with a great big question in his eyes. Being that I was his momma pro tem, I nodded in the affirmative, prompting him to gush, "That would be great, Mr. Tucker! Can Gramma come, too?"

"Why, Mark," I said, "Clem's Porsche is a tiny little thing. I'm not sure we could all squeeze in."

Clem looked straight at me and said, "It would be my pleasure. Unlike their elders, young boys are flexible. I'm sure we'll all fit in. If the weather's nice, I'll put the top down, too."

Mark asked, "It's a convertible?"

"Yes it is, son. Why in the world would a man own a ridiculously fast car unless he could put the top down?"

Apparently, Mark took this as a rhetorical question because he never answered it. Instead, he went streaking into the parlor to tell his big brother the news. While he was on his way out, Mr. Moore was on his way in, but at a more even pace.

"Will you walk me to my car, Vernon?" Clem asked.

"Of course. What's on your mind?"

"The true identity of Vernon Moore."

Mr. Moore smiled broadly and said, "That is an interesting topic. I sometimes wonder myself."

"Excellent. Would you be interested in discussing it further?"

"Sure. Right now?"

"I have a meeting at the bank until four. Could you meet me there afterward?"

"I'll be there with bells on."

Mr. Moore arrived at the bank early, of course. He was shown into the executive conference room on the top floor and supplied with iced water. A few minutes later, he was joined by Clem Tucker and none other than Mr. Buford Pickett.

Clem made the introductions, then he and Buford sat down directly opposite Mr. Moore. Clem began by saying, "First, Vernon, allow me to explain Buford's presence at our little get-together. Buford is the senior vice-president in charge of commercial loans here, so the bank's research department reports to him. Early yesterday morning, I asked him to get me a detailed report on your background and he and his people have been at it ever since."

Mr. Moore smiled and said, "That's very flattering, Clem."

"You don't object?"

"Of course I don't. Why would I? Perhaps we'll both learn something. What have you found out so far, Buford?"

Clem answered, "That's the problem. This is the Internet Age. It's not like we have to send for information by Pony Express, and Buford and his research assistants are very good at what they do. They have to be; the future of the bank depends upon their abilities. However, they've been working hammer and tongs on your background for two business days, and they can't seem to find out one single thing about you that makes even a lick of sense. How can that be?"

"Well, I'm sure I don't know. Maybe I can help out. What have you found out so far?"

Buford answered, "Not very much, Mr. Moore, I must say. For instance, we know you have a Visa card. We have your number because we clear for the Come Again, but we can't trace your card back to any U.S. bank. Can you explain that?"

"Of course. I'm an importer. My bank is overseas. It's a very, very private bank; that's why I bank there. I bet Clem has one just like it. What do you say, Clem?"

Buford didn't wait for a response. "Your business address is just an answering service," he said. "They wouldn't tell us anything about you, either."

"Why would they?"

"Don't some of your customers request financial information from you before they agree to do business?"

"Yes they do, but you're not a customer. You didn't try to impersonate one, did you?"

Buford decided to move on quickly. "How about fulfillment, Mr. Moore. I understand that you're a salesman. Your orders must be fulfilled from somewhere."

"They are."

"May I ask where?"

"Yes."

After several seconds of silence, Buford asked, "Where is it?"

Mr. Moore replied, "Offshore, of course."

Buford looked at Clem. Clem growled back and then smiled at Mr. Moore. Buford pressed on, "We traced the URL of your Web site back to a Cayman Web service, but we can't seem to get any further than that."

"That corporation is privately held. Why should they tell you anything about me? In fact, they don't know anything about me except that I pay my bills on time. What else would they need to know?"

Buford started to open his mouth again, but Clem interrupted, "As I remember, Vernon, you told me that you went to school in Ohio. But Buford's team hasn't been able to find a single Vernon L. Moore with a degree from any college or university in Ohio between 1950 and 1990. Can you explain that?"

Mr. Moore leaned forward, smiled and replied, "Yes." Then he took a sip of his water and sat back again.

After a second or two, Clem laughed out loud and said, "Would you, please?"

"Not quite yet. Is there anything else you're missing?"

Buford answered, "Lots. Everything is probably more accurate. We can't seem to find any trace of your career after your job at RSA."

"Well, that shouldn't be so surprising. I can tell you that a traveling salesman doesn't make a lot of headline news."

"I understand, Mr. Moore, but we can't find any information

about your career before RSA, either, and the records of your employment at RSA, which must have included your credentials, remain sealed by the court. We can't find a picture of you either, so we can't even ascertain that you are the same Vernon Moore that worked at RSA."

"But didn't you recognize me, Clem? I thought you said you did."

"That's what I thought, but I'd rather be sure."

Buford added, "The bottom line is that we're flat stumped, Mr. Moore."

"That's a shame. Do you mean to tell me that you haven't been able to find a single Vernon Moore out there?"

He replied, "No. That's not right. We've found eleven Vernon Moores who were born in the state of Ohio between 1900 and 2000. All of them are either dead or accounted for except one."

"Who's that?"

Buford looked over at Clem. Clem waved his arm in the air, which Buford interpreted as the go-ahead, so he said, "Have you ever heard of the *Lady Be Good*?"

"Yes."

"Then I assume you know the story."

"As it happens, I'm familiar with it."

"Then you know that Vernon Moore was the only member of the crew who was never found."

"Yes I do."

"Really? You already knew that?"

"Yes."

"Well, there you have it. He's the only Vernon Moore that we can't account for. Coincidentally, his middle initial is L, just like yours. He was also born in New Boston, Ohio, which is where you said you went to school."

"That's very interesting. If he's the only one left, then there can only be one possible conclusion, can't there? Isn't it right there on the table? I must be that Vernon Moore."

Buford looked at Clem, who sighed and said, "Read it. Read it all."

Buford opened up his notebook and began, "The *Lady Be Good* went down in April of 1943. That was more than sixty years ago. Vernon Moore was the radioman for the aircraft, a young man in his twenties at the time. All nine crewmembers bailed out, but they landed smack dab in the middle of the Sahara desert in southern Libya. One crewmember's chute failed to open but the other eight survived the jump. Over the next ten days, they walked due east more than eighty miles, even though they had exactly one half of one canteen of water between them. Five of them died there from heat, dehydration, and exhaustion, but the other three, including Vernon Moore, went on. I guess the last one made it one hundred and seventeen miles. Over time, the bodies of eight of the original nine crewmen were discovered, mostly by inexplicable luck, but not Vernon Moore. His remains have never been found."

Clem added, "They were hundreds of miles from anywhere, in the middle of the Sahara desert. No one could have survived the heat and the cold and the lack of food and water. Even if that Vernon Moore had survived by some miracle, there would be some record of his return, and he would be more than eighty years old by now."

Mr. Moore said, "Am I to take it, Clem, that the preponderance of evidence has persuaded you that I am not that Vernon Moore?"

Clem laughed. "That would be correct. One of Buford's researchers has postulated that you changed your last name to your mother's maiden name after she divorced your father. That happens a lot around these parts. Buford watches a lot of TV. His theory is that you're in the Witness Protection Program. A third idea here at the bank is that Vernon Moore is a well-paved alias, and that you use it to cover your true intentions. Which one is it, Vernon?"

Mr. Moore did not say anything and neither did Clement. Buford started to, but Clem shushed him up. After a time, Mr. Moore smiled and said, "Are you sure you want to end this little contest right here, right now? You must have a few more threads to follow. Do you want to give up?"

Clem responded, "That's a good point, but the road from here gets mighty rough. Expensive, too. We don't have much to go on."

"Then I'll make you a deal. If you'll do me a favor, I'll let Buford copy my driver's license."

Buford sat forward quickly and said, "Do you carry health insurance, Mr. Moore? That would be real helpful, too."

Mr. Moore nodded but continued to look directly at Clem. "Do we have a deal?" he asked.

Clement squirmed. "What exactly is this favor of yours?"

"I need two hours of your time. That's how long it will take me to explain why Calvin should wake Lucy up and be truthful to her."

"That little girl was in so much pain that Doc Wiley had to put her into a coma. I can't see how you could be doing her a favor by waking her up, and you certainly won't be doing her a favor by telling her that she's going to die."

Mr. Moore said, "Hank Wiley may have a solution for the pain, but it's usually used for a mother during birth, and it's expensive. Calvin's insurance probably won't pay for it. He may need some financial assistance from you."

"Calvin Millet won't take a wooden nickel from me. I promise you that."

"Not even to help his daughter? All I want is two hours of your time. What have you got to lose?"

Clem thought about Mr. Moore's proposition for a minute and then he stood up and said, "If I have to stay in here for two more hours, then I'll need to visit the facilities first. Buford, you make copies of Vernon's driver's license and health insurance card, and send one of your people in here with some things to drink. Make sure no one interrupts us, either."

Mr. Moore waited in the conference room while Clem and Buford left together and walked down the hall. When they were out of earshot, Clem said, "Where do we stand on callin' in Calvin's loan, Buford?"

"We're almost ready to go, Mr. Tucker."

"Almost ready?"

"That's right. I've been working on Mr. Moore's background full tilt for two days. We haven't budged on the paperwork for Millet's."

"Well, budge."

"No problem, Mr. Tucker. I can be ready to go on Monday."

"Were we in the same meeting? That's not fast enough. I want to go tomorrow."

"But Mr. Tucker . . . "

"Didn't you tell me that Calvin is more than ninety days overdue on that loan?"

"No sir. I said he would go over ninety on Monday. Not 'til then."

"Well, what about the other covenants? Is he in violation of any of those?"

"Yes, but . . . "

"Which one?"

"The inventory line requires a minimum cash balance of twenty-five thousand dollars."

"Twenty-five thousand dollars? Is that all?"

"That loan has been in place for more than twenty years, Mr. Tucker. Back then, twenty-five thousand dollars was a lot of money."

"But he is in violation of the covenant."

"Yes."

"Then call the loan."

"But . . . "

"Call the loan, Buford. Tomorrow. I've got to go back and meet with Mr. Moore again. I made a promise."

"Dammit, Mr. Tucker. Hear me out. If we call Calvin's loan, then the value of his store will drop off the face of the Earth."

"I know it will. That's the point."

"But what if this Mr. Moore is a buyer? Couldn't you just be lowering the price for him, or maybe some other outsider?"

"You're a good man, so I'm going to explain this to you, but only once. Calvin will never let the call become public. He can't because the value of the store will implode. He'll have to phone me instead. Under the circumstances, I'll give him a much better price than anyone else, including Vernon Moore."

"Are you sure?"

"Call the loan. Do it before the end of business tomorrow. Is that clear?"

"Yes sir."

LATE THAT AFTERNOON, Mona came back from the Bold Cut looking like a new woman, from the neck up anyway. Loretta had given her a complete makeover. Not entirely satisfied with the balance of her appearance, Mona went straight upstairs and bathed, and then she changed into fresh jeans, black cowboy boots, and a red silk cowboy blouse with white trim and buttons.

The next thing I knew, she was coming down the back stairs with those old sweat clothes bundled up in her hands, walking outside, and stuffing them into the big black trash can in the back. Thank God she didn't set them afire; that trash can is made of plastic.

Well, I suppose my questions about second thoughts were answered then and there, but we talked 'til dinnertime anyway, just the two of us. We didn't discuss what had already happened that day; we talked about the things that were going to happen: the divorce; the custody fight; retrieving Macbeth; splitting things up; initiating Mona into the Circle; finding her a good job; taking the boys to Easter services on Sunday; getting them enrolled in school on Monday and making sure they met the right children.

Meanwhile, Mr. Moore and Clem were finishing up at the bank. I don't know what they actually said to each other. I'm not sure that Mr. Moore always explains the Benevolent God Paradoxes in exactly the same way, but I do know that Clem called Buford Pickett at home immediately after they said their good-byes.

He said, "When will you be ready to call Calvin's loans?"

"Just before close of business tomorrow, Mr. Tucker, like you said."

"That's good, Buford. I appreciate the effort. But I don't want you to present the letter to Calvin until you get the green light from me."

"May I ask why?"

"No."

"Does this mean you've changed your mind?"

"No. I just want to make sure that I have the timing right. You call me on my cell phone tomorrow, but not 'til you're ready."

"Yes sir."

Chapter 15

A Pet Before the Storm

AFTER HIS MEETING with Clem, Mr. Moore left the bank and walked over to the Bold Cut to see Loretta. She lives in a two-story, Craftsman-style home that was originally built for the town pastor more than one hundred years ago. We both see some irony in that. Loretta recently had it painted springtime-yellow with white trim, and it has a lovely, two-tiered front porch that overlooks Main Street. The downstairs is Loretta's salon; the upstairs is her home.

Loretta unlocked the front door to let Mr. Moore in, then said, "Welcome to my store, Vern. Would you like to step into my office and check out the lay of the land? It's dark and cozy back there, and I have some things to drink in the refrigerator."

Mr. Moore replied, "Thank you, Loretta. I can always use a cold drink."

"But you don't drink alcohol? Is that right?"

"No I don't. Booze clouds my mind. It's weak enough as it is."

Loretta smiled like the coquette she is and said, "Sometimes, darlin', a shot of vodka or bourbon can also free the spirit."

"Believe me, my spirit is about as free as it can get."

"Is that a fact, Mr. Mystery Man? You hold that thought for a minute while I get us something to drink. What would you prefer?"

"Iced water."

"Perrier? Pellegrino? I have 'em both, darlin'."

Mr. Moore smiled and replied, "My preference is the Pellegrino. With some ice cubes in it."

Loretta squeezed him on the chin and said, "You can have anything your heart desires. Anything at all. You just have a seat. I'll be right back."

Mr. Moore used the time to look around the room. Lo's office was paneled in fake wood just like so many others in these parts; don't ask me why. Her desk and chair were near the back, facing the entryway. There was a black-leather foldout sofa running along one wall, sitting behind an elliptical mahogany coffee table. I have been there a hundred times, though, and I can tell you that the first thing Mr. Moore saw when he entered Loretta's lair was her black-leather massage table, which was pushed up against the other wall. It even has a padded circle at the top for your head.

Mr. Moore sat down on the couch facing Loretta's massage table; there was no place else to sit except up on the massage table itself or behind her desk. Presently, she came back with his iced water and her vodka whatever, and then she perched herself on the couch sideways so she was facing him and said, "So, darlin', I have proposed marriage. What's your answer?"

"I already said yes, Loretta. What can I add?"

"You were just fibbin'. You know you were."

"Well, to tell you the truth, I'm not sure I can pass your IQ test."

"That's not the test you have to worry about passing. Why do you think I invited you here? To give you the SAT?"

Mr. Moore smiled. "I may be an optimist, Loretta, but I've learned that it's best not too assume too much from a woman's invitation."

"That alone makes you a very unusual man." With that, Loretta took a long swig from her vodka.

Mr. Moore thought about what she said for a bit and then he remarked, "Once again, Loretta, I sense that you have been disappointed by the male of the species. Would that be the case?"

Loretta laughed out loud and said, "Did I ever tell you about my cat?"

"No. I don't think you have."

"Well, he was a black, furry thing with a right angle near the end of his tail. I came home from work one winter night—I was living in Omaha at the time—and I found him huddled up against my back door. I guess that door was leakin' heat; everything in that old clapboard house leaked somethin'.

"I let him in and gave him some tuna; what else is a girl supposed to do? Naturally, he stayed. I would let him out in the morning before I went to work, and then he would come back in the evening. I never knew what he did during the day, although he did bring me some dead mice a few times. I'm sure they were supposed to be gifts, but they made me angry and I told him so, as if it ever made a difference.

"The rest of the time, all that cat did was eat my food, mark my clothes, scratch my upholstery up, get cat hair on everything I owned, and sleep. No, that's not true. Every once in a while he would sit on my lap while I was watchin' TV. That's what I got out of it; a cat on my lap once or twice a week, plus the occasional dead rodent at my doorstep.

"One night, he just didn't come home. Fool that I am, I drove all over the neighborhood looking for him. I even put an ad in the paper but I never saw him again. To this day, I don't know if he got killed or he found himself a house with central heating. Do you know what I named that cat, darlin'?"

"No, Loretta."

"His name was Metaphor. And you know what else? I still miss that big, mangy cat and he has been gone for more than ten years. Wilma tells me that you're good at explaining things. Maybe you can explain why you cats are so damn difficult to put up with."

Mr. Moore shook his head. "I might be able to, but it's a bit of long story; more like a parable really."

"Well I just told you one, and I've always been in favor of tit for tat. It's your turn. Why don't take your shoes off and relax. I'm not goin' anywhere. Do you have a date tonight?"

"No."

"Yes you do, Vern, and I'm it. Now tell me your story."

Mr. Moore kicked off his loafers, put his feet up on the coffee table, and began his tale. "Just like the Bible says, man's troubles began with food. It wasn't an apple, though. That's an inaccuracy. Mankind's problems started when lightning struck a chicken."

"What did you say?"

"When lightning struck a chicken. There have always been thunderstorms, even before the recording of history, and on this fateful, primordial day, lightning struck the pet chicken of a local cave dweller. Until that time, men and women had been vegetarians, but that roasted chicken smelled mighty good, even if it had been a pet before the storm. Well, the local caveman and his spouse got over their deep sense of loss and fried it up with some rice and salt, and it tasted so good that the word spread quickly throughout the land. Do you know what happened next?"

"No, darlin', and I can't wait. What happened next?"

"For the next one thousand years, prehistoric men and women tied chickens to metal poles during thunderstorms. As you might expect, this did not produce a reliable stream of chicken-fried rice. Eventually, though, an enterprising young man discovered how to kill a chicken on purpose.

"It turned out that murdered chicken tasted just as good as the accidental death variety, and the man and wife could eat it whenever they wanted, so the next thing they did was tell their neighbors. Well, they told their neighbors, and so on and so on and so on. So, it came to pass that human beings became omnivores, men became chicken killers, and women became expert chicken cooks."

Loretta frowned and said, "You're a strange man, Vernon Moore. Are you tellin' me that I shouldn't eat chicken. I like chicken."

Mr. Moore smiled and answered, "No, Loretta. That's not my point at all. Even back then, Nature could not leave well enough alone; chicken was just the beginning. A few millennia later, lightning struck a water buffalo. That first water buffalo produced enough barbecued ribs to feed a dozen families, so word of the new discovery quickly spread far and wide. This time, though, the men didn't wait for lightning to strike again; they went straight out to hunt more water buffalo. That's when tragedy struck. It turned out that water buffalo were a lot harder to kill than chickens and, I might add, they were not the least enthused about the prospect. Guns hadn't been invented yet, nor had bows and arrows or even spears, so the first buffalo hunters were massacred by their prey.

"Humans, however, have never quite known when to quit, so they persisted and persisted. Eventually, this presented a dilemma to God, who was much more involved with our progress back in those days. Having no other choice but to protect the Dwindling Few, He decided to intervene in a way that only God can intervene, meaning by divine chemistry."

"What does that mean?"

"He started tinkering with the formula for man. First, He made the men bigger and stronger, but that wasn't enough. They were still slaughtered by the water buffalo, which made the women unhappy.

"Then God made men smarter, but that didn't work either. Instead of making weapons and heading out onto the savanna to risk their lives in pursuit of dinner, the men stopped hunting altogether and hung around the cave all day, telling stories and doodling on the walls. Well, that made the women even more unhappy, so they stopped having babies."

"Good for them, Vern."

"Perhaps, but that put God in a box because he was back to the Dwindling Few. Having no other option, he finally made men stupider. In His wisdom, though, He didn't want men to be utterly stupid all the time, just some of the time, so He invented a new chemical. This chemical, which is now called testosterone, caused all higher brain functions to cease any time that the male of the species was in the hunt—any kind of hunt.

"As we all know now, God is a chemist par excellence. The third formula worked to perfection. Newly motivated, the men went out and attacked with mindless abandon. Water buffalo started dropping in droves. Subsequently, of course, we men attacked lions, tigers, and bears, endangered species, the environment, our enemies, our neighbors, opposing teams, the opposite sex, anybody else's ideas, and convenience stores. To this day, in fact, we men are still on the attack, regardless of whether the quarry is male or female, animal or vegetable, friend or foe, or none of the above. Then, when we're done attacking the prey of the day, we like to head back to the cave for dinner and a nap. Because we're still stimluated by the thrill of the hunt, a new cave is often more enticing than an old cave, regardless of how comfortable the old cave was. In other words, we have not evolved one iota since God made us stupid enough to kill the water buffalo."

Mr. Moore stopped and took a sip of his iced water. Loretta reflected on his story for a moment and then replied, "What are you sayin'? Are you trying to tell me that men are too stupid to control these urges?"

"Not completely. It's all a matter of degree. The men that most women prefer tend to have more testosterone than most, although the flow subsides with age. Over time, intelligent thought eventually becomes possible for all of us."

"What age is that?"

"Scientists have shown that hormone flow usually begins to recede around the age of twenty-five, but it takes scientific instruments to detect it. Deliberate male thought is not normally discernible by the laywoman until at least five years later."

"Age thirty? I know little boys who are sixty-five."

"I said it was all a matter of degree, Loretta, and considerable regret. For us men, impending rationality is a death sentence for some of our favorite parts. We fight it."

"Are you saying that men prefer the little head to the big head, Vern? Even you?"

"I know it sounds strange, but being a purely hormonal creature has a certain, devil-may-care allure. I miss it. All older men do. Have you ever seen the walls in Clem Tucker's River House? Now there's a man who refuses to give up his little head."

Loretta smiled sweetly and said, "That's all very interesting, darlin', but what about you? Have you given up? That doesn't seem like you."

Mr. Moore sighed. "Before I pass on, I have to learn when to give up. That's the one thing I have to learn to do. Even a salesman has to know when to throw in the towel and move on."

"Really? Is that so? Is that the right thing to do? Maybe there's something I can do to recharge that hormone battery of yours."

"You're an enticing woman, Loretta, but . . . "

"But what, darlin'? I got your message. Consider my offer of marriage null and void. I know you're leavin' Ebb after your work is done, whatever it is. But while you're here, why don't you just enjoy yourself and let me enjoy myself? In fact, why don't you come on over here and sit on my lap? Metaphorically speaking, of course."

Then she smiled and said, "What have you got to lose?"

• • •

Mr. Moore did not get back to the Come Again until after closing time. I made him some iced tea after I let him in, but he would not tell me much about his evening with Loretta. In fact, I couldn't even get him to tell me how much money he won from Clem Tucker at gin rummy. Instead, he asked me a lot of questions about Mona and the boys, which always gets my motor runnin'.

Speaking of my Mona, Marv Breck didn't call her until nearly eleven o'clock that night. Mona sent the boys upstairs and took the call in the study, where she could close the door and be by herself. Mr. Moore went up to bed, too; he looked plumb tuckered out. I had to stay up, though; it's what a mother does, so I made some pumpkin bread for Hank because we had eaten his banana nut bread for lunch. While I was waiting for it to cook, I checked my email. As I hoped, there was a note from Clara, an atypically lengthy one. It said, "Tell me more."

After I sent her back a response, I turned on the TV to see what was on the Discovery Channel. It was some show about the mysterious forces of Nature, but they left the most mysterious force out: static cling. One dry winter day, I strolled into Lulu Tiller's clinic wearing navy-blue wool slacks with silver studs and a matching long-sleeved cotton blouse, and I walked out ten minutes later looking like I was wearing grey angora from head to toe. You have never seen so much animal hair attached to one single person in all your life. My advice: when you visit your vet, always wear gray.

I was still brooding about static cling when Mona came back into my kitchen, dry-eyed as an Indian scout. All she said was, "It's over, Mama. I have to go tell the boys now."

So much for cling. I gave her a great big hug and then she went upstairs to tell Matt and Mark the whole story. I knew that the boys would be hurt but that they would get over it. Ebb is chock-full of children who have already crossed that divide, but I was still worried about my Mona. You see, we Porters don't follow the standard denial/anger/ bargaining/depression/acceptance cycle. As a matter of fact, I don't know anybody who does.

My ex-husband, Al, had a cycle that was more like denial/ anger, denial/anger, and then more denial and anger. Denial and anger were that man's forte. Like a lot of men in these parts, he was particularly good at weather denial, accompanied by anger. In my mind, I can still see him heading off to shoot skeet one April morning—right into the teeth of a howling, horizontal hailstorm, cursing every step of the way, as if God was ruining his day for spite.

Myself, I am an anger/depression/revenge person, and I don't do it straight through either. I can loop through anger and depression over and over before I finally get to revenge. That was how I was with my marriage. I probably had to repeat that cycle a gazillion times before I finally figured out that I was going to have to leave my husband if I was ever going to get to the third plateau.

My two girls are half like Al and half like me: not as much

anger or revenge I expect, but lots of denial and depression, and they can jump back and forth just like we did. I also know from personal experience that depression and acceptance can look a lot alike, which is why I was worried about my Mona. In my heart I knew she had made the right choice for the long run, but I figured that she was still in depression.

I guess old Silas the Second was worried, too. Just before I closed up, I noticed him drifting up the staircase to see about our new arrivals. He was carrying a single, long-stemmed red rose. I swear to God he was. I even looked for it the next day in Mona's room, but I couldn't find it.

Sometimes, old Silas seems so real to me that I think I should cook him a meal, but other times I wonder if I'm just making him up in my head. Is that acceptance, or is it denial? I guess I'll never know for sure.

Chapter 16

The Odds of God

MR. MOORE HAD to leave early for Carson the next morning so we only had a minute or two to visit. I wished him good luck and made him promise to spill the beans when he got back. He swore up and down that he would.

After he left, I fixed Clara's breakfast and took it up to the top floor. In case I haven't told you before, Clara is a tall, pale, gray-haired woman who looks like she has lived every single minute of her sixty years, whether she has or not. On that specific day, she was jogging on one of her machines and watching an old Lucille Ball rerun on TV. Her hair was done in a ponytail and she was dressed in a black leotard, white support hose, a lavender headband, and gray-green athletic shoes. You could see right there why she never entertained.

I put her breakfast down on the butcher-block table and sat

down to wait, but Clara hopped over as soon as I caught her attention. She took a big, long swig of her cranberry juice, and then she looked straight into my eyes. That was my cue. She was ready for me to talk.

Well, I tried again to explain what Mr. Moore had said to Hank and me, but after a minute of listening to myself make no sense at all, I gave up and said, "You need to talk to this man yourself. He has a philosophy that could change your life."

Clara didn't reply so I tried to answer the question that a woman was most likely to be thinking. "I don't know where he comes from. I'm not sure what he does either; nobody is. But I believe he was sent here to help us. He can help you, too. You should listen to this man."

Clara still did not answer. Now, I am not the smartest woman, but I concluded that she was still on the fence. I said, "Whatever or whoever he is, Clara, he is an honest man. He wouldn't harm a fly." Then I took a page from Mr. Moore's book and added, "What have you got to lose?"

Clara didn't answer again, but this time I waited. We sat through an entire commercial for the latest miracle skin lotion, but then she finally said, "Yes."

I grinned and replied, "You'll like him, Clara. I'll set up a mutually convenient time by email." Clara smiled and then stuck a spoonful of oatmeal in her mouth, which I interpreted as the termination of our chat.

Like I said, having a conversation with Clara is a bit of a chore.

• • •

Calvin met Mr. Moore at the door of the Carson house and the two men went directly into the kitchen. Before they had even sat down, Mr. Moore asked, "How's Lucy?"

"Hank started reducing her medication last night. She'll be conscious soon, and then we'll see what kind of pain she's in."

"What's the prognosis?"

"No surprises there. Hank is noncommittal; Louise is optimistic."

"How about you?"

"It's Good Friday. I choose to be optimistic."

"Me, too, which means that you'll be able to tell Lucy about her condition."

Calvin stammered, "I don't know, Vernon. I just don't know."

"You don't know? I thought we had a deal."

He shook his head and replied, "I was up all night thinking about the three paradoxes. It seems to me that there could be a flaw in your thinking."

"Really. What's that?"

"Well, the core question is the existence of God, not his benevolence. Isn't that true?"

"Yes."

"But isn't it also true that we reached a benevolent conclusion because we began with that assumption?"

Mr. Moore steepled his hands, bowed his head slightly and answered, "Yes, grasshopper. We began by assuming that there is a benevolent God, and then we attempted but failed to disprove His existence. Very good."

"Okay, Yoda. That's fine with me. But I never really agreed with the first premise. What would have happened if we had started somewhere else, someplace other than the first paradox?"

"Philosophy is logic without the comfort of proof, Calvin, but it is logic just the same. Like all forms of logic, the end depends upon the beginning. We began with the first paradox. If we had started from a different place, then we might've reached a different destination."

Calvin grimaced and said, "Well, that's what I thought. That is just what I fucking thought. We're right back where we started, aren't we?"

"No, Calvin, we most certainly aren't. We went though one logical door, the very same paradox that has created millions of agnostics and atheists, and we found a solution to the paradox and a very happy ending. We found hope."

"Okay, but we went through one goddamn door. One. Pick another. Pick one more door, but not one that presumes the existence of God at the beginning. No religious claptrap, that's still the rule, and no more paradoxes either."

"Okay, but are you absolutely sure? Will one more argument for the existence of God really give you hope?"

"Absolutely. I'm still a buyer. In fact, I'm looking to buy hope in bulk quantities. I just want to make sure that you aren't selling me a pig in a poke."

"Fair enough, but this is an objection that I wasn't prepared to handle. Can I have a little time to think about it?"

"Sure. How much time do you need? Five minutes? Ten minutes?"

Mr. Moore laughed and answered, "I need to take a walk. Is there a river or a stream close by? I know there's a river between here and Ebb. I crossed it on my way here."

"That's the Nemaha. It's not the most scenic river in Nebraska, but if you take the road out front due east for a quarter mile, you'll run smack into it. Don't worry when you hit dirt; that just means you're gettin' close."

"That'll be perfect. I'll be back in thirty minutes or so. Will that be soon enough?"

"Of course it will. You take your time. I'll call Lily and see what's going on at the store."

On his way to the river, Mr. Moore stopped at his car to make a call.

I picked up the phone at the Come Again. Mr. Moore asked, "Is Clem there?"

"Not yet, "I answered. "He should be here any minute, though. Are you on a cell phone, Mr. Moore? I thought you said you didn't own one."

"I said I don't carry one, Wilma, but I do keep one in the car for safety's sake. Will you do me a favor, please?"

I nodded my head and answered, "Of course I will."

"Will you ask Clem to meet me at Starbucks or the River House this afternoon? I don't care which one."

"Is there a special time you have in mind?"

"No, as long as it's after two."

"Will he know why you want a meeting? You know he always says he's a busy man, whether he is or not."

"Just tell him that I have an answer to his proposition."

"That's all?"

"Yes."

"Is there any more I can say, Mr. Moore? Are you sure he'll know what you mean?"

"I'm never sure of anything, Wilma. If he wants to meet, just ask him to leave me a voicemail at this number with the time and location of his choice."

Mr. Moore gave me the number of his car phone, but that was all I could wheedle out of him. Clem arrived at the Come Again about ten minutes later and I gave him the message, which I had written down on a pink sticky-note. He thanked me kindly, which was a bit of an eyebrow-raiser, and then he went outside to call Mr. Moore. Mona brought the boys down for their ride a little later, and then she talked with Clem and me for a while. She wanted to make sure that Clem didn't drive too fast, and she wanted me to know that she was going back to the Bold Cut for a manicure.

The boys climbed in the back of the Porsche, which was tight but they managed to squeeze in, and there were some seatbelts back there that I had never noticed before. That particular day was glorious and warm, so Clem put the top down and we headed back through town and on down to the River House. Clem took a twisty county road and he didn't drive too fast. Well, maybe he did once or twice, but I always felt safe. The boys were in hog heaven.

Marie Delacroix was waiting for us with homemade cinnamon buns and orange juice and coffee, and Clem had to explain every single head on his wall to Mark. Matt was more interested in the gun rack in the den, which worried me some, but Clem said the boy had acquired a good knowledge of them from his father. Before we headed back into town, Clem and I took a walk along the river by ourselves. We talked about old times and little Lucy Millet. There was a moment or two when I thought he was going to tear up, but he didn't. I did—when he took my hand. Until that moment, I don't believe that he had ever touched me before dark.

When Mr. Moore got back to the Millet rental, Hank Wiley and Nurse Nelson were sitting in the kitchen with Calvin. Mr. Moore turned his chair around backward before he sat down and then said, "How is she?"

Hank replied, "Lucy's pulse is coming up and her blood pressure is fine. Her temperature is still on the low side, but it's not too bad. Still, we won't know how she feels until she wakes up."

"When will that be?"

"In the next hour or so. Maybe a tad earlier, maybe a bit later." Hank turned to Calvin and said, "I have to run back up to Ebb to see another patient, but I'll be right back after that. Nurse Nelson will keep an eye on Lucy while I'm gone."

Nurse Nelson smiled broadly and asked, "Perhaps you'd be interested in a rematch a little later, Mr. Moore?"

"We'll see. If I have time, then I would enjoy another game. At just this moment, though, I have to speak to Calvin."

"Come on, Louise," said Hank. "You can take Mr. Moore's money when I get back from town."

After they had left the room, Calvin said, "Well, did you come up with another door?"

"I did. Why don't we go for one with numbers in it? There's a lot of comfort in numbers, wouldn't you agree?"

"I have no idea what you're talkin' about, Vernon."

"Didn't you tell me that you had a degree in accounting? You must have studied probability theory."

"Yes, but . . . "

"Then let's calculate the odds of God. Are you game?"

"That is completely and utterly insane."

"It's just another door; a door for a numbers man. Are you game or not?"

"Okay. Fine. Let's calculate the odds of God."

"Just so I know in advance, how high do you need them to be? Eighty percent? Ninety percent? How high do the odds have to be before you have hope?"

"Well, I don't want to make things impossible for you. How about ninety-nine percent? That should do it."

Mr. Moore said, "Fair enough."

"Really?"

"Absolutely. Have you ever seen a ghost?"

Nostradamus himself could not have seen that question coming. Calvin replied, "Excuse me. Would you please repeat the question?"

"Have you ever seen a ghost? A simple yes or no will do."

"It's a damn unnatural thing to ask, Vernon, but the answer is no. I've never seen one. Wilma Porter says she's seen Silas the Second in the Come Again a bunch of times, but that's Wilma."

"In other words, she can't prove it."

"Right."

"Can you prove that she hasn't seen Silas?"

Calvin rolled the question over in his mind. Before he could answer, Mr. Moore said, "I saw a ghost once."

"You did?" Calvin replied. "Seriously?"

"Yes. A few years ago, I was staying at a plantation-style bed and breakfast in an area of rural Virginia where a lot of Civil War battles were fought. One Saturday afternoon, I got up from a nap and went into the bathroom before I went downstairs. For some reason, I looked back into the bedroom while I was washing my hands, don't ask me why, and that's when I saw him. He was a tall, older man, possibly in his late fifties or early sixties, but weary looking. He was dressed in a long gray coat with an erect embroidered collar, red-and-gold insignia, red cuffs, and gold buttons. He also wore a gray homburg with a red ribbon around it. There was a strand of gold around the band, tied at the front. He was looking at my bed, longingly, as if he wanted to sleep there.

"I turned back toward the mirror, either out of fear or to reestablish my grip on reality. When I got up enough courage to look back into the bedroom, he was gone."

"Don't you think he could have been an illusion?"

"He might have been; or he might not have been. To this day,

I don't know. Certainly, I'll never be able to prove it one way or the other, even to myself."

"Okay, but is that your reason for God? Is that it?"

"No, but we are getting there. Tell me this: throughout history, how many people could have had an experience like mine?"

"I don't know, Vernon. For sure, I've never had one like it."

"But you know at least two people who have: Wilma and me."

"True, but that's only two out of maybe a thousand."

"Fair enough. But there are six billion people on the planet today. Doesn't that mean that as many as three million of us could have seen a ghost?"

"That's a hell of a stretch. How can you say that?"

"It's a simple proportion, Calvin."

"You can do numbers like that in your head?"

"Yes."

"Well, I still think it's a stretch."

"Throughout history? How about a million sightings throughout human history?"

"Okay. But like I said: not one of them has ever been proven."

Mr. Moore said, "An excellent point. Let's follow your train of thought. Out of one million ghost sightings, what percent would need to be proven in order to establish the certainty of life after life?"

"I don't know. I suppose you do."

"Yes. The answer is one ten-thousandth of one percent, or zero-point-zero-zero-zero-zero-one percent."

"Okay. I guess that's a pretty small number."

"It is. It's the equivalent of exactly one confirmed sighting out of a million. In comparison, what percent would have to be disproved in order to establish that there are no ghosts?"

"I suppose you're going to tell me."

"The answer is all of them, one hundred percent, and that still would not eliminate the possibility of other forms of life after life. From a logical point of view, in fact, it wouldn't even eliminate the possibility of ghosts. It would just mean that none had ever been seen."

"I'm starting to get dizzy, Vernon. Add this up for me. "

"If my experience with the Civil War ghost was genuine, even if it was the only honest-to-God paranormal encounter in the entire history of humankind, it would prove beyond a shadow of a doubt that there is some form of life after life. The reason is that it only takes one legitimate paranormal event to prove it. Just one."

"Go on."

"However, to eliminate any possibility of the existence of life after life, we would have to disprove every ghost sighting in the history of man, every single one, and that would still be insufficient. After that, we would have to find a way to eliminate every other possible form of life after life. In short, we would have to disprove an infinity of possibilities.

"We only need one legitimate experience to prove life after life, Calvin. We need an infinity of negatives to disprove it. In practice, though, we can do neither, which means that we can never know for sure. Therefore, the critical question is this: given what we can infer from the very large number of potentially genuine ghost sightings throughout history, which of the two is more likely?"

Calvin chose to ponder rather than to respond. Mr. Moore said, "You take your time."

Calvin was still thinking when Nurse Nelson rapped on the inside of the doorframe leading into the kitchen and said, "Yoohoo! Am I interrupting? I need to get a glass of water for Lucy."

Calvin stood up and said, "Is she awake now?"

Nurse Nelson put some water in a small glass and answered, "No, not yet. She's starting to fidget a little, though. That's good. It tells me she'll be coming around soon. She'll want a sip of water when she does. Her little throat will be parched."

"I have to go in and see her."

Nurse Nelson put her hand on Calvin's shoulder. "Not yet. It could be another half hour before she wakes up, and I absolutely have to be in there when she does so I can take down her vitals. I'll come and get you the moment I'm done."

"But I have to be there when she comes to. I have to know if she's in pain."

"She won't know how much pain she's in herself until her mind clears. As soon as she wakes up, I'll let you know."

"Louise . . . "

She pointed to his chair and said, "Sit."

"Louise . . . "

"Sit, Calvin," she repeated. After he sat back down, she turned her head toward Mr. Moore and said, "Don't you forget that you promised me a rematch." Then she bounced out of the kitchen with that little glass of water in hand.

As soon as Nurse Nelson left the room, Calvin got back up and began to pace. After about seventeen trips up and down the length of the tiny kitchen, he stopped and said, "Fine. Okay. I guess I'm stuck in here. Where are we?"

"You tell me, Calvin. You used to play baseball. Which is more likely: one hit in a million at bats or an infinitely long no-hitter?"

"I'm not sure it's the same thing, Vernon."

"It's not. If it were the same thing, we could prove what we needed to prove. This is philosophy; we are denied the comfort of proof—but which alternative is more likely?"

Calvin answered slowly, "I guess life after life . . . "

Mr. Moore came forward in his chair and said, "What did you say?"

"Life after life. I suppose."

"No more supposing, Calvin; it's time for you decide. Either God is likely or He is not. Either life after life is likely or it is not. Either the odds are ninety-nine percent in your favor, or they're not. This isn't about Lucy's hope; it's about yours. Choose, and choose now. Do you have hope, or not?"

After a few more seconds, Calvin responded, "Fine. Okay. Yes!"

Mr. Moore inhaled deeply and said, "My God, you were one tough customer. Now let's discuss what you're going to tell your daughter."

Calvin immediately sat down and slumped in his chair. "I don't know," he said. "I just don't know. I don't want to tell Lucy that she's going to be a ghost. What kind of future is that?"

"I thought you wanted to tell Lucy that she would be going to heaven."

"I do, but . . . "

"Then why not tell her that? But also tell her that she didn't get a fair chance this time, so she will get to come back to Earth and live at least one more long, full life before she goes to heaven. No paradoxes, no percentages, no paranormal phenomena. Do you think you can handle that?"

Calvin carefully considered Mr. Moore's question and then replied, "No."

"Yes you can, Calvin. Yes you can. All you have to do is sell it. Have you ever had any sales training?"

"Sales training?"

"Sure. All you have to do is sell your daughter some hope. It's the easiest thing in the world. Have you ever had any sales training at all?"

"No. Well, maybe. I've read a few books about the subject, presumably to help me handle people like you—well, not exactly like you, of course, but the manufacturers' reps and distributors who try to call me twice a day every day."

Mr. Moore shook his head in sympathy and said, "After being on the wrong end of so many sales calls, Calvin, you may think you know us, but we salesmen have a lot of trade secrets. One of them is the very essence of selling. Do you know what the essence of selling is?"

"That's easy. The essence of selling is talking. It's persuasion; it has to be."

"That's exactly what most folks believe. A lot of salesmen believe it too, but not the best of us. The essence of selling is asking good questions. Do you think you can do that?"

"I don't know."

"Well, I'll tell you another secret about salesmen. We practice; especially when the call is going to be a nail-biter. Are you up for a little practice?"

Calvin brightened up and replied, "That's it. That's precisely what I need."

"Okay. I suggest we role play. To start, I'll be you and you can be Lucy. Later, we'll reverse the roles. How would that be?"

For the next thirty minutes, Calvin learned his sales pitch. The men were interrupted by Nurse Nelson, who burst in and said, "Lucy is awake!"

Calvin jumped up from his chair. "How does she feel?"

"She's groggy, which is to be expected, and she seems to have a bit of pain in her lower back. Anyone would have to be sore after lying in bed for so long. But her vitals are strong and she looks much brighter than I expected she would."

"So I can go in and see her now, right?"

"Of course you can. She's waiting for you. Just don't expect too much conversation for a while. Why don't you let me get some ice chips that you can take in with you. She's had some water, so ice chips will be the best thing for her now."

Calvin looked at Mr. Moore and said, "I'm not ready to tell her yet. I'm just not ready. I'm afraid I'll blow it."

Mr. Moore smiled and replied, "Don't tell her now, Calvin. Just be with her; enjoy her company. Practice over the next few weeks. When you're ready, do what you just did with me: ask her good questions and let her do the talking. She's a smart little girl, and you're a smart man. Have confidence in yourselves."

Nurse Nelson handed Calvin the ice chips from the freezer. He said, "Thank you, Vernon," and left the kitchen without another word.

Nurse Nelson remarked, "Calvin and Lucy should be allowed to spend some time on their own now and Doctor Wiley won't be back for an hour. How about that rematch?"

"If you could indulge me for a moment, I have a slightly different proposition."

"Ooh, that's interesting! What's on your mind?"

"I want to teach you how to deal the cards."

"Teach me how to deal? I'm a good dealer. You saw me."

"You're very good, but you don't deal the way that I want you to be able to deal."

"What do you mean? Are you going to teach me how to cheat, Vernon Moore?"

Mr. Moore smiled and replied, "That's one way to look at it. I'd rather say that I'm going to empower you to disrupt the laws of probability, but only for the benefit of others. That means that they must never, ever know you're doing it."

"Okay. But just exactly who is 'they'?"

"'They' is Lucy Millet. If you have the time, and I have every confidence you will, I want you to teach her to play cribbage, but I want her to be incredibly lucky. I want twenty-fours and sixteens and twelves to rain down on her from the heavens in quantities that could never be explained by the laws of probability. Do you understand what I mean?"

Nurse Nelson smiled and said, "Yes I do, Vernon. I certainly do. Now show me what to do."

"I will. I just need to check on my next meeting." Mr. Moore excused himself, and went outside to his car so that he could make a phone call to Clem.

By then, of course, the boys and I were all back home and Clem had accepted my invitation for dinner, so Mr. Moore and Clem agreed to meet at the Come Again. Clem dallied in the kitchen for a while after that. He does enjoy my pumpkin bread so, especially when I have baked it for somebody else. Then he jumped into his Porsche and headed over to the bank to see Buford Pickett.

Chapter 17

Men in the Den

WHILE MR. MOORE was sitting in the kitchen with Calvin and I was at the River House with Clem and the boys, Mona was at the Bold Cut, getting a manicure from Loretta. At least, that's what I thought she was doing. Actually, Loretta was teaching her Manicure 101. By the time Mona came home, she had the most lovely, rose-colored, French-cut nails you have ever seen, plus matching lipstick—and a job. I didn't want her to harm those lovely nails so I did the cutting and the chopping for dinner while Mona told me all about her new situation.

Without ever saying one word to me in advance, Loretta had asked Mona to take over reception and bookkeeping at the Bold Cut, which were the same things she had done for Marv and his daddy at the dentistry up in Omaha before Mark came along. In addition, Loretta offered to teach Mona to manicure, pedicure, and cut men's hair which, as every woman knows, is a plain simple thing to do. Also, she said Mona would only have to work from nine to three during the school year so she could be with the boys, plus nine to five on Saturday, so she could get away from the boys. I swear, that Loretta thinks of every little thing.

Of course, I called Loretta right up and thanked her seventeen thousand times from the bottom of my heart. I asked her to dinner, too, and I may have mentioned that Mr. Moore would be there. Whatever it was, Loretta was in my kitchen about two blinks later, just jabbering away with Mona and me and sipping a glass of my best Iowa wine.

Mr. Moore showed up around two-thirty and I have to say it was the second time in two days that I had seen him tuckered out. Little Mark was all over the poor man, telling him about Clem's Porsche and asking for another ride. Mr. Moore had to fight off Loretta, too, so he could go upstairs and freshen up. Naturally, she offered to help him, right there in front of Mona and little Mark. That woman has no shame. Thankfully, he declined her offer, but I sensed some hesitation. I'm certain that Loretta caught it, too. I could see it in the smirk on her face.

Before he could get up my stairs, I grabbed Mr. Moore by the elbow and ushered him into the dining room so I could tell him about Clara. Bless his soul, he said he wanted to meet her as soon as possible, so I went straight into the den and called, Mr. Moore in tow. In case you were wondering, she says "yes" when she answers her phone. Luckily, she said she was available, too, so Mr.

Moore went directly up to the third floor. I offered to go with him but he said it would probably be better if he went alone. I had my doubts at the time but I also had a lot of cooking to do, so I didn't object. Not too much, anyway.

About three hours later, Mr. Moore came down the back stairs into the kitchen and fixed himself a glass of iced tea, just as Clem was getting back from the bank. I wanted to know what he had said to Clara, but I never had a chance to ask. Those two men went straight into my den and shut the door, and they didn't come out until almost seven-thirty. It's a good thing dinner was late, because what they said in there turned out to be important.

Mr. Moore held the study door for Clem, and then he closed it after both of them had entered the room. Clem took my office chair, which is right in front of an antique rolltop desk that he let me keep when I bought the place. He just sat there for a moment or two, admiring my desk, and then he said, "Isn't this magnificent, Vernon? It was originally bought by my great-great-grandfather. I have no idea how old it is, and I have no idea what I was thinking when I let Wilma keep it."

Mr. Moore sat down in my reading chair, a comfy burnt-orange loveseat with a genuine Lakota Indian blanket over the cushions to hide the wear. He replied, "I know exactly what you mean. I'm an antique myself."

"We both are, Vernon, although we may end up having to carbon date you to get a reliable date of birth."

"I take it that Buford and his team at the bank have not made a lot of progress in that regard."

"Not as of this morning. According to Buford's researcher, your driver's license is from New Boston, Ohio, the same place that the radioman on the *Lady Be Good* was born. It says you were born on May fifteenth, 1943, which is exactly forty days after the *Lady Be Good* went down. Would you have us believe that you wandered in the desert for forty days and forty nights before your rebirth? How very Biblical."

Mr. Moore smiled gently and replied, "I guess this means that I'm no longer in consideration for the post of Tucker Foundation investment funds manager."

"I don't want you to take this in the wrong way, but you never were. A few days ago, I was concerned that you might be a buyer for Millet's so I wanted to know more about you. I'm not the least bit worried about that anymore."

"If I may ask, why not?"

"Because you could never survive due diligence. Hell, if I can't find out about you, then nobody can this side of the CIA."

"You're absolutely right. I have no interest in buying Calvin's store. I do have a few ideas, though. For instance, I may have another candidate for your funds manager."

Clem's eyebrows shot straight up. "Is that the truth? Do you know someone who might be willing to do it?"

As you may have noticed by now, Mr. Moore often answered a question with a question. "Present company excepted, who's the best businessman in Ebb?"

Clem broke off eye contact and replied, "I don't exactly know for sure. Maybe Buzz Busby, but I'd have to think about it for a while."

"Well, I'm not as well acquainted with the local talent as you are, but I have another nominee."

"Who?"

"Calvin Millet."

"Calvin?"

"Think about it. He's managed to run a successful department store when every other within a hundred miles has folded. How do you think he's done that? By luck?"

Clem sat back in his chair. Mr. Moore continued, "He has a degree in accounting. Did you know that? You said you needed someone to help you with the taxes and the paperwork, and I'll bet you a dollar you also want someone who can keep the bank and your mutual funds honest. That means someone who can read financial reports. Isn't that the case?"

Clem still didn't answer, so Mr. Moore pressed on. "I'm not suggesting that you turn over all of the reins to him right away. He's still young and his experience has been a bit narrow."

Clem said, "What about Millet's? Who'll run the store?"

"You'll have to recruit someone."

"I thought you had a solution. That's a problem."

"Which problem is smaller: bringing someone in to manage the family trust or bringing someone in who can manage an independent department store under Calvin's supervision?"

"Point taken and I'll think about it. But the issue of store ownership remains."

"Yes it does. My guess is that you've been planning to take a majority ownership in Millet's for some time; at a minimum to protect your other property interests in Ebb."

Clem replied, "Congratulations, Vernon. You've hit the nail on the head. My interests have nothing to do with Calvin; they have to do with insuring the future of Ebb. To do that, I have to own a majority interest in Millet's. I'm the only man in town with the capital to make it go."

"Really, Clem? The Millet family has run that store for decades."

"They have, but they've always been undercapitalized. I'm not."

"But wouldn't a smaller investment, say thirty or forty percent, provide Calvin with enough money to fund the store's future operations?"

"It would, but I never invest unless I have control."

Mr. Moore rubbed his chin and then relied, "Is that so? Do you own controlling interest in Wal-Mart?"

"That's an entirely different thing. You know it."

"I also know that Calvin will never sell fifty-one percent, not to you or anybody else."

"Wrong. I have him. He can't have his cake and eat it, too. He doesn't have the cash."

Mr. Moore laughed. "You know, that particular saying has never made one bit of sense to me."

"Why the hell not?"

"Let's follow the train of thought. Would it be logical to say, 'You can't have a car and drive it, too'? How about, 'You can't have a house and live in it'? Or, 'You can't own a coat and wear it'? Who would ever say such a thing? Karl Marx? Groucho Marx? The IRS?"

"What are you trying to say, Vernon?"

"There is no point in having a cake, none whatsoever, if you can't eat it."

Without waiting for a reply, Mr. Moore continued, "I seriously doubt that Calvin Millet will have much interest in retaining a minority stake in the family cake precisely because he won't be able to eat it anymore, at least without your permission. More importantly, he has an alternative. I know for a fact he does. I have insider information."

Clem shot forward. "Insider information? What in the devil are you talking about?"

"I have it on very good authority that there's another suitor for the store, a serious, well-heeled bidder who is willing to take a minority stake."

"Goddammit, Vernon. I knew you were fronting for some out-of-state buyer. Who is it?"

"Think what you will. There is another qualified bidder in the game. Coincidentally, their interest appears to be in a minority position."

"Who, goddammit?"

"Well, Clem, I could tell you, but it would be more fun to introduce you. It'll only take a moment."

"What?"

"It'll only take a minute. Sit back and relax."

With that, Mr. Moore picked up the phone, dialed a number, and said, "We're ready." Then he put the phone back on the hook.

Clem said, "What was that, a code? Is our mysterious guest on his way?"

Mr. Moore replied, "Yes. The trip will take no time at all. While we wait, I think we should discuss a related topic."

"What's that?"

"Win or lose, you have to sell your Wal-Mart stock."

"Win or lose what?"

"Millet's Department Store. To the other party."

"First off, Vernon, that's not going to happen. I'm not going to lose, and I will keep my Wal-Mart stock, regardless. It's a fine company."

"It is a good company but, whether you become a significant investor in Millet's or not, your bank will continue to be a lender to Millet's. That's a conflict of interest."

"Now, just hold on for a minute."

"Why? Why should I hold on? You know you've thought about all of this before. Any investment you make in Millet's, regardless of what form it takes, is much more important to you than any investment you can make in Wal-Mart, no matter how large, and you damn well know why."

"Humor me."

"It's obvious. What happens to the bank if Millet's fails? If the bank goes under, what happens to property values all over town? If property values drop just ten percent, how much money do you lose?"

"That's confidential."

"And it should be, because there would be a lot of zeros between the dollar sign and the decimal point, wouldn't there?"

Clem harrumphed but did not respond. Mr. Moore continued, "There's another reason you should divest."

"Why is that?"

"Half the town knows that you've invested in Wal-Mart. As long as you hold that stock, they'll be afraid, especially if you become a prominent investor in Millet's."

"Are you telling me that I should manage my portfolio based upon what other people think?"

"No. That would be a mistake. But fear is a different matter altogether. If what you do frightens people, then you need to reconsider. A strong man doesn't make people more afraid, he makes them less afraid."

"Dammit, Vernon, that investment is personal. The townspeople shouldn't even know about it."

"Sunk cost, Clem. They do know."

"And how will they find out if I divest?"

"Do you really need me to answer that question? Unless I miss my guess, spontaneous celebration will break out within an hour."

Clem harrumphed again and said, "I'm still waiting for that

backdoor bidder of yours to show. I thought you said he was right around the corner."

Mr. Moore was trying to figure out how to buy some time when Clem's cell phone rang. He said, "Hello."

Buford Pickett answered, "The lawyer approved the call letter, Mr. Tucker. I'm delivering it now."

"Where are you?"

"I called to see if Calvin was at the store but Lily said he was at home. I'm driving down to Carson as we speak."

"Did you say anything about your purpose?"

"No, Mr. Tucker. I just told her that it was urgent bank business."

Before Clem could reply, there was a knock on the den door. Mr. Moore said, "I believe our mystery guest has arrived. I'll get it." He opened the door and in walked none other than Clara Tucker Booth Yune, freshly made up and dressed in her shiniest Cornhusker-red sweat suit and white New Balance trainers, looking for all the world like she was ready for the health-club prom.

I guess Clem was taken a bit unawares. He jumped up from the chair and said, "Clara, is that you?"

She smiled and replied, "Yes."

Mr. Moore said, "Please, Clara, have a seat on the settee. I'll stand."

Clem said into his phone, "Buford, are you still there?"

"Yes sir."

"Pull over."

"What?"

"Pull over, dammit, and wait there 'til you hear from me. Is that clear."

"Yessir."

"I mean it, Buford. And don't you call me again either. I'm in an important meeting. You just wait where you are."

"Yes sir."

Clem closed his phone slowly, then he fixed his eyes on Mr. Moore's, and then he said evenly, "To what do we owe the pleasure, Clara dear?"

Mr. Moore answered, "She still says only yes and no. I'll have to answer that one for her. Clara is interested in becoming a minority investor in Millet's."

Clem continued to glare at Mr. Moore and said, "Is that true, Clara?"

She smiled sweetly again and responded, "Yes."

"Are you confident that this outsider, this salesman, has told you everything you need to know about the situation?"

Again she replied, "Yes."

"Fine. Do you have any idea, any idea whatsoever, what this act of charity is going to cost you?"

Mr. Moore answered on her behalf, "We haven't exercised all the numbers, but I think I've given Clara a fair idea of what the investment will cost her and what kind of return she can expect."

"I suppose you also disclosed to her that the business is out of cash and Calvin is damn near broke. Did he tell you those things, too, Clara?"

She said, "Yes."

Mr. Moore added, "My suggestion is that Clara give Calvin a small bridge loan secured by the property where his house used to be, something in the neighborhood of forty to fifty thousand dollars. That should give him time to crunch the numbers with Clara's representatives and set a fair price. What do you think?"

"I think you just hijacked my deal, Vernon."

"Now, how could you possibly think that? All I did was introduce another interested party. The bidding isn't over. In fact, it hasn't even started. As an experienced investor and the owner of the local bank, I would think that you'd have an enormous advantage in the negotiations, wouldn't you?"

"Vernon . . . "

"Come on, Clem. How much of an advantage do you need?"

Clem just sat there, shaking his head. Eventually, he said, "You know, I can't remember the last time I was this pissed off. This is my town; I run it the way I see . . . "

Well, I guess Clara had had enough company for one day. She stood up and said, "Dammit, Clem, you were always such a whiner when you were little. I'm a bidder for the store. Either get in or get out, but stop whining." I swear to God that's what she said, and then she walked out without another peep.

The two men gazed at the open door for a second or two, then Clem looked at Mr. Moore and said, "Millet's is the linchpin of the county. That's why I'm going to control a majority interest in it and my wacko sister isn't going to own a single share. I hope you understand that."

Mr. Moore responded, "I have no doubt that you will prevail in the end, Clem, no doubt whatsoever. All I've done is introduce a dab of uncertainty. The deal will be a lot more interesting for you now."

"Do you know what more uncertainty means in business, Vernon? It means more expensive."

"Maybe so, but the beneficiary will be the father of your granddaughter, and he's a man who needs your help."

Clem grunted something unintelligible and then said, "Before we go eat, do you have any other surprises for me?"

Mr. Moore smiled and replied, "Well, I do have another idea or two. Speaking of Calvin, I think you should move him and his daughter into the River House. I can think of no prettier place for her to live out her final days. Leave Marie there, too, so she can cook for Calvin and Louise."

"Now that's something I can buy into."

"Not so fast. I want you to make the offer conditional."

"Conditional? On what?"

"On what we discussed last night. Calvin has promised that he will let Lucy make her own decisions in her final days, but that will require him to tell her the truth about her prospects. I know he still has cold feet, any loving father would, so I want you to make your offer of the River House conditional upon his promise to give her the chance to determine her own destiny."

"You told me that he's already promised you."

"You're her grandfather. A promise to you carries more weight. Don't you agree?"

"Yes."

"Good. After that, you should bundle the River House into your offer for a minority position in Millet's. Frankly, I don't see how Clara will be able to compete—unless, of course, you persist in pursuing majority ownership."

"Would you run that by me again?"

"Calvin needs a house. You have two. Do the math. But I think you'll have to move the trophies. I don't see Calvin or Lucy being fond of all those animal heads."

"Why in the hell would I do that? I love that place and I'm sure as hell not looking for an heir."

"Is that a fact? If my radar is picking up the right signals, then I think you've already got a plan in motion. Regardless, Calvin needs a house and some help with his personal finances. You have a spare house, more money than Croesus, and a personal interest in making sure that Millet's succeeds. That's all that's on my mind."

"Is there anything else?"

"Well, now that you mention it, there is one more thing. I want you to get a law passed."

"A law? You're a walking work of art, Vernon. You have to be joking. How in the hell am I going to get a law passed?"

"You're an influential man, Clem. You have access to everybody in the state who matters. They'll pass this law; I promise you that. It'll be great PR for everybody."

"What is it? I can't wait to hear this one."

"I have a lawyer working on a draft right now. You'll get it before the end of next week."

"Is that all you're going to tell me?"

"That's all for now."

Clem shook his head and said, "That is probably the most outrageous request I have ever heard of."

"Perhaps, but will you do it?"

"I'll look at what your lawyer sends me, Vernon. I can't commit to anything more and you know it. Now, is there anything you want from me today? An invitation to dine at Buckingham Palace perhaps?"

"That's a nice offer, and I'm sure you could arrange it, but I don't want anything else. You're on the right track; I could see that when we met at the River House. With the exception of the legislation that is being drafted for your review, there probably isn't a single thing I've suggested here that you haven't already thought about yourself."

Clem responded, "Maybe so, but have I given you the impression that I've agreed to any of your proposals? Except for letting Calvin and Lucy use the River House, of course."

"Yes. As a matter of fact, you have."

"What? When?"

"Do you remember the question I asked you over breakfast at the River House?"

"You asked me a lot of questions. Which one?"

"The important one—the one about your three best moments?"

"Yes. So what?"

"None of those moments had a thing to do with money, Clem. I think that was news to you, too, wasn't it?"

Clem didn't answer. Mr. Moore went on, "But as I remember, one of your top three was the first day you had sex. Now, I don't want to diminish that moment a bit—every man remembers it with pride and more than a touch of sadness—but for a man of your age and resources, it ought to be out of your top three by now. Saving the father of your granddaughter would be much more memorable, don't you think?"

Clem grumbled, "Are we finally done?"

"I do have one more little question for you."

Clem shook his head and said, "Mercy! What else could you possibly want?"

"Just one little thing. It's personal. Wilma talks about seeing a ghost on the front stairs named Silas the Second. I know you were raised in this house. Did you ever see him?"

"Confidentially?"

"Of course."

"I mean it, Vernon. I don't want this going to Wilma or anybody else."

"Cross my heart and hope to die."

"Then yes, I probably saw him a dozen times. It was always at night, and it scared me half to death when I was little. It seems to me that he came around every time something important was happening."

Vernon smiled and said, "Thank you, Clem. Thank you very much. I won't breathe a word. Scout's honor."

"Okay, but why did you need to ask about old Silas? Since

you're a ghost yourself, I figured that you and old Silas would be pals by now."

Mr. Moore replied, "We never met, which I regret."

"What on earth for?"

"It's my theory that there are a thousand possible outcomes after death, but I am pretty certain of only three. That would make a fourth."

"I thought you told me that we could never be sure of life after death."

"We can't, Clem. That's one of the possible outcomes."

CLARA REFUSED MY invitation to dinner that night but it was still an energetic affair. Clem sat at the head of the table like he always does, even when he is eating in somebody else's house, and I sat at the other end. Mona sat between her two boys on my left and Loretta sat next to Mr. Moore on my right. Hank Wiley showed up unannounced halfway through the salad course and sat to my right between Loretta and me. By the time dinner was over, you could not have slipped a credit card between Loretta and Mr. Moore. I suppose I have already mentioned that that woman has no shame.

For the main course, I served roast pork with cranberry sauce, which Matthew wouldn't eat, dirty rice, which Mark wouldn't eat, and Brussels sprouts, which neither Clem nor Mr. Moore would touch with a ten-foot pole. Hank Wiley, bless his soul, will eat anything that was once alive as long it is served hot, cold, or at room temperature.

Most of the dinner discussion revolved around Lucy and her successful return to consciousness. I worried some about how Matthew and Mark would take it all, but Mark was very sympathetic. He even asked if he could visit her, and Clem said he would drive them both down. Matt, on the other hand, was sullen. Go figure.

Afterward, Clem and Mona helped me clean off the table while Mr. Moore taught Loretta and the boys how to play a card game called fan tan. Then something inexplicable happened: Clem Tucker rolled up his sleeves and helped Mona rinse the dishes while I put them in the dishwasher. As I live and breathe. I had never seen a man do such a thing, much less a feudal lord. Once I got hold of myself, I had an almost irresistible urge to call the county news desk. In the end, I decided not to ruin his reputation because of one good deed, but he'll never know how close he came to having the soft underbelly of his persona revealed.

As soon as the dishes were done, Clem gave Mona and me a kiss on the cheek, and then went into my den without asking, as if it was still his, and called Calvin Millet. When Calvin came to the phone, Clem said, "How's Lucy tonight?"

"She's eating some soup right now. She's talking so much that I can hardly get a word in edgewise and seems to be in very little pain. We're all tickled pink."

"I am, too. That's wonderful news. It's all I needed to know."

"What about the store?"

"What about it?"

"You knew that Buford threatened to call my loan, didn't you?"

"No, I didn't know, but don't worry about it for a minute. Buford doesn't run the bank; I do. We'll have plenty of time to discuss the store later on. In the meantime, you send Lily back to the bank to cash that ten-thousand-dollar check. I'll make sure they take care of it. If you need more, you just let me know."

"Clem, are you all right?"

"I don't know if I am, Calvin. I think I may have caught some kind of bug from a traveling salesman. It's probably a temporary condition, so you do what I tell you to."

"Fine. Okay. I'll have Lily take care of it."

"Give Lucy my love."

"I will, Clem. And thanks."

"You're welcome. Good night."

Clem came back into the kitchen and told us all the good news about Lucy. Loretta broke out another bottle of my wine and we all sat around the kitchen table talking and laughing. It was just like things used to be before TV was invented.

AROUND TEN-THIRTY I got a call from Dot Hrnicek. She said. "One of my deputies just called in to report that Buford Pickett is pulled over on the shoulder of Highway Seventy-three just west of Carson. Apparently he's all right and his car is running fine. He said he's waitin' for an important call, but he won't say what. Do you know anything about it?"

At the time I didn't, so I said, "I don't, Dot, but Clem Tucker is here. I could ask him about it. He probably knows."

"Before you do, let's think this thing through, Wilma. Where would Buford be headed at this hour of the night?"

"Are you thinking what I am thinking?"

"Yes I am. I'm thinkin' that he was on his way to Calvin's house and something stopped him."

"Well, what should we do?" I asked.

Dot thought it over and then she answered, "Whatever it is, I doubt that it's a social call. I've never heard of Buford makin' one. Since he's stuck, why don't we just leave him where he is? I'll have the deputy check on him every half hour or so."

"That's probably a good idea. Will you let me know what happens?"

"Of course, dear. You have a pleasant evening, okay?"

"You too. Thanks for calling."

Mark had to go to bed shortly after that, and Matt disappeared into the parlor around the same time, but Clem and Hank and Loretta stayed so late that I thought I was going to have to ask them to sign the guest register. They finally all went home after midnight. Clem gave Loretta a ride in his Porsche. Mona dragged Matthew up to bed, too, and that left Mr. Moore and me alone in the kitchen.

He said, "Wilma, I've had a wonderful time here at the Come Again, but it's time for me to go."

"Must you?" I asked.

"I have to move on. Calvin will be spending almost all of his time with Lucy now, which is the way it should be, and I have to be in Trinidad on Monday morning."

"Trinidad. As in the island?"

"As in Trinidad, Colorado. It's a lovely town, not unlike Ebb but set at the foot of the Rocky Mountains."

I guess I wasn't ready to give up. I asked, "Did Calvin ever buy any of your games, Mr. Moore?"

"No. No, he didn't. Maybe he will later, though. I don't always expect to make a big sale on my first visit."

"But are you sure you should go? Has Calvin spoken to Lucy about her situation yet?"

"No, Wilma. He hasn't yet, but I'm confident he will. If his feet get a bit too cold, I know that Clem and Hank will remind him of his obligation. You should, too."

"I will, Mr. Moore, I will." Then I said, "You know that you'll break Loretta's heart when you go."

He looked into me with those twinkly blue eyes of his and answered, "I don't think so, Wilma, and neither do you. Anyway, I'm going to see her right now. If I break her heart, it will be one-on-one."

I said, "Then I suppose you will be needing a key to the front door."

I didn't even wait for an answer; I just went and got him a house key from the rolltop desk and then I asked, "What time are you leaving tomorrow?"

"At first light. You have my card imprint. I'd appreciate it if you could just email my receipt to me."

"What about your home address? Can I send it to you?"

"You could, Wilma," he answered, "except that I don't have one. I'm a traveling salesman, you know. If you ever need to mail me something, you can send it to my business address."

We both stood up and I started to get teary. Mr. Moore tried to give me a peck on the cheek, but I grabbed him and gave him a great big hug—and then I called Loretta the second he walked out the door.

Chapter 18

The Last Oasis of Nice

When Mr. Moore got to Loretta's place, she was waiting for him in a long black robe that buttoned from chin to toe—or, more accurately, that could be buttoned from head to toe. Loretta looked lovely in black, but she wasn't much for buttoning buttons below the knee or above the crevasse between her breasts, if you can see what I mean. She led Mr. Moore upstairs to her parlor, which looks more like a nineteenth-century English library than a living room. She must have ten bookshelves in that room, some of them eight-feet tall and all of them filled to the gunwales with hard-cover books.

Mr. Moore sat himself down on one end of a lovely pearl-colored Queen Anne sofa that sits in between two matching end tables in a conversation island in the center of the room. Loretta sat down at the opposite end of the sofa with her legs underneath her bottom, facing Mr. Moore.

He looked around the room and said, "You have a lovely home, Loretta. Such beautiful furniture; so many books."

She replied flatly, "You could've told me last night."

Mr. Moore smiled and answered, "I didn't know for sure last night, but would it have made a difference?"

"No, but I would've liked to know. How soon are you going? Are you leaving tomorrow?"

"This morning, actually. As soon as I return to the Come Again. I'm all packed up and ready to go."

"And where are you headed, may I ask?"

"Trinidad."

"The town in Colorado? I have a cousin who moved there."

"No, the island in the Caribbean. Near South America."

"Hmmm. I don't suppose that you'd care for a travel companion?"

"That's a lovely offer. If I had a choice, I'd surely take you along, but I have to go alone."

"Why?"

"It's what I do, Loretta. I am a traveling salesman. I work alone."

"Vern darlin', there is not a soul in Ebb who believes you're a traveling salesman. I would've started a pool on your real profession in my shop, but I was afraid that we would never learn the truth. Now I guess we never will."

Mr. Moore smiled gently and said, "Okay, Loretta. Fair enough. What would you like to know?"

Without hesitation she replied, "I want to know what you really do."

"That's easy. I'm a salesman."

"Okay, then what do you really sell? It ain't games, darlin'."

Once again, Mr. Moore answered a question with a question. "Tell me, do you think things are getting better or worse?"

She thought about it for a second or two and then answered, "I don't know. Do you mean for me personally, or do you mean for everybody?"

"Everybody."

"That's easy. Things are getting worse."

"Why, Loretta? The environment? The cost of living? Taxes? What?"

"I can answer that one. There was a time when children could walk to school without being worried for their lives. There was a time when I could get onto an airplane without undressing. There was a time when I could turn on the TV and I wouldn't see things that would make a longshoreman blush. There was a time when at least some of our Congressmen wouldn't sell a million acres of virgin forest for a thousand-dollar campaign contribution.

"I moved to Ebb because I wanted to be around people who are nice. Ebb is the Last Oasis of Nice. Everywhere else, people are getting meaner and meaner. Meanness is the new culture. That's why things are getting worse. Don't you think I'm right?"

"I do, Loretta. I think you've hit the nail right on the head. But why? Why do you think people are getting meaner?"

"I haven't thought about it much. I suppose you have an answer, though."

"It's more of a working theory."

"Uh-oh. Is this like that chicken allegory, or is it more like the Paradox of the Benevolent God?"

"Who told you about that? Wilma?"

"Yes she did, and I think I get it. I get the chicken bit, too. Because of that, I'm thinkin' about becoming a lesbian, but not tonight. Right now, I'm just hoping for one straight answer."

"Fair enough. The reason is that we've lost our blind faith."

"Blind faith? What in heaven's name do you mean by that, Vernon Moore?"

"It's gone. For two thousand years, blind faith was at the very center of our behavior. By promising to reward our good deeds and punish our bad deeds in an eternal afterlife of one extreme or the other, our blind faith told us how to act. It taught us what was good and what was bad. Most of all, the threat of eternal damnation helped us control our baser impulses."

"That's true, but most people don't believe in that old-time religion anymore."

"That's my point; it's gone now. As a species, we've lost our blind faith, especially those of us who live in the western world. Along with it, we've lost our honesty, our honor, our compassion, and our consideration for others. That's why things are worse now. Instead of becoming a kinder and gentler species in the last fifty years, we have become meaner and more self-serving."

Loretta shook her head and replied, "I know you're right, darlin', but this is starting to sound like a Sunday sermonette. As we say in the pen downstairs, why don't you just cut to the nape?"

Mr. Moore looked her in the eye and replied, "There are four kinds of people in this world, Loretta. The first are people who need assistance to survive: the young, the elderly, the sick, the poor. The second kind are those who take care of themselves. The third kind are people who care for themselves and for others, too. They are the lifeblood of society: giving parents; genuine leaders; people who devote their lives to medicine, law enforcement, fire fighting, national defense, and charity. Of all the people on Earth, they are the essential ones, because they take care of those who cannot care for themselves.

"Sadly, though, there is a fourth kind. They are the people who take from others to survive. They are the weakest among us: criminals, con men and, regrettably, many of our nation's leaders. One reason that things are worse now is that so many of our business and political leaders take from their constituencies for their own personal gain. In other words, they are no longer our strongest; they are our weakest. I could give you a thousand examples, but I don't think you need any."

"Amen to that. But what's the solution? Do you think we need our blind faith back?"

"No. We need to evolve. We need to move beyond blind faith."

"To what, Vernon? What in the world could replace blind faith?"

Mr. Moore sat forward and replied, "Reasoned faith. I believe . . . No, I have reasoned that life after death makes sense. Therefore, faith in God makes sense."

"So that's what your Benevolent God paradoxes are all about: reasoned faith?"

"Yes. That's it exactly."

"So you're telling me that you sell reasoned faith. Is that what you sold Calvin Millet?"

"I sold Calvin some hope. I used reasoned faith, not blind faith, to sell it."

"Hmmm. That was real clever of you, Vern darlin', but did he buy some? I think he needs a lot of hope. Did he buy a lot?"

"We'll know for sure in the next few months."

Loretta whistled and said, "I hope he did. If Millet's fails, Ebb will turn into a ghost town. And we don't need a junior Clem Tucker runnin' around town causin' more trouble."

Mr. Moore replied, "Don't sell Clem short, Loretta. Give him another chance. His early adulthood was eerily similar to Calvin's in some respects, but I think he's begun the process of graduating from 'me' to 'we.' If he can complete the course, it will be a boon to the entire county."

"I suppose you sold him some reasoned faith too."

"I did my best."

"Did you tell him about the four kinds of people, too? That man could be the international poster child for the fourth kind."

"I did, Loretta."

"You did? All four parts?"

"All four; just like I told you."

"How did he react? Did he get angry?"

"No. He seemed to take it pretty well."

"That's good. God knows he needs to be interested in something besides the numbered etchings of dead presidents." Then Loretta stuck out her lower lip and said, "But now I'm hurt, darlin'. Why didn't you sell me any of your reasoned faith?"

Mr. Moore laughed and answered, "It's not what you needed. You're already a loving and caring woman. All you needed was a little insight into the male species. That's why I told you that story last night."

"I got it, Vern. You told me what I already knew, that any man I ever love is going to leave me. Isn't that right?"

"Yes."

Neither one of them knew what to say after that, so the two of them sat there in silence. After a short while, Loretta stretched out her arms to yawn, and she took her sweet time at it. I don't know if you men have ever noticed, but when a woman stretches out like that, it's a come-hither sign. After she was done, she said, "I know it's late, but are you up for one more little challenge?"

Mr. Moore smiled and answered her question with a question, "What did you have in mind?"

She touched the bodice of her robe and replied, "There are twenty-four buttons running down the front of my dressing gown, darlin'. I've given you a head start because half of them are already undone. Now, how many more do you think you can undo before the sun comes up?"

Mr. Moore laughed and answered her question with, you guessed it, another question. He said, "Well, I'm a bit short of time. Do you want a written estimate, or can I just give it a try?"

My guess is that there was a lot of laughing after that, at least for a while.

WHEN I CAME down to start breakfast at 6:30 A.M. on Sunday morning, I found Loretta Parsons sitting in my kitchen drinking red wine out of a cheap old water glass. I could see right away that she'd been up all night with you-know-who. I started to say something, but before I could get a word out of my mouth she said, "He's gone, Wilma, just like you said. But he left this for you."

Loretta pointed to a present sitting on my kitchen table. It was wrapped in light-blue paper and tied with a bow of pewter-colored ribbon. I'm sure it wasn't the mature thing to do, but I opened it up then and there, right in front of Loretta. It was the most lovely black lacquered box I have ever seen. On each side, there were tree branches and blossoms inlaid in mother-of-pearl. On the top, a single crane was taking off from an oblong pool that reflected a yellow-gold moon. Inside the box, there was a folded piece of roughhewn stationery with a handwritten note from Mr. Moore. All it said was:

Uncertainty is the spice of life.

At exactly that moment in time, I had no idea what he meant, so I showed the note to Loretta and then I broke down and cried. I must have been saving some up because I cried like a baby. Lo cried too, but just a little, and then she poured herself some more wine and told me everything about her final hours with Mr. Moore, at least until the lights went out. After that, she went upstairs to get some sleep and I went into my study to hide my black lacquer box. That was when I got another call from Dot Hrnicek.

"This is Wilma," I yawned.

"Dottie here. That deputy I told you about—the one who found Buford down on Seventy-three near Carson—she just signed off her shift about ten minutes ago."

"What happened?"

"She said Buford was still sleeping in his car at sunrise, so she woke him up and told him to go home. Do you know what happened then?"

"What?"

"He refused. He said he couldn't leave until he got an important call."

"What did the deputy do?"

"She breathalyzed him, of course."

"Well?"

"He was stone sober. He's not breakin' the law. There was nothing else she could do."

"He's still there?"

"Yep. Doesn't that beat all? The day deputy is going to take him some coffee and an Easter egg with my compliments."

Well, all I could do was shake my head and wonder what shenanigans those men would get up to next, but shenanigans did not come next.

Chapter 19

On the Privilege of Being a Seal

MY GRANDFATHER, GOD rest his soul, used to say that the porch was his favorite place because it was just like being outside, but you never got sunburned or wet. After Calvin moved into the River House, the porch was where little Lucy Millet spent most of her waking hours. It was a large, wooden, screened-in affair with a thick old rug on the floor and antique white-wicker and dark-hardwood furniture everywhere. She could see across the river to Missouri in that room and pick up the breeze from three points on the compass.

There was a well-cushioned white-wicker chaise lounge in the center of the porch where Lucy liked to sit. It had a high back, which had the effect of making her IV apparatus and TV monitors less intrusive. Calvin liked to sit in a fanbacked wicker chair close by and read to her, and Nurse Nelson taught her to play cribbage on the coffee table. To hear Calvin tell about it later, Lucy was incredibly lucky, but that little girl deserved a run of good luck, even if it was only at cards. I guess Nurse Nelson never told Calvin about her secret skill. I never did either.

Around sundown on a perfectly clear day in early May, Calvin asked Nurse Nelson if she could leave him and Lucy alone to talk for a while, and of course she said she would.

After she had gone, Calvin sat down on the chaise next to Lucy and said, "How do you feel, honey? Can I bring you another blanket?"

"No, Daddy. I'm warm. Honest. Sometimes I get too hot from all these things."

"How about something to drink? I can ask Nurse Nelson if it's okay."

"Uh-uh. I'm fine. Really. I might want to watch some television in a while."

"You just say the word, honey, and I'll help you move into the great room."

"Why does Grandpa call it a great room? I think that's a funny name."

"I guess he calls it a great room because it's so big. It's the biggest living room I ever saw."

"Me, too."

"Is the pain okay, sweetheart? Is it better? Worse?"

"It's not too bad. I just don't like to talk about it. It doesn't hurt so bad if I don't have to talk about it."

"Okay. But there's something else we do have to talk about."

That got Lucy's attention. She looked into her father's eyes and said, "What, Daddy?"

"Do you remember what happened to those baby seals on TV the other night?"

Lucy's lower lip stuck out just a bit when she replied, "They were just babies. The sharks ate them. It was very sad."

"Yes it was, honey, but that's the way Nature is sometimes. After the baby seals passed on, what do you think happened to them?"

Lucy did not answer quickly, but when she did, she said, "Didn't they go to heaven?"

Calvin smiled and responded, "That's an excellent answer, sweetheart. But if you were God, is that what you would do?"

"What do you mean?"

"It just seems to me that being a seal would be a lot of fun. You could travel across oceans, and swim on your back, and see things that no man or giraffe could ever, ever see. I think that being a seal would be a great privilege, don't you?"

Lucy's eyes lit up and she answered, "Oh yes! I'd love to be able to glide through the water like that. It would be so much fun."

"I think so, too, honey. But if they die as babies, they don't get the chance, do they? Isn't that kind of unfair, even if they do get to go to heaven?"

Lucy had to think about her father's question for a minute,

then she said firmly, "I never thought about it that way, but you're right. It is unfair. They never got their chance."

"So what would you do if you were God, sweetheart?"

"I wouldn't let them die when they were so young," she replied.

"That's a good answer, but it's against the rules. That would mean that you would have to stop the sharks from being sharks, and you made those sharks the way they are. You have to let them be sharks, don't you?"

"Do I have to? I like the seals a lot better."

"If you're God, then you have to love the sharks as much as the seals, and you mustn't tell any of them what to do. That's against the rules, too."

Lucy considered her dilemma and then said, "Then I don't see how I can help the baby seals, Daddy."

Calvin replied, "You underestimate yourself. You're God now. Why don't you just give the seals another chance?"

"Another chance? How?"

"Why don't you give them another life as a seal?"

Lucy thought again and then said, "That's a very good idea, Daddy. That's just what I'll do."

"Good. How about baby kangaroos and baby giraffes, Lucy? Would you do the same for them, too?"

"Don't be silly. I have to love them all the same. You said so."

"How many chances would you give them?"

"If they were good, I'd let them have as many as they wanted. If they were bad, I'd have to think about it. We would have to have a talk."

"That's another good answer. You're a very fair God. Now, how about little boys and girls? If they didn't get a fair chance at life, would you let them come back, too?"

Lucy started to answer, but then she fell silent. As he had been trained to do by Mr. Moore, Calvin waited. After many seconds, Lucy's mouth twisted slightly and she asked, "Am I going to die, Daddy?"

For the second time, Calvin Millet faced the Moment of Truth. He hesitated.

Lucy had not been trained to wait by Mr. Moore. She said, "Daddy?"

Calvin replied, "Where did you ever get an idea like that, sweetheart?"

Like an impatient parent, Lucy repeated, "I'm a big girl. I want to know the truth."

Calvin had practiced and practiced and practiced, but he just couldn't help it. He tried as hard as he could to hold back the tears, but he couldn't do it. He began to sob as only a grieving parent can. It is a cry like no other, because the pain is worse than any other. After a time, he managed to inhale deeply and answer, "Not now, sweetheart, but . . . " Then he began to cry again.

Little Lucy didn't cry. She put her hand on her father's and said, "Will you be okay?"

It was a long time before Calvin could answer. "Yes, sweetheart. I'll be all right, but I'll miss you so badly." And then he took Lucy in his arms and held her while he tried and failed to choke back his tears again.

This time, Lucy cried, too, but softly, and then she said, "When, Daddy? When am I going to die?"

Calvin sniffled, but he managed to gather all his courage and answer, "I don't know. Dr. Wiley doesn't know, either. No one knows. But if you want, you can decide."

Lucy looked up at her father and said, "What does that mean?"

"The pain is going to get worse. There will come a time when there will be no way that we can stop it except by giving you so much medicine that it will put you to sleep again."

"That's what Nurse Nelson does now, every night before I go to bed. She told me so."

"But she doesn't kill all the pain, does she?"

"No, but I'm used to it now."

"I know you are, sweetheart. You're an incredibly brave girl. But if we had to kill all of your pain, we would have to put so much medicine in your IV that you couldn't wake up."

"I couldn't? Not even if I wanted to?"

"No, sweetheart."

Lucy was quiet again for a long time, but then she looked her father straight in the eye and said, "I'm not going to get better, am I?"

Calvin teared up again but he managed to say, "No, sweetheart."

Lucy said, "I knew it. I knew it when Grandpa said we could stay here and Nurse Nelson came too."

Calvin lifted Lucy into his lap, blankets and all, and rocked her gently. After a while, she asked, "What will happen? How will I die?"

"That's what you can decide, if you want. Dr. Wiley says the pain is going to get worse and worse. He says it may also get harder for you to breathe and swallow, maybe even to hold your head up."

Lucy replied swiftly, "I don't want to be a lump. I want to be able to sit on the porch with you, and watch TV, and play cards with Nurse Nelson."

"I want that, too, sweetheart; I want it so bad. But the time will come when none of that will be possible anymore."

"But I get to decide when? Not you or Dr. Wiley?"

"The pain will come on its own, but you'll get to decide when we stop it for good. That will be your decision. I promise."

Lucy put her arms around her father's neck, she kissed him on the cheek, and she said, "Thank you, Daddy."

After that, she closed her eyes and sat perfectly still in her father's lap with her arms still around his neck. They stayed that way for a long time, long enough for Calvin to regain some control of his emotions. Eventually, though, Lucy opened her eyes again and said, "Do you believe I will get another chance? Honestly and truly?"

"Yes I do, honey. With all my heart."

"Will I get to be with you again?"

"I don't know. If you start over, then I think you'll need new parents."

Lucy thought that answer over some and then she asked, "Does that mean I can be anything I want?"

Calvin smiled and answered, "Yes. I'm sure you can."

"Anything?"

"I think so, sweetheart. I don't know why not."

Lucy looked her father right in the eye, grinned, and said. "When I come back, Daddy, can I be a seal?"

Lucy Millet lived longer than any of us could have ever expected. Her father read to her, she played cards with Nurse Nelson on the porch, and Clem visited her every single day. He even took Mark down to see her several times, and Mark taught Lucy and Clem and Nurse Nelson how to play fan tan.

As spring turned into summer, though, Lucy's condition deteriorated, just as Hank said it would. Although it was hard for her, she did manage to sit up with us for the Fourth of July. Clem sent a special man to the River House the day before to set everything up, then we all went down on the morning of the Fourth, including Mona and the boys, Hank, Loretta, Clem, and me. Marie cooked us all up an amazing Cajun meal including gumbo, prawns, and red beans and rice, and then Clem's special man started shooting off the fireworks just after sundown. It seemed like it took him an hour to light them all. I don't think I've ever seen so many pretty, red-white-and-blue explosions in all my life.

After we all left the River House, Calvin and Lucy went up to the porch to be by themselves. She sat in Calvin's lap for a long time, until it was very, very dark outside and there was no sound left except for the crickets and the breeze, and then she put her tiny little arms around her father's neck, she kissed him on the cheek, and she whispered, "It's time for me to go, Daddy."

Nurse Nelson found them in the same position at dawn the next morning. Little Lucy Millet had died quietly and painlessly during the night, but Calvin Millet had never moved, as if by his stillness he had preserved their final moments in a photograph of time.

Postscript

Return to Bluff's Edge

I TOLD YOU at the beginning that there are only about two thousand people in Ebb, but at least that many must have come to Lucy's memorial service at the church. The parking lot was full to the brim, and cars and pickup trucks were parked on both sides of the road for half a mile in either direction. A bunch of those cars were from Lincoln, and some of them were big black limousines with state government plates.

There was standing room only in the church itself, including the balcony, and there were people standing outside who had to listen to the proceedings on speakers. One of mourners who stayed outdoors was Lulu Tiller, who must have brought fifteen dogs along to the service. Not one of them made a fuss, but I hear that some of the out-of-towners were amused by certain aspects of her behavior.

Inside, the church was floor to ceiling with flowers: lilies and red roses mostly, plus every other flower I could name and a couple of varieties that I couldn't. Three of the arrangements were the size of hay bales: one from Clem; one from his sister, Clara; and one from the governor. I had known that Calvin Millet was an important and popular man in Hayes County, but I didn't get the whole picture until the pastor turned the pulpit over to none other than Clement Tucker.

Clem, who was one hundred percent dressed in black, walked up to the pulpit with a somber, serious air. He opened up an official folder, he looked down upon Calvin and smiled, he cast his eyes slowly across the congregation, and then he said, "One thing all of us believe is that Lucy Millet will come back to a fuller, fairer life. If any little girl ever deserved a second chance, it was Lucy. When she comes back, though, we all want the world to be a better place for little girls to live in. Accordingly, the state legislature of Nebraska, the nation's only unicameral, has unanimously passed a new law."

Clem looked down at Calvin again and continued, "It is called the Lucy Millet Memorial Statute and it reads as follows:

> Being unfair to all parties concerned and of considerable heartbreak to mothers and fathers everywhere, it is hereby forbidden by law from this date forward that any Nebraska child, whether male or female, shall precede his or her parents in death. Any child who attempts to disobey this act in any way shall be loved and cared for ceaselessly, as was Lucy Millet of Ebb, Nebraska, by her father, Calvin."

Clem looked up and went on, "This bill was passed by affirmation in the state unicameral and signed yesterday by the governor. As such, it has officially been entered into the body of Nebraska law. Given its unanimous support, I expect it to be vigorously enforced throughout the state."

He closed the folder, walked down to the front pew where Calvin Millet was sitting, and said, "This is your official copy, Calvin. It was also signed by the governor, who asked me to pass along his personal condolences. Another copy, in brass, will hang in the entryway of the Rutherford B. Hayes County Courthouse."

Calvin cried his heart out. Everybody cried, even Clem and Doc Wiley. I swear to God.

After the memorial service, Calvin and Clem, Mona and the boys, Loretta and Lily, Hank and Nurse Nelson, and yours truly went back to the River House for the wake. Marie Delacroix made another nice meal for us, including bread pudding with homemade chocolate sauce, but no one was very hungry or very talkative either, not even that perky Nurse Nelson.

At sunset, Calvin picked up Lucy's urn and walked over to the bluff's edge. We all gathered around him and he said, "Bring my heart back with you, sweetheart." Then he opened it up and let her ashes float down to the Missouri River on the wind. He began to cry again, and Clem walked up and put his arm around him. They stood there for a long time; we all did.

MILLET'S DEPARTMENT STORE was never put up for sale. Clem bought 49.9 percent of it for cash, which gave Calvin more than enough money to put the store back on a sound footing. I know that Clem also offered to pay for Lucy's medical bills. Out of kindness, Calvin let him pay for half; I guess the actual figure was closer to 49.9 percent. Clem told me later that he had to sell his Wal-Mart stock to cover his share.

About a month ago, Calvin hired in a new general manager for Millet's, a woman if you can believe that. She seems to be a real nice person, and the cosmetics section in the store has already improved by leaps and bounds. Nowadays, he spends most of his time helping Clem manage the Tucker family trust, in which he is now a minority owner.

Shortly after Lucy's death, Calvin moved into Clem's modern place on the other side of town, funny angles and all, and Clem moved back into the River House. After dinner the other night, Calvin told Mona and me that it was growing on him and that he might buy it if the price was right.

Nurse Nelson didn't leave Ebb after Lucy's death. She now works for Hank Wiley on a permanent basis and she's become a card-carrying member of the Quilting Circle. Naturally, Hank has taken a shine to her, but I think she has Calvin Millet in her sights. Half of the women in the Circle do, as near as I can tell, but they will all have to reckon with me before that match is decided. I have Calvin over for dinner at least once a week, and I make sure that he and Mona always have some time for themselves.

After we found out why Buford Pickett was parked on the side of the road all night, the executive committee of the Quilting Circle decided that he needed round-the-clock supervision. Lulu Tiller volunteered of course, she always does, but Lily Park eventually agreed to take the job. That woman is made of nails. Buford has already lost ten pounds, the comb-over is gone, and he has bought Lily a Husker-red minivan with four-wheel drive. To be exact, he leased her one. He said it was a better deal from a financial point of view.

In case you're wondering, Clara still says just yes and no. In a way, I guess you have to admire her for it. Oddly, though, Mark goes up to visit her a lot. He says they play cards. We played gin rummy the other day and he kicked my behind. He is turning into a cardsharp; I suppose we have Mr. Moore to thank for that. Nobody knows what his big brother Matt is getting good at, but we all have our fingers crossed.

Mr. Moore was in Ebb for only six days and then he disappeared without a trace, on Easter Saturday no less. We still sit around my kitchen table and debate whether he was a salesman or not. He never sold any games and his Web site now says "Under Reconstruction," but at least he sold Calvin some hope. He sold me some, too, and Hank and Clem. Now that Millet's is healthy again, you might fairly say that he sold the entire town some hope.

Loretta is a different story. Mr. Moore broke her heart in two when he left, and it stayed broken—until she found out she was pregnant. Hank says the child is due the last week of December;

Loretta says it will be Christmas Day. The three of us are driving up to Beatrice next week to find out what gender it is. She says she wants a Vernon Junior, but I'm hoping for a Lavern instead. Loretta has never had good luck with men.

It's been such a long time since anybody I know has been truly lucky in love. That's why you could have knocked me over with a feather when Clem proposed about a month ago. Half of me was inclined to accept his offer on the spot—very inclined, as in hop-a-plane-to-Vegas inclined. But my past adventures with Al and the institution of matrimony made my other half afraid to take the chance—real afraid, as in flee-to-Mississippi afraid.

Well, I mealymouthed my way out of giving Clem an immediate answer and then I put him on hold for two more weeks while I vacillated back and forth like a teenaged girl: yes, no; yes, no; yes, no; yes, no. I know I drove Loretta and Mona mad, and the boys must have thought that I had devolved into the Gramma from the Nether Reaches. Then, during the deepest depths of my indecisiveness, I recalled the message that Mr. Moore left for me in my black lacquer box.

I know where he lives now. He lives in the State of Second Chances. And I am certain he is right: uncertainty is the spice of life.